WHIPPED

WHIPPED

CHEF'S KISS SERIES

E. J. Hopps

For Mom and Katie. You know what you did.

Prologue

Theo watched as small hands pulled an espresso with surgical precision. Those hands skipped over the proper towel, a minor problem and one that could be trained out of the right person given time. His gaze traveled from fingertips to soft features bracketed by thick, corn-colored locks. Shannon's hair was in its usual state of adorable. Half up, with a light gray ribbon tied around the pony, its loops forming a perfect little bow on top of her head while the rest disappeared in the mass of blond strands. The look brought those sapphire eyes straight to the forefront where they belonged.

Stopping the shot at the wrong time, Shannon lifted the small ceramic cup without wiping the tray beneath it, holding it up to him with a smug grin.

"Try this, Sexy Brit."

"Shannon, if you start working here, you really have to stop calling me that. In fact, you should stop regardless."

The pout she pointed in his direction was a weapon, even if it did nothing to sway his resolve. He knew that hiring

Shannon would come with its challenges, but he needed someone to replace Evie. The woman herself had nothing but remarkable things to say about her roommate.

And best friend, he reminded himself. Her opinion was most definitely biased. He didn't necessarily trust his former sous chef—he didn't trust anyone, really—but he couldn't deny that of the seventeen applicants that already tore through his café, Shannon was proving to be the most qualified.

He winced at the scent of the over-extracted espresso, resigned to the fact that he was about to have the most bitter, astringent bean juice drain all moisture from his tongue. Most qualified did not equal skilled. Not yet, anyway.

"This position will involve training in the kitchen as well," he said, barely holding back a grimace as he choked down a sip.

"Not a problem. I have some prior experience and would love to learn more," she answered, her gaze holding his in a way that had always made him uneasy. The problem with hiring your friends, or more accurately, your previous employee's friends, is you already have a pretty good idea of who they are. So he knew that Shannon was an unapologetic flirt, who possessed far too much charm for a human body to hold. And wouldn't you know it? She loved tormenting him of all people. Pushing his buttons until he found himself avoiding her whenever Evie was working, a tactic that had worked well for him for a solid two years.

So, hiring her as his manager was obviously a great fucking idea.

"I saw your management experience, so I'm not worried there. You seem more than capable of handling the small team we have here. Aside from baking, roasting the coffee beans keeps me fairly busy, so I'll rely on you for most guest interaction."

"Absolutely," she responded without pause. Arguably the most professional he had ever seen her. "I'm great with

2

guests and a fast learner. I have no doubt that I can fill Evie's extremely large shoes." Her voice rang strong though she played with a gold band around her finger, twisting it over and over again and revealing her nerves.

Eyeing her warily, his eyes roamed over the mole just above her cupid's bow, to the cut of her stubborn jaw, over blushed cheeks and back to those ocean eyes. Devastating, a face like hers. The stuff of fairytales and myth. The kind of face that had him searching relentlessly for signs of deception. The type of face that would easily distract from the malice within.

Wow, maybe he'd see if his therapist could squeeze him in for an emergency session. His paranoid delusions seemed to be breaking the surface of his mental pool, Shannon's angel face notwithstanding.

You're being creepy, he told himself, silence thick between them, stares unblinking. Finally, he asked the question that every single one of his previous applicants failed to answer correctly. "Why do you want to work at Bloem?"

Shannon smiled, her eyes breaking from his to meander over the small café. Had her eyes softened, or was it just him projecting how he would react after sweeping his gaze over the space he created?

"Because this place that you've built…it calls to me. You ever get the feeling that life is just missing one little puzzle piece that you most likely lost in the couch cushions, and every day you search and search for that one missing piece as if it will make everything complete?" He blinked, completely taken aback by the thoughts that spilled from her tongue. She went on as if his silence was an answer. "Well, that feeling? It goes away when I'm here. As if the space itself is telling me to stop searching and just…be. You know?"

Theo nodded, his jaw clenching as he fought back the response that immediately sprang to his mind at that baffling declaration. He did know what she meant, had felt that same way about the café once before he realized there would always be missing puzzle pieces to search for.

The silence sat crisp in the air between them, her terrible espresso shot still held in his hands as their eyes stayed glued together. Who the hell was this woman?"

"Plus," she added, a rosy tint rising to her cheeks. "I'll finally get to perfect my British accent."

Theo ignored that last bit, all too familiar with Shannon's taunting. Sometimes it made her appear a little out of sorts, as if she were nervous or uncomfortable. Like maybe her random inappropriate ramblings weren't so random after all. And he wasn't really sure if it was the twist of that ring on her finger, or the oddly intimate answer she had word-vomited at his feet, either way, he found himself extending a hand to the woman, a foreboding shiver coursing through his spine as their hands clasped.

"How often am I going to regret this decision?"

She grinned, solidifying that foreboding where it rested in his chest.

"Every day for the rest of your bloody life, Guv'na."

cHapter one

It was one of those San Francisco days where the fog said, "Okay, fine!" And allowed the sun its hard-earned glory. July was nearly over, and beams of perfectly warmed light caressed Shannon's SPF-smeared skin, warming her on the outside as the company she held warmed her little guts on the inside. Her roommate, Ben, luxuriated next to her on a bright pink blanket, his red hair unbound and spread over the wool in a shocking contrast. A beer bottle sweated in the midday heat, leaving several dark rings on his shirt from its travels.

Evie sat cross legged on his left, fanning herself with an empty prosciutto sleeve. Her brown hair flopped whenever she turned her head too quickly, the bun atop it messy and lopsided as always. At the exact moment Shannon decided to pause and lovingly gaze at her two besties, Evie was two seconds away from murdering Ben and enlisting her help to bury the body.

She loved them so very much.

"I'm simply saying," Ben said, sunglasses hiding the mischievous gleam in his eyes. "That neither Shannon nor I will look good in yellow. I know you want this wedding to be all Good-Day-Sunshine-Yellow-Submarine-She-Loves-

You-Ya-Ya, but can we tone it down a bit? I'd rather be a Blue Meanie than be subjected to canary yellow."

Shannon scrunched her nose. "What's a Blue Meanie?"

Evie paused an impressive glare, turning devastated eyes on her. "Are you serious?"

"Add it to the list," Ben sang, still sprawled on his blanket.

"We can't," Evie said, shaking her head in defeat. "At this rate, the list of movies Shannon hasn't seen will take our entire lives to get through. If we started now, we'd be halfway through by the time our eighties rolled around."

"Can you imagine the three of us in our eighties? We'll be the bitches of the retirement home. Max will trail behind us with that disappointed dad look he does so well." He sounded absolutely smitten with the idea.

"My fiancé does not make a disappointed dad face. That's just his face."

"And we all agree that it is a stunning face," Shannon chimed in.

"Right. Which circles me back to the Big Bird bridesmaids' dresses. I don't want his perfect face to morph into *you're not leaving the house in that* energy on your wedding day. Because trust me, when he sees my ginger ass in yellow, that's exactly what is going to happen. I've come too far in therapy to rehash that sort of trauma."

"I'm going to have to side with Ben on this one Evie-Jean. Yellow is...bright."

"This from the woman whose wardrobe is a pastel fever-dream? You're literally wearing yellow right now."

Shannon glanced down at her soft corn-colored shirt. It had a vintage look to it with its faded hems and dainty fit. Especially when tucked into the ivory lace skirt she had paired with it. It was adorable. Her hand found the silk ribbon tied into her mass of blonde hair and ran the length of it. Yellow, to match the shirt. Again—adorable.

6

"I'm in my loungewear, not Maid of Honoring your wedding," she said simply.

Ben snorted, sitting up with impressive grace for someone his size. The man was living for the rugby bod and looked like he belonged in a biker bar rather than on his pink blankie in the park.

He pointed a glare directly at Shannon's face. "You're right, because *I* will be Maid of Honoring her wedding."

Shannon laughed freely, her ribbon catching on a small breeze and flowing over her cheek.

"That's adorable Benjamin, but we all know that I am the honorary maid of Evie's dreams. I'm the one who helped her and Max along. The best match I ever made," she said with a wink at her friend.

Evie rolled her eyes, grinning like a goon. "I would say that your matchmaking skills played a minor role in this production."

Ben snorted, choosing a song to play before passing the phone to her. He would have just played an artist whose name started with K, so Shannon would have to choose an L before passing her phone to Evie. They almost always made it through the alphabet but as Shannon saw a notification from her boss, chances of that happening were slim.

"Ugh, the devil knows how to use a phone, and he chooses to text me? My virtue is constantly tested," she said without further explanation.

"Theo? Great, ask him what he thinks of yellow bridesmaids' dresses."

"No, you know what? We've discussed this for far too long already," Ben said, finally at his wits end though his deep voice remained teasing. Just one of the many reasons he and Shannon had bonded over the years. In appearance, they couldn't be more different. But they had always leaned into humor and fun rather than seriousness or conflict. She hoped it worked as well for him as it did for her. "Shannon and I, as Honorary Maidens—"

"I'm not sure these words mean what you think they do."

"It is our duty," Ben said over Evie's attempt to reign them in. "To tell you the truth. And the truth is, I would rather listen to Creed than wear a yellow tux."

Shannon decided that playing "With Arms Wide Open" was truly more important than sticking to the rules of their game. She hit play next without a second thought before pocketing her phone. They wouldn't be playing for much longer after her text from Theo.

"Fine," Evie finally conceded, and although her tone was sharp, Shannon could tell she was enjoying herself. "Harper is going to join us at some point today and she can be the tie breaker."

"I'm so excited that she agreed to be a bridesmaid," Shannon squeaked before Ben could retort. "She could use a little happiness right now."

Harper had joined their little threesome a little after Evie and Max finally stopped being stupid and admitted their undying love for one another. Another Michelin chef to add to their collection. Harper was quiet and shy and scary as hell in the kitchen. A real Dr Jekyll/Mr. Hyde situation. When she joined their group, she was so tightly wound you could barely glance in her direction without spooking her. So naturally, Shannon made it her life's mission to break her out of her shell so they could become best friends and share their deepest secrets.

Unfortunately, being the chef owner of a three-star Michelin restaurant kept her insanely busy until about a week ago. Burnout was a hell of a thing.

A sigh escaped her lips as she resigned herself to the fact that she would be missing Harper's life update. One did not keep the devil waiting.

"I have to go. I'm being summoned to the underworld," she said, handing over her beer to Ben's already extended hand. His lack of tact was astounding.

"Boo," he said with very little feeling. "It's Tuesday. Tell Theo to go play cricket or sip a cheeky cup of tea in his study or whatever sexy Brits like to do in their free time."

"Theo's the type of sexy Brit that probably sips two fingers of fine whiskey while reading a memoir by the fire," Evie chimed in, snagging the licorice from their pile of candy and ripping into one.

"God, yeah. Sexy Brit is probably busy gazing out the window of his library, wishing for the rain and writing poetry." He sounded a little too wistful at the idea.

"Shocking no one, you're both wrong. Sexy Brit had a barista no-call no-show and literally didn't even ask me to work. He just sent me a text that says quote, 'Big roast. Sadie didn't show, threw a spanner in the works. You free?' end quote."

"What does 'threw a spanner in the works' mean?" Ben asked in a truly terrible British accent.

Shannon shrugged. "I don't speak demon."

"Doesn't matter anyway. Tell me you at least made a joke at the way he asked if you were free." Her big blue eyes sparkled with mischief as she flipped the phone to show Ben her response. His laugh rumbled alongside the cool breeze as Evie groaned, burying her face in her hands.

"Job security only lasts so long," she mumbled, prompting another round of chuckles from Ben. Stuffing her things into her bag, she moved quickly, already picturing the scowl Theo would wear when he read her message. The thought made missing Harper only slightly less annoying.

Weaving through park-goers, she dodged soccer balls and frisbees, her grin unwavering. As she slid into a waiting Lyft, she tilted her face to the sky, soaking in the last bit of sunshine while Creed drifted from the speaker she left behind.

CHaPTer TWO

Shannon Perry: You free? A little early for a booty call, isn't it?

Theo eyed his screen with little to no surprise whatsoever. The fact that he was running the espresso bar and interacting with guests clearly meant very little to the manager of his café if her only response to the crisis was mocking. If his message had been a bit too staccato it certainly wasn't his fault—it was Sadie's. In hindsight, it may not have been a great decision to hire a high school student with no experience and an appreciation for gingerbread lattes—whatever the fuck that meant.

The number of times he had caught her filming TikTok videos rather than working had been almost impressive.

Yet even with her professional shortcomings fresh in his mind, Theo was contemplating a few of his own as well. He had typed and deleted a reply to Shannon about ten times including but not limited to:

"Daydreaming again?"

"Is that on the table?"

"Don't she-devils like yourself sacrifice their partners after sex? Not sure I should risk it."

"Booty calls can happen at any time of day."

And his personal favorite, a simple, not even remotely sexy or flirtatious, "No."

Even after all these years Theo couldn't quite wrap his head around the woman. She was flirty and inappropriate, grossly optimistic, and her smile rivaled any star in the sky. She was infuriating. She acted like a sweet little tease and looked like a waking dream. A cinnamon roll in human form. Warm and comforting and spicy and…approachable. Delicious.

Theo despised cinnamon rolls.

He found them to be too much work for something so soft and sweet. Kinda like Shannon. Normally, he was resigned to her antics, but with his mind in a dark place lately, he had really needed the day to go smoothly. Not have a seventeen-year-old ghost her job, keeping him shackled to the espresso machine instead of the roasting room where he belonged.

The look of longing he sent to the viewing window where the roaster remained still and silent was felt bone deep. He didn't do guest interaction very well. That was why he had hired the she-devil in the first place. Her flirtatious nature and sunshiny personality had people eating out of the palm of her hand and eagerly returning for their daily caffeine boost. Unlike his brand of customer service which consisted of curt nods and prompt service.

Also, why would anyone want to add vanilla syrup to their single origin Guatemalan? People were puzzling. He wanted them to have the best experience when they walked in his door, which was why he kindly kept to the confines of the roastery instead of attempting to smile through an explanation of a proper macchiato.

Theo plucked a portafilter from the espresso machine, knocking out the old coffee grounds before giving it a quick wipe and locking it onto the grinder for the next round. The machine kicked on, its slightly high-pitched racket soothing him as it annoyed everyone else. His movements were crisp and efficient, completely contrasting the delicate tattoos covering his hands and fingers. His gaze caught on one of his favorites, a small, single stem rose that ran just along his thumb. The line work was incredibly fine, each thorn and petal as clear and crisp as the day he got it.

The day everything in his life changed.

It was an odd thing, to have something so soft and lovely be a constant reminder of something devastating. To have an attachment to this scribble that only forced him to think about subjects that brought on anger and bitterness. A painful memory forever etched in delicate ink. Maybe that was why he loved the damn thing so much. It reminded him how strong he could be. It reminded him of his promises and responsibilities.

An oddly serious path for his thoughts to travel as he made a sugar-free vanilla latte—with whip.

His mind was too full of worry to even argue with the man who ordered it. Did whipped cream have sugar in it? Yes. Was it worth it for him to wade through the financial spreadsheets and numbers currently occupying his thoughts to come up with a proper argument to express that point? No. No, it was not.

"Brady," he called, dolloping the beverage with softly churned cream and really giving a kind expression his best effort. The way Brady snagged his to-go cup and practically ran out the door told him he failed at that task.

It wasn't Brady's fault. After going over the financials for what felt like thirty hours that morning, Theo had already been in a pretty foul mood. Combine that with the fact that Shannon's terrible ex had walked in as if he had the right— as if he hadn't been a complete prick who deserved whatever brake fluid they were serving at the new chain up the street— and his temper was heated. Theo's face must have conveyed the message for him because after sweeping his gaze over the bar once, the twat spun on his heel and walked right back out again.

He felt good about that. That his scowl had been enough to scare him away. But it didn't change the fact that he had tried to come in, clearly looking for the woman he had somehow broken months previously. She had just started to gain back some of that lost light, so seeing his smug face waltz through his door had launched Theo even further into his terrible mood. Brady just happened to trail in behind him with his stupid order.

The click of a camera sounded through the soft piano and strings echoing around the café. Then another, and another. Annoyed by the sound, Theo glanced up to find a mass of blonde hair, the sight softening him in an instant. He recognized the back of that head. The unmistakable honey-color and the silk ribbon nestled into soft looking strands. His relief lasted all of two seconds as he realized his own face was on her screen.

"Smile," Shannon sang as she captured a selfie of her sunshiny face, Theo scowling in the background.

"Why with the selfies? You don't post them; you don't print them. I'm almost certain you save them for demonic rituals that involve burning my face out of each one. Somehow shackling me to a life of high school students as applicants and a rapturous blonde for a manager."

"How do you know I don't post them, stalker?" His gaze begged the ceiling for patience as Shannon turned to face him, remnants of a smile still visible on her face. "I needed proof that you're the kind of Sexy Brit that broods over having to make flavored lattes."

He blinked, understanding evading him.

She could have clarified but, why break her routine? Instead, she circled the bar and joined him at the espresso machine. Standing way too close, looking way too dressed up, and holding way too much eye contact.

"Did you just come from church or something?"

Shannon snorted, grabbing the portafilter and helping herself to an espresso. No new guests came walking through the door, a fact he was painfully aware of as he released the other handle and began making his own beverage. His tatted arm almost brushing Shannon's smooth skin. The contrast their skin made annoyed him to no end.

"*Wow Shannon, you look lovely*. Why, thank you Theo. I just came from the park with my friends. In fact, I left right before Harper arrived, just so I could be here with you. Now I'm missing all the tea on how her sabbatical's going."

"What could she possibly report about a sabbatical? Knowing Harper, she's probably bored out of her mind."

Shannon steamed milk as her espresso poured smoothly into one of the café's soft blue mugs. He followed suit, his hands dwarfing the milk pitcher. He could feel Shannon's eyes on his tattoos like he did every time. Catching her looking was always a highlight of his day. She loved to feign disinterest for someone who stared as much as she did.

"Like what you see?" he asked, his face completely neutral as they both cleaned the steam wands and tapped the bubbles from their milk. "Oh and, wow Shannon, you look lovely."

"Thank you," she said with a wide smile. Fresh latte in hand, she turned to give him the full force of her perfect face. Blue eyes glowed with mischief as she sipped her beverage, staring at him over the cup's rim. He held the contact, lifting his own mug with one hand and sampling. He wasn't sure why they tortured themselves, he just new that when they got into these staring contests, they were usually completely random, had no clear rules, and he always lost. He hated losing, but at some point, her cerulean gaze would break him.

He should thank her for coming in on her day off. Offer up as many free pastries as possible so she continues to show up and save his ass. He knew what he *should* be doing, but instead he sipped, and stared. Contributing to their little power struggle for unknown reasons. He was doing pretty well too, until she said, "For the record, I like that you're the type of sexy Brit that broods into a vanilla latte."

Eyes closing on a sigh, he reluctantly accepted defeat.

CHAPTER THREE

Matchmaking is a delicate art form. It requires subtlety—grace. Small nudges and nonchalant words that, when delivered properly, ignite sparks between two people without them ever having noticed someone else's involvement in the first place. Two oblivious people finding love organically and experiencing their happily ever after. They would call it fate. Destiny. A gift from a higher being.

It was a humble expression. This at least, Shannon knew, valued, and practiced very well. One did not simply play with fate just to boast about it to any listening party. The illusion would be shattered.

Which was why, instead of screaming in the middle of the café and thrusting triumphant fists in the air, she widened her icy blue eyes, gazing at Harper in shock.

"You what?" she squeaked, voice rising at least two octaves. Her thick, blonde braid swung over one shoulder as she froze her clearing of a table, giving her friend the entirety of her focus.

Harper eyed her warily, hazel eyes tired and *almost* brimmed with moisture. If Harper Walsh ever cried, Shannon was sure tears were a heartbeat away. As it was, her friend was the chef owner of a three-starred Michelin restaurant with a work ethic that rivaled the Energizer Bunny. Her brand was terrifying and stoic, so tears would not be falling from those green eyes. Hell, she barely even ran a nervous hand through her cropped brown hair.

She couldn't believe Harper was opening up to her in the first place, but who was she to question the gifts of the universe? After ten years of living in San Francisco, one would think that Shannon would have more than two friends and a boss she semi-liked. She had always thought that was enough until Harper joined the fray. With Evie planning her wedding while running The Lennon and Benjamin working nights, she had been spiraling a bit. Harper joining their little group three years ago helped ease the trajectory of that spiral. Gave Shannon some purpose. She barreled into her life without warning, and although her walls were nearly impenetrable, she had been slowly chipping away at her new friend's stony exterior.

A thrill nestled into her chest as one of those walls collapsed and Harper said, "I sort of asked him to show me how to…" With a groan, she allowed her head to fall into her palms. "Shannon, I think I drunkenly asked my best friend to act out amorous scenes from his fairy-tale romance novels with me."

"Oh my fucking God," Shannon exclaimed, her eyes growing ever rounder in her head. That surprise was genuine. Her outburst drew more than a few glances from her guests as they sipped from light blue mugs.

She knew that pushing friends together was a dangerous game. What if it all went to shit and she ended up ruining a friendship forever? But Harper and Elliot belonged together. Everyone with literal eyes could see how she affected him— everyone but the woman herself, of course. Who better to bring Chef No-Nonsense out of her shell than her romance writing best friend? That, in itself, was a romance novel!

It is important to add that Shannon had read every single one of Elliot's novels, and if that man had half as much talent in the sheets as his characters did, Miss Walsh was a rich woman.

Her friend's eyes darted to the roasting room where Theo was undoubtedly glaring at the back of her head. He could glare all he wanted; it would not ruin her triumphant moment in the least.

"Tell me every, single, detail," she breathed, emphasizing each word.

As if Theo called upon demons from the underworld, the door to the café opened, bringing with it four highly under-caffeinated guests, their feet dragging as they made their way through the sage green chairs and oak tables. Maintaining eye contact, Shannon backed toward the counter, willing herself to ditch the matchmaking and do her actual job. She threw one parting glance at Harper, demanding she tell her in vivid detail exactly what her and Elliot discussed, before circling the bar and stepping behind the counter.

"Attend to your guests before you burst into flame," Harper said with a pointed look towards the roasting room.

She followed her gaze to the viewing window where Satan incarnate glowered over his monitors, a clipboard in hand to go along with that perma-frown. The machine was active, freshly roasted beans churned in the cooling drum while a batch of green coffee waited its turn. From the looks of it, Theo had a good four hours of roasting ahead of him. Maybe that was why he was particularly grumpy today.

She gave him her sweetest smile, her spirits rising when his frown deepened, and blew him a kiss before ignoring Lucifer completely and turning that saccharine smile to the guests.

Grumpy owner aside, Shannon loved working at the café. The space was small and intimate. Sage and natural wood worked harmoniously with the dark concrete walls and floors. It was always a little dark but like, aesthetically. She always thought it looked like a cozy, rainy afternoon in the space, regardless of the weather outside its large front windows. The main attraction was certainly the roasting room. All shiny stainless and intricate controls. The shelves lining the back were so organized, they could have been a simulation, and nothing beat the smell of freshly roasted coffee.

Then of course, there was the absolute beefcake of a roaster. Theo had no idea that most people sauntered into Bloem to watch him work, their morning buns merely a perk. Shannon could admit, he wasn't bad to look at. Being taller herself, he had to be at least six four the way he towered over her, with arms that could have been written about in poems, songs, salacious erotica—whatever. Large, muscled, and tattooed. Ink ran from his neck down to each finger, drawing the eye more than any of his actual work did. The fact that he always looked a bit disheveled only added to the allure. Although his auburn hair was clean-lined and begging to be cast as a Peaky Blinder, it was always slightly mussed.

Kinda like the man himself, Shannon thought as she began pulling shots of espresso for her sleepy guests.

The fact that her boss was hot as sin was great for business. Anytime his piercing, amber eyes deigned to rise from his work, an audible sigh moved through the café like the wave in a baseball stadium. She loved it for a lot of reasons, chief among them being that Theo would hate it if he knew. Anything that vexed Lucifer—or as she liked to call him, Lulu—generally made her exceedingly happy. The man had no idea how many of their patrons pined over him as he ignored every single one of them, roasting and baking his days away.

The thought pulled a broader smile to her face as espresso poured from both group heads, milk steaming in her held pitcher simultaneously.

If Theo Abbott ever decided to give up devil worship and actually be nice to people, they were all in trouble. She rested easy knowing they were all safe from his charms because frankly, he didn't have any. Broody, impatient, stubborn, and just about a hundred additional unsavory adjectives could be used to describe her boss, but his baked goods brought her closer to heaven than even her vibrator could, and the man knew coffee. Every espresso pulled was arguably the most perfect two ounces of liquid ever produced.

This is why after six years of dealing with his surly, British ass, she still loved her work. A lot could be said about Lulu, most of which was lukewarm at best, but no one could ever say he wasn't insanely good at what he did. But as it turned out, *what he did* excluded customer service. The café ran because Shannon showed up every morning at six a.m. to hedge any guest's questions about caramel macchiatos before Theo overheard. If any of their patrons actually spoke to him, it would take about five seconds before they stopped swooning over his accent and started frowning at his complete lack of charisma.

Snagging a light blue mug from the drip tray, she expertly poured steamed milk into the awaiting espresso, breaking up its crema and warming with pride as a perfectly layered heart bloomed in the foam. It never got old, seeing her hands create something beautiful and delicious and life-bringing and completely temporary. That tiny little latte was going to lend someone joy for about fifteen minutes—then it would be gone—a brief moment of happiness and relief provided solely by her.

And one she could actually take credit for.

She never meant to become a matchmaker—it just kind of happened. One of her regulars had been ranting about the hellscape of online dating while simultaneously gushing over an audiobook she couldn't stop listening to. Well, guess who knew the voice actor. And guess who *just so happened* to have tickets to a panel he was speaking on. Now guess who doesn't have to hear another word about Tinder Ted ghosting her after date three.

It had been a successful connection. One that Shannon had planned, set up, and executed all without anyone being the wiser. The feeling had been as intoxicating as that first whiff of espresso in the morning and damnit, she just couldn't quit it.

"What are you thinking about?"

Shannon jumped, the empty milk pitcher falling from her grip as she startled at Theo's familiar lilt. The sound that reverberated through the gentle typing and quiet chatter of the café was near deafening, drawing several startled glances her way.

"Christ, Shannon, are you trying to scare our clientele straight into the arms of Starbucks?"

"I'm sorry," she stammered, attempting to stop the pitcher from rolling beneath the sink with her foot. "If only you had announced your hulking presence before blasting into my daydreams." Despite her attempts, the pitcher rolled beneath the sink and out of sight, drawing an impressive sigh from her lungs.

"Daydreaming? I didn't realize that was part of your job description."

Narrowing her eyes, Shannon met the devil's gaze with barely contained annoyance. Nobody knew how to push her buttons quite like Theo Abbott, and even as her baby blues fought the urge to check out his crossed arms and the ink that covered them, she couldn't help but hate the sight of his furrowed brows and that fucking scowl.

"Daydreaming is good for company morale, Lulu," she said with the brightest smile she could fake. His frown deepened at the nickname, giving her more encouragement to push rather than serve as the warning it should have been. "It helps me push through the sadness that I feel anytime I actually catch sight of you through the viewing window. Would it kill you to crack a smile every now and again?"

"I'll crack a smile when its earned, *Lily*." Shannon's hackles rose as he threw her own nickname back at her. Lilith being Lucifer's demonic consort and all that. Although the idea of her being compared to a she-devil was absolutely ludicrous. Her life revolved around making people's days and the promise of happily ever afters.

Plus, she wouldn't marry Theo if her sin-filled, demonic, under-the-cover-of-darkness life depended on it.

Okay, so maybe she enjoyed pushing his buttons, but it couldn't be helped. Half the time, she truly didn't mean to press those buttons and the other half, he deserved it. It wasn't her fault that she was an unapologetic flirt with boundary issues...well, maybe it was, but the point remained that if he leaned into her flirtatious nature, they would all have more fun. Instead, she ended up with countless selfies of him scowling at the back of her head and nothing but staring contests to fill the time. An arrangement that had seemed to work for the past six years.

Still, she had to admit that his comment was the perfect, most strategic way to get under her skin. It grated on her that she was unable to pull a smile from his stony exterior.

"Is there something I can do for you Mr. Abbott?" she asked, knowing damn well how much it would annoy him. Sure enough, his jaw tightened, a tic in his tatted neck drawing her attention before it darted back to amber irises.

"I was just wondering if Harper was okay," he managed.

Shannon softened as she wrapped her head around the conundrum that was Theo. He and Harper knew each other of course, but she never thought it went beyond business. She purchased his coffee for the restaurant and was arguably his most loyal customer aside from Evie. That damn matchmaking itch tingled her skin because, why would he care if she was okay when he barely gave her a second glance most days?

Unfortunately for him, she had already made a match for Harper, and it certainly didn't involve him. None of her matches did.

"Why don't you ask her yourself? She…" Shannon trailed off as her eyes landed on the empty table where Harper had been on her video call seconds before. "That little snake!"

"What?"

"She was supposed to give me super juicy details about her *almost* hook up with her best friend," she whined, turning back to him in exasperation and *just* managing not to stomp her foot.

"I'm missing more of a story than I care to commit to," he said slowly, completely uninterested in the drama of the story like a full-on sociopath. "She just looked a bit upset, and I really don't want to lose another regular."

And there it was. More concerned about losing another coffee drinker than he was about her actual wellbeing. Typical Lulu behavior.

"Harper would rather sift through Yelp reviews than buy coffee from anyone else. Besides, she's asked me almost every day whether or not you're rolling out those pumpkin cinnamon rolls again. She's not going anywhere."

This earned her an eye roll and a frustrated hand through auburn hair.

"Seriously? It's barely August for Christ's sake."

"Speaking of," Shannon said without skipping a beat. "Where did you hide the fall decorations? I wanted to get a head start on turning this place into an influencer's wet dream." Knowing that phrase would earn her another wicked scowl, she returned to her work, dropping to her knees in search of the dropped pitcher. One hand just shy of touching Theo's boots, she felt around underneath the sink for the familiar feel of the stainless cup.

Theo's voice reached her from above. "Can we skip the circus act this year? We're trying to discourage the wide-brimmed hats from ordering crème brûlée lattes, not shower this place in décor that begs them to be obnoxious."

"It's not our job to yuck someone's yum, Mr. Abbott," she said, her fingers searching blindly for the pitcher. "If someone wants to pay you eight dollars for a sugar free pumpkin spice latte in their very own Yetti cup, you take the eight dollars and rest easy knowing it's the best damn PSL to ever touch their tongues. That's why you need me around."

"So you keep saying," he murmured, and that reluctant indifference was as big a win as she was gonna get.

"And it's true, I know how to do something you don't. Swallow…" Finally, her fingers connected with the handle of her downed milk pitcher. Snatching it up she rose to her knees; eyes closing on a sigh as her neck straightened in delicious relief. She stretched, head shifting from side to side until comfort was provided. "My pride."

Opening her eyes was a very strange experience. For one, she was face-to-crotch with her boss. It wasn't necessarily a bad view, but…well she didn't know what it was. Did Satan usually don well-worn jeans? If he didn't, he absolutely should.

The silence somehow broke the silence, and Shannon was suddenly hyper aware of her position. Slowly—mercilessly—her gaze wandered up, past the soft, dark cotton of Theo's shirt. Over the swirling ink on his neck, the stubble on his clenched jaw. Her eyes collided with his, severe as they stared down at her. She didn't move. Even as her knees screamed at her to disconnect from the hard concrete, she remained locked in a staring contest with Theo from her knees.

He swallowed, and her attention snapped to the bob of his throat. Without blinking, he held his hand out to her. Should she take it? Outside of their handshake upon her hiring, they had never really touched. It bothered her that all of their progress was happening while she was kneeling before him, but wasn't that typical? Or maybe it bothered her that she liked the view—just a little.

She-devil indeed.

"Excuse me?"

They both jumped out of their stare, Shannon slapping his hand away before launching to her feet. Theo tucked the hand directly into his stupid jeans before swiftly turning to the bakery case. Snagging a clipboard from the shelf, he began taking inventory of the baked goods as she turned to the guest that had interrupted…

Nothing.

Absolutely nothing had been happening, she told herself vehemently.

"Sorry about the wait," she said with a smile. "What can I get ya?"

Shannon fought back a groan as the woman set the largest Stanley she had ever seen on the counter. "Could I get a salted caramel macchiato with a pump of hazelnut—no whip?"

"A macchiato is a three-ounce beverage that—"

"Absolutely," Shannon exclaimed, cutting off Theo before he could lean into the pretentious barista stereotype too much. "That'll be eight seventy-five, please."

cHapTer Four

Theo had a few regrets in his lifetime. After thirty-eight years of rollercoaster hikes and dips, maybe he had more than a few. Luckily, most of his regrets either had a temporary effect on his life, or at least a solution to work for. That tattoo he got when he was eighteen came to mind, now covered by a delicate rose on the back of his bicep. Or he often thought about the year he allowed his seven-year-old nephew to eat every single piece of Halloween candy instead of dispersing it to him in manageable payments. After watching Sebastian Spider-Man through his living room for an hour, Theo had bucked-up, built the most ridiculous blanket fort and committed to an Avengers marathon in order to get the kid to come down from his sugar high.

He'd had his fair number of drunken nights, a couple of disastrous dates, and once attempted to change his own oil. Attempted, is the takeaway word from that sentence.

The point is, his regret never lingered too long. A solution would present itself in one form or another, and he would move on with his life without issue.

Until the day he hired Shannon Perry.

That regret still lingered in his bloodstream like a new cell, mutated from his constant annoyance and reluctant affection for the woman he spent more time with than his own family. Who knew the Devil would present as a sunshiny blonde with disgusting amounts of optimism and a cold-weather kink? He knew it was inappropriate at best to be thinking about his employee's kinks but inappropriate seemed to be the title of their relationship handbook.

It certainly was for him. The week had stretched on like any other with him stressing over accounting software and staring into the drum of the coffee roaster to unwind. But this week had provided a new thought that wedged itself between the budgeting and marketing strategies already roiling around in his relentless dome. Shannon. On her knees, *I know how to swallow* having just left her annoyingly pouty lips. The pause after that statement had lasted about a thousand years, tugging at a spot low in his stomach as he grappled with the view, her words—fucking everything that was Shannon.

The woman had officially reached expert level when it came to pushing his buttons. The reality of that hitting him hard as she accused him of hiding the fall décor from her for the tenth time in as many days.

"We have reached the third sunrise of August. The holidays are literally around the corner," she complained, her blue eyes round with shock. As if she couldn't believe he wasn't dropping everything to dance around the café, singing and throwing fake fall leaves around like a deranged flower girl.

"First of all, don't threaten me with the holidays unless you have a Xanax at the ready, my mental stability is hanging on by a thread." Theo weighed out ground coffee to a perfect eighteen grams before tamping them with just enough pressure. "And second, why do you always start speaking like a witch the minute the leaves begin to fall? Has it been two fortnights since you last charged your crystals or are you just in need of the ritual candles in that box so you can finally get back to hexing people?"

Locking the portafilter onto the machine, he pressed the brew button and watched as creamy espresso flowed from the spout, the aroma swirling to his nostrils with intoxicating affect. It never got old, the feeling that flooded his senses after he successfully processed coffee from start to finish. Not every roast was a success story, but they all had a special place in his heart. This one in particular was a roast he had handled with immense care. The green beans had been purchased from a sustainable, woman-owned coffee farm in Ethiopia. His intention was to donate to Grounds for Health with each bag sold, and Theo couldn't wait to see that stamp proudly displayed on each bag.

"Third sunrise!" Shannon sounded a bit hysterical, her eyes growing impossibly larger. "A hex will be the least of your worries if you keep withholding those candlesticks I bought last year."

"That wasn't an approved purchase," he grumbled before taking a sip from his espresso.

Christ, but it was delicious. Rich, creamy, and tart with notes of cherry and blueberry on the nose. The acidity was perfectly bright and balanced with a nice, sweet finish.

He pushed the cup toward Shannon, wordlessly offering her a sip. Without hesitation, she lifted it to her lips, drinking from the same spot he had. His gaze lingered as her lips closed over the rim, and a quiet hum of approval vibrated in her throat. A trace of crema clung to her cupid's bow, holding his attention a beat too long before he forced his eyes upward, fixing them on the rafters above her head. A small office could be found there, along with the dreaded fall décor. You had to cross the beams to get to the storage area and there was absolutely no way Shannon would be doing that anytime soon. The woman was barely able to get over her fear of heights to hang out in the office, let alone cross the distance of the café on planks of creaky wood.

She narrowed her eyes at him, the icy blue growing icier as she glared.

"You hid my candlesticks in the dusty, unstable attic, didn't you?"

"I didn't hide anything Shannon, I stored them. In the storage space." He paused as a grin spread across his face. "Where things are stored."

Shannon licked the foam from her lip, pulling his gaze again because apparently self control was a thing of the past.

"Well, can you go get it for me? I want to have the place decorated before the weekend."

Just then, the front door of the café burst open, and a flurry of activity cut off the "no" he was about to hand his employee with the biggest shit eating grin he could muster that early in the morning. He had to do something to take the power back.

Still glaring, Shannon's attention darted to the front door and immediately softened as his sister-in-law's voice cut through the empty café.

"I will only say good morning after at least three sips of coffee. Please tell me the machine is calibrated and ready to provide."

Krista Abbott balanced three bags as she made her way to the counter, a sleepy, gangly boy dragging behind her. Sebastian's auburn hair pointed in eight different directions, sleep lines still covering one cheek, and Theo was pretty sure his shirt was inside out. He supposed at twelve years old, six in the morning was a god-awful time to have to be awake and functioning.

"Yowza, what's this zombie creature you brought with you this morning?" Shannon asked, a smile brimming in her voice.

"A grounded one," Krista replied with a glower. Theo's attention snapped to her; brows raised in question. "Your

29

nephew decided to stay out with his friends until," she turned to Sebastian and clapped him on the shoulder. "What was it? Two?"

"In the morning?" He and Shannon asked simultaneously.

Krista nodded; her eyes scary as they burned holes into her son.

Theo fought back his concern as he casually took in the kid's appearance, looking for any sign of distress. His father was out of the picture, a train of thought Theo had to beat back more times than he cared to admit. The way his brother walked out of their lives would burn through his bloodstream if he let it, scorching the walls he had carefully constructed and burn his resistance to the ground. He needed that boundary. Needed the safeguards he had built around himself. Without them, the injustices in the lives of the people he loved would be too much to fully comprehend.

"I told you, I lost track of time," Bast grumbled, avoiding eye contact with Theo at all costs. The kid glanced around the café, before focusing on Shannon. "Where are your weird pumpkins?"

"See?" Shannon asked as he fought the urge to facepalm. "Even sleepy, grounded Bast misses my weird pumpkins."

Shannon began pulling a double espresso for Krista's usual quad shot latte. Her hands worked gracefully and efficiently, and Theo always had to fight the temptation to stare as her movements captivated him. It was like watching a ballet or something, each move executed perfectly.

"You can change the subject all you want, mate," he told Sebastian. "But I'm afraid we're having a little chat about this after school."

Shannon set a paper cup on the counter, Bloem's logo stamped proudly on one side. Maybe he was a big softy, but the delicate lines of the tulips, along with the sweeping cursive of his café's name always drew a sigh from him. For

30

someone who dodged aesthetic culture like snowballs, he couldn't deny the romance behind that logo. It drew you in.

Lately, it just hadn't drawn *enough* people in.

Refusing to go down that path without at least one more cup of coffee, he focused his attention on glaring at Sebastian who, not only broke curfew, but had the nerve to encourage Shannon's certifiable pumpkin obsession.

"I'll see you at three," he told him before adding sternly, "Right at three. If you aren't walking through those doors on the hour, I'll send Shannon after you."

"You wouldn't," Bast said, a look of mock terror on his face.

"He would," Shannon teased as she pumped chocolate sauce directly onto a spoon and popped it into her mouth. "And I plan on getting especially hopped up on sugar today."

"The horror," the kid mocked as he and his mom turned to leave. Krista merely shook her mane of black hair, clutching her coffee as they moved through the tables and chairs.

"Two in the morning," Shannon murmured as they watched the pair leave. Theo tried not to focus on the fact that no one came in behind them. He most likely wouldn't see another guest for a full hour or so. "Can you imagine staying out that late? To be around people?" She shivered, drawing his gaze.

"No offense Lily, but you don't exactly come off as the antisocial type. I'm pretty sure you've charmed, made friends with, and been asked out by ninety-five percent of the people that walk in here."

Shannon rolled her eyes as she straightened some pastries in the case. He had just finished baking the first round of scones and cookies, while the smell of those fucking pumpkin rolls wafted into the café as the new batch baked to golden.

"It's my job to charm people. If I didn't, walking in here would be like traversing the dunes of hell. Would you even put music on?"

He bristled. "Of course I—"

"I don't mean Bach's greatest hits, or whatever classical snooze fest you like to bore your eardrums with."

He ground his teeth. "Classical music has been shown to reduce stress, improve brain function, and decrease blood pressure."

"Would you say that's working well for you? She accompanied the question with fluttering lashes, and his jaw clenched ever tighter. "Because you can't even hear the word *caramel* without a persistent eye twitch to go along with your scowl."

Just in the nick of time, an alarm for the rolls began beeping from the large kitchen at their backs. That was perfect. The last thing he needed was an early morning brawl with Shannon when he had a million other things to do— including the hour he had carved out for budgeting.

Still, one more jab wouldn't hurt.

Standing to his full height, he took a step closer as she stocked the case with a reverence only reserved for his baked goods. The way she delicately transferred the items from tray to case nearly softened him enough to walk away. Nearly. He knew she could feel his closeness, saw it in the way her skin rippled with little bumps. "I thought it was your job to be charming," he murmured. Her thick blonde hair was twisted into a perfect bun on top of her head, giving him a clear view of the delicate skin now peppered with goose pimples. It was fascinating. He stood a good foot away, yet it was almost as if she could feel his eyes on her. He hoped she could, his glare was a particularly nasty one.

"It's my job to charm the guests, Lulu. There's nothing that says I have to be charming to you."

Closing the case, she stood straight and met his gaze. A smirk threatened his features as he watched her subtly stretch to her toes to gain a few inches. Losing battle. She could work in three-inch heels, and he would still have a couple of inches on her.

"Interesting concept for someone who can't seem to locate the fall décor." A grin worked its way over his mouth as Shannon gaped. "I would think that you would desire the favor of whoever could provide you with that disgustingly orange box of whimsy."

The timer could not be ignored any longer, and Theo felt the familiar jolt of happiness that came with a victory over the she-devil. Her glare could be felt on every inch of his back as he made his way to the kitchen whistling one of his favorite pieces from Debussy as he pulled a tray from the oven, the smell of pumpkin spice filling the air.

**

The man was infuriating. Shannon stared at the empty café over an induction burner; her eyes drawn to the sweet little bookshelf behind a cozy green couch as she mindlessly stirred pumpkin spice syrup. The day was perfectly cast in shadows, rain cascading in sheets beyond the large windows at the front of the space.

She liked what she did, managing the café. Things had slowed a bit over the past year or so with a larger chain opening around the corner, but taking on more of the workload truly didn't bother her. It was work she was good at. And lord knew Theo needed her help. The man was one pump of vanilla away from bursting into hellfire.

Actively avoiding the viewing window and glimpsing the man himself, she continued stirring the syrup with determination. If she wasn't going to be allowed to transform the space into a scarecrow's spank bank, she would at least raid the recipe books for every fall inspired syrup and blend she could find. Seeing those pumpkin cinnamon rolls had only fueled her need for kitsch even more.

The rain continued its steady downpour as she plucked the pot from a small electric burner and ran the syrup through a strainer, her movements clean and efficient. Maybe that was what drew her to the café so much. Everything had a place, a procedure, and a purpose. Theo may be a curmudgeonly old Brit with no vision and even less enthusiasm, but the man was organized. When he trained her on the espresso machine, every single thing had a place. Every towel, every pitcher. She loved that about her work. It was the ideal job for someone raised on the idea of perfection.

Shannon grew up with two older siblings who both followed in their parents' footsteps in one way or another. A surgeon and a lawyer which, aside from giving her the shivers every time she thought about it, made her practically crack her jaw from yawning. She loved her family, but the idea of poring over paperwork and jabbing people with needles made her recoil. Though her sisters often told her how proud they were and how much they enjoyed seeing her happy, Shannon could sense their confusion over her life choices.

Hospitality work wasn't real work in their eyes. And no matter how hard Shannon fought to be perfect, she couldn't shake the feeling that she was letting them down with each pull of espresso.

Rain hitting the sidewalk threatened to overtake the Bon Iver sailing through the café as the door opened and she finally had a guest to focus on.

"Hello," she threw over her shoulder, setting the hot pot safely aside.

"Hello yourself."

Shannon spun around, her gaze colliding with the soft brown eyes and chocolate hair belonging to that painfully familiar voice.

"Ryan," she breathed, her heart pounding a steady rhythm in her chest. "It's been a minute."

"Too long," he crooned, swaggering up to the counter with little to no self doubt. Never mind the fact that the last of his features to grace her line of vision was his back as he dressed in record time. Forget the detail that the last thing he said to her was a measly, "This was fun!" exactly as his phone pinged with an arrival notification from an Uber driver.

No, he looked like he didn't remember at all how he strung her along for an entire fucking year before taking her to bed, only to leave her empty and vulnerable.

"Can I get you a coffee?" she asked through a smile that hurt to produce.

"Soy milk latte," he replied with a wink. "And a promise."

"A promise?"

"Call me when you get off today."

It was a demand more than anything, and Shannon hated the little flip in her gut. A flip revealing her thrill at the idea of him wanting to talk to her, a detail she would absolutely never share with her friends. Benjamin had to console her for a full two months after Ryan left her high and dry, and Evie had threatened to wait outside of his workplace and put her kickboxing skills to good use. It wasn't a joke. Shannon knew that Evie would punch a man square in the jaw for less than what Ryan did to her, and one tear from her usually dry eyes had sent fire dancing in her bestie's irises for a full month.

But she didn't say any of that. In fact, she ignored her hurt feelings and skepticism, launching straight into smug satisfaction that he recognized his mistake. He wanted her back, and she absolutely loved it.

"Call you for what? Don't tell me you need help with the crossword again," she teased as her hands made quick work of his latte.

He chuckled, and she felt a small sense of triumph at having pulled the sound from him. For reasons unknown, she thought of Theo. Of how she never managed to force that scowl into a quick grin. "Not this time, although I had a particularly nasty one the other day that made me wish for your company. I've missed you."

Shannon couldn't help the smile that plumped her cheeks at that. God, she had dreamed of the day she saw him again. How she would swagger past without giving him a second glance. In her daydreams she had been clad in black leather—it didn't have to make sense—and had a large, tattooed man on her arm for emphasis. In her fantasies, she had always been bad Sandy to his fuckboy Danny.

In hindsight, she should have known her guts would betray her and get all mushy as soon as he flashed one of those lopsided smiles. The second that stupid dimple appeared she was cooked like the pumpkin syrup behind her. Melting into a puddle of fall spices and brown butter.

"Then what could I possibly do for you?" she asked in a voice that may have been a little embarrassing had anyone been around to hear it. No, Evie would never EVER know about this interaction as long as she lived.

"Well," he said, drawing out the word.

"Alright mate?" Shannon's mind nearly turned to Swiss cheese at the sound of Theo's monotoned greeting cutting through her magical moment. What the hell was he doing out from the confines of his roastery?

Ryan nodded to a space behind her in greeting before kindly ignoring that spot and focusing on her once more. He made a show of sipping from the latte and stuffing a dollar tip into a vase next to the register. The smile she sent him was super impressive, it wanted to be a frown so badly.

They didn't take tips at Bloem, a stance that Theo had insisted on from the beginning. In his opinion, the tipping system was an ancient American custom built solely on racist foundations. Shannon had been sold the minute he told her he wanted to be a positive change for the industry in any way he could. She had practically swooned at the way "Oppressive wage gap" and "Dismantle archaic restaurant policy" had flowed from his lips in that damn accent.

That had been before she knew him. Before he embraced darkness and let his inner demon out of its cage. After working with the man for years, she saw right through that ridiculously deep British accent, past the promise of a tip free income and straight to the heart of her recurring nightmare—the one where he denied her God-given right to slather the café in cinnamon sticks and hay. Straight through to the realization that Theo Abbott, although admittedly a great mentor, was a fucking bummer. He frowned at puppies, scowled at children, and despised the holidays.

And—shocking no one—he was bulldozing what had been a very promising reunion.

"I was hoping you could help me out with something," Ryan said, his lopsided smile returning in all its glory.

"Sure," Shannon said way too quickly. Her cool was officially depleted as her gaze ran over the face of a man who had put her through hell. She wasn't dumb. She knew what he wanted from her. But maybe this time would be different. He seemed genuinely happy to see her, and lord knew she was in a drought from hell. There was no way she would be admitting to a soul that she hadn't slept with anyone since he left her naked and alone in that ritzy hotel. She didn't need that kind of negativity in her life.

"Can't I'm afraid."

Shannon nearly choked on air as she registered that Theo was not only still there, but he had just inserted himself into their conversation. Wide eyed, she snapped her head around to gape at her boss.

"What?"

"You have to stay late tonight," he said casually, leaning against the counter as his gaze found everything but her eyes. He crossed his arms over his chest and Shannon fought weird urges like she did every time. Urges that begged her to drink in tattoos covering flexed muscles.

"For what?"

A muscle ticked in Theo's jaw just before he narrowed tawny eyes on her.

"To decorate," he said through gritted teeth.

She smiled her most sugary smile at him, praying it blinded. "I thought you didn't want to decorate this year."

"I changed my mind," he said, smiling sweetly back. It was the fakest smile she had ever seen in her natural born life, there and gone as if she had imagined it.

"I'm sure that can wait, right? Doesn't seem like this place has a line out the door..." Ryan trailed off as his gaze drifted around the empty café and she experienced an involuntary wince as his insult landed. "Shannon will have plenty of time to do it tomorrow."

That's when she knew she hadn't been working in hell after all. Because as Ryan confidently told her boss that his business was a joke, she felt the ground open and swallow her into its inky black depths.

Her eyes drifted back to Theo, so she saw the rage burn through his features. Witnessed him slowly stand to his full height and tracked his every step toward the register. His arm brushed hers as he stood right next to her, towering over them both, an odd look covering his face.

Shannon fixated on swirling ink instead. Stars and constellations that spanned one side of his neck all the way from jawline to where they disappeared below his crisp black shirt. Like the universe being swallowed by a black hole. A delightful alternative to her current circumstances.

"That's okay," she said, eager to get Ryan away from the ticking time-bomb beside her. She suddenly didn't feel all that excited about their meeting. In fact, she felt an overwhelming desire to defend the café and the man running it. "I'll call you tomorrow."

"She won't be doing that either," Theo said cheerfully.

Shannon's spine felt ready to snap.

"What?" Apparently, that was the only response she could pull off as she searched for a reasonable explanation for whatever was happening. All she was really taking in was Ryan's annoyed face and the fact that Theo's odd expression turned out to be an actual smile. The Devil was smiling.

Nothing good could come from that.

To his credit, Ryan kept his mouth shut as Theo pressed a couple of buttons on the register. "Yeah, Shannon won't be calling you. And after you pay for this drink, you are never welcome back, so she also won't be seeing you. You're going to need to build that vocabulary up since she will never be around to help you with those crossword puzzles again. Feel free to start that journey by snagging a book from our free library on the way out.

"Now, we don't take tips because generally, that implies that we need you to tell us we've done a decent job—which we don't. I already know that Shannon is exceptional at what she does, the same way I know, deep in my marrow, that she is way too good for some finance bro with bad manners and even worse dairy preferences." Theo made a show of plucking the dollar from her vase and setting it on the counter as Shannon's eyes felt ready to pop from her head. "So, putting that towards your beverage, you owe me four dollars. Unless you'd like to tack on one of our delicious pumpkin cinnamon rolls."

Shannon was fully aware that her mouth was hanging open but fuck if that mattered in the slightest. Theo still held his smile firmly in place, venom practically leaking from his mouth. What was this behavior? He was a pit viper wearing the face of a friendly barista. Service with a smile as he handed out vague threats and not-so-vague insults.

"What the hell, Shan?" Her shocked face found Ryan; his cheeks red as he pulled more money from his wallet and tossed it on the counter.

"I'm sorry…"

"Cheers," Theo responded, his voice sugar coated.

She finally snapped out of her trance in time to watch the familiar sight of Ryan's back as it moved farther and farther away from her. As if on cue, lightning lit the streets outside, thunder following close behind as the door closed behind a very angry, very rigid man.

Her Swiss cheesy brain simply could not.

"What the shit?" she asked at the same time Theo said, "*Sorry?*"

"Why would you ever apologize to that soy milk of a human?"

"That doesn't even make sense," she spat, her anger finally managing to break through the stupor.

"The hell it doesn't. That man is bland, bitter, and probably can't remain stiff long enough to be satisfying."

Shannon's lip twitched despite herself. Who was this man? The morning had been chugging along like any other. Starting with her fighting with Theo over fall décor, and she had hoped it would end with her getting what she wanted like she did every time. Never had she expected whatever hellscape she had wandered into now, where her boss was privy to her embarrassing past and making dick jokes.

"Ryan is a friend of mine, and you just went all Gordon Ramsay on him."

"Friend." Theo somehow managed to make the word sound utterly disgusting. "That man has the personality of a fucking crumb."

"Remember when I asked for your opinion? Me neither." She ran an agitated hand over her bare neck. "You had no right to kick him out of here like that, what did he ever do to you?"

"I think we both know it's what he did to you that bothers me, Lily girl."

Her anger flared even brighter because, fuck this guy. Her and Theo weren't close. There was no thread of reality in which she would have shared how her heart was broken as he braided her hair. The two of them consuming inhumane amounts of Twizzlers.

"First of all, this is my life, Lulu. It is none of your business how I spend my time outside of these walls. If I want Soymilk to warm my sheets, then I'll do just that. You didn't have a problem with it before." She hadn't realized that they had moved even closer, the toes of her shoes nearly connecting with his as she glared up at him. No trace of that idiotic smile remained on his evil face, just the familiar scowl she had seen every day for the past six years. Thankfully, his arms remained at his sides, not a single muscle rippling and drawing her attention.

"Additionally," she said before she could focus on how her voice was one hitch away from yelling at her boss. "You clearly think you know what happened here, and that's fine. Make your judgements. But I don't understand why you're so worked up when you have literally never cared about me before."

A strange look overtook his features before he schooled them again and damnit, crossed his arms at the chest. Those ink covered biceps were a weapon. They should come with warning tags and flashing lights. *May cause distraction while attempting to win an argument.*

"Nothing to say? No apology for barreling in here and ruining whatever chance I had of…" she searched for a safe-for-work term for fucking. "Reconnecting with Ryan?"

A star pulsed on his neck; no doubt caused by the vice-like clench of his jaw. He leaned in even closer, and the air left the room. He was crowding her. Sucking the available oxygen into his own lungs instead of saving some for her struggling airways.

"I'm not going to apologize for getting in between you and that little prick," he said quietly, precisely. "I saw the way you moped around the café last time, as if he had any right to breathe the same air as you let alone steal the sunshiny rainbow spears you blast into every single one of our guests."

Shannon's brows straightened out as confusion spread through her chest. Moped? Yeah, she fucking hated that he said that, but the follow-up was too unexpected. She could do nothing but stare as Theo continued on through clenched teeth, looking for all the world like the words were causing him pain.

"Why you even gave him an ounce of your light is beyond me, and maybe this is me overstepping, but I won't watch you flicker out again." His words clipped off, The Lumineers suddenly the only sound filling the space aside from the gasp that escaped her parted lips.

"What the fuck, Theo?" She was never one to mince words, but this question whispered from her throat rather than demanded the answers she sought. An alarming desire to touch him tingled her fingertips as she watched his jaw work, mouth stubbornly drawn shut without any sign of opening and spilling more damning words over her again.

And it didn't.

Without another word, as if it were the most natural thing in the world for him to spit his feelings at her—to say she had *sunshiny, rainbow spears*—he spun on his heel and stomped away. Leaving her alone with affections that had no business warming her body.

CHAPTER FIVE

His fury was alive and well. After watching Shannon's ex saunter into the café, Theo felt the familiar beast rage in his gut, caged until he could no longer stand the sight of him leaning into her space, touching her hand, looking in her general direction, breathing her fucking air.

He knew more of their history than he cared to…how could he not? Aside from the fact that Shannon didn't take a single selfie that week, didn't joke or prod or call him Sexy Brit once, her friends had made it his problem whether he wanted to get involved or not. And annoyingly, what should have been a relief inducing break from her incessant teasing became a loss he couldn't describe. Comparing it to a loss of limb was a bit extreme, but…

He had decided to stay out of it. Keep his thoughts to himself like he always did and hold Shannon at a very platonic, very safe distance. Until Evie swung into the safe space of his café and blasted his staying-out-of-it to dust.

"It's like he's doing voodoo or something," Evie had exclaimed. "He's hypnotized her into thinking he's a French fry when he's actually one of those shriveled potatoes with that green hue that will most likely poison you."

"Uh huh," Theo had said. "And why is this any of my business?"

"Because I need you." She replied while pulling her dark hair into a lopsided bun on the top of her head. It was a move he had seen a million times while she worked at the café. "Shannon must be protected."

"I'm fairly certain she can take care of herself."

Evie waved a hand in dismissal. "So can I, but that doesn't change the fact that she has shown up for me when I needed guidance. Whether I asked for it, or not."

He had met her rich brown eyes directly, completely unfazed by the intensity he found there. Although he didn't care for the little prat, there was no way he was getting involved in Shannon's personal life. It was inappropriate and wholly out of character for him.

"He told her she needed a real job," Evie threw at him.

Theo's blood went from tepid to a rolling boil in one point five seconds. He leaned over the café table, completely ignoring the new guests that walked in the door.

"He what?"

"Yes," she breathed, her eyes shifting from side to side as if Shannon would pop out at any moment and catch her in this betrayal. "After talking about himself for a thousand dates, he asked her if being a barista was her *real job*. He couldn't believe that she worked here for a living. Kept asking if she was going to school or what she intended to do in the future. Remember when she started those evening classes at the community college?"

"She took those classes because some potato asked her what she wanted to be when she grew up?"

Evie responded by throwing her hands in the air, point proven. "His male-rage brain can't process the idea of hospitality as a career. He treats her like she's beneath him, and I can't watch her lose her confidence again, Theo. She is so much better than—"

"I'll take care of it," he had cut in before adding, "With pleasure."

That was how he ended up in the roasting room after exposing way too much and saying far too little, cheeks still burning with anger from watching Ryan drop that dollar into Shannon's vase. The asshole just wanted control over her. As if his opinion was worth a shit. He probably couldn't even consume a chocolate covered coffee bean without choking on it, let alone manage any task Shannon pulled off seamlessly on a daily basis.

That thought actually brought a small twitch to the corner of his mouth as he continued to monitor his progress. Coffee shuffled in the machine as toasty aromas drifted all around him. Even their mesmerizing shift as they slowly roasted didn't soothe the ache left behind by Shannon's sad eyes. Dvořák's "Serenade for Strings" soared from the corner speakers, echoing off the walls and over the sounds of turning drums and mingling beans.

Haunting string instruments couldn't even bring him out of his roaring anger.

Having already spent a good chunk of his morning poring over the books, punching numbers, and actively trying not to panic, the last thing he had needed was potato boy waltzing into his failing café. Theo knew that he would be involuntarily pulling up the image of that smug face looking around his empty business with disdain. In his daydreams, he pummeled that smirk from his mouth before tipping his hat (he's wearing a hat for some reason) to Shannon and strolling back to the roasting room.

In reality, he had left about a hundred things unsaid before storming off like a man-child.

A dramatic sigh heaved from his gut as he watched the ever-shifting color of his roasting green beans, his thoughts shifting from his Shannon conundrum to his failing business conundrum. What was he going to do? He had chatted with Krista for hours over the weekend, discussing the very real possibility that he may have to cut his losses and sell the roastery. His chest ached at the thought. Putting a price tag on his life's work, on twelve years of pushing, sacrificing, and alienating himself from his friends and family, seemed like an impossible task.

What would his mum say when he told her all her efforts to get him to America were for nothing? Well, with all the uncertainty in his life Theo at least knew exactly what she would say. Something starting with how proud she was no matter what and ending with him moving back to the UK. He knew he was in trouble when that idea didn't elicit his usual reaction of shivers from his head to toes.

The number of turtlenecks his mum would force him to wear would be insufferable. She never did take a liking to his tattoo obsession.

Another indulgent sigh wrenched free as the roasting reached its critical moment. The machine would require his absolute focus for the next ten minutes or so as the chances of over-roasting the beans were high in the last leg. No more thoughts could be spared for his miserably low bank account or his dwindling savings. Selling the café would have to be pushed aside along with the burning ache he felt when he thought about missing the space in the dark hours of morning. Missing the sound of the espresso machine coming to life. Of Shannon's snarky, candy-coated greeting—always the first one to walk through the door.

He shoved it all aside, and didn't even notice the dimming of the café or the echo of his music as it cut off to a silent space. Didn't notice his manager leave without saying a word.

***

46

Shannon loosed her hair from its bun, raking cold fingers through the strands before she walked into the bar. It wasn't Ben's bar. He worked in the Castro—a fact that she relentlessly kept reminding herself of as she stepped through the ancient wood door and scanned the bar stools in search of Ryan. After Theo's…let's say *confusing* reaction, she didn't need a run-in with her roommate to top things off.

A sweet little voice echoed in her head. It asked her why she was so adamant about not bumping into her friends. Could it be that she feared their judgement? And maybe if she recognized that, she could recognize that what she was doing was moronic and the literal definition of insanity. That maybe what she was feeling was guilt about leaving the café without a single word to Theo after he clearly just thought he was helping, and…

Shannon's attention snagged on a familiar waffle knit polo. The baby blue stood out in a sea of black and gray. This bar was notoriously packed with industry folks, and the familiarity of the neutral uniform gave her confidence as she skirted patrons complaining about lunch services and needy guests. Her rain-soaked shoes squeaked slightly on the sticky floors, drawing more than a few eyes her way. She avoided them all like a coward. Anyone could be a spy for Evie…

That was an insane thought.

"You look like you're on another planet," she teased, taking the stool next to him. The bar was dark and quiet save for the Wu-Tang echoing from a brightly lit jukebox that clashed with its dark surroundings. The perfect setting for her strange mood.

"I've never been to this bar before," he admitted before taking a sip. He didn't smile at her in greeting and barely managed to look her way at all. Clearly, he was still upset by his interaction with Theo. She didn't blame him. And although she had her own issues with Lulu at the moment, the annoyance she felt earlier in the day didn't resurface.

When she tried, all her brain managed to produce was Ryan's bored face glancing around the empty café.

Clearing her throat, she stiffly shuffled that reel from her mind. "Thank you for meeting me. I wanted to apologize for Theo's behavior. I swear, I don't even know why he said those things, and it—"

"He seemed to think I had done something wrong," Ryan cut in. "Jesus, he said I didn't deserve you, Shan. Why would he have said that?"

Oh, she didn't know. Maybe it was because he had ghosted her after a year of buildup. "I have no idea, I swear." She lied; the words tasted bitter on her tongue. Fixing whatever had broken between them was rapidly shifting lower on her priorities list. "He and I don't talk about personal stuff, so I've genuinely—"

"I mean, what did you say to him, then? Because he seemed to have a lot of opinions about me. It's like he thought we were dating or something. Like I broke your heart, as ridiculous as that sounds."

Shannon blinked, either from the second interruption or from his statement, she wasn't sure which was causing more surprise.

"Right," she murmured. Catching the eye of the bartender, she ordered a gin and tonic, hoping to hell it was a strong one. "Like I said, I didn't tell him anything about you. I'm just as confused as you are."

"Okay," he said slowly, still refusing to look at her.

"The man can't even be bothered to tell me I have food in my teeth," she snapped, her words growing frantic as she wrestled with conflicting feelings of anger and tenderness towards her boss. "He's never been interested in what happens to me. Ever," she added, driving her point home more to herself than anyone. "Last spring, when I had that flu from hell and was bedridden for five days, he called me once. And the lead topic was when I would be returning to work."

She had been miserable. Aside from the fact that every hair follicle hurt, she couldn't stand being that still for that long. Feeling useless was not an option for Shannon Perry.

"But I didn't come here to drone on about Lulu. I'm sorry he made you uncomfortable, I promise you the devil works in mysterious ways because I have no idea where that came from—"

"He wants you. He clearly feels threatened by me."

Shannon nearly shot gin from her nose at *that* interruption. Palm slapping at her chest, she coughed as his words fell flat one by one into her brain. She didn't know where to start. Every fiber of her being wanted to begin by debunking the theory that Theo could *ever* feel threatened by Ryan—a man he had compared to soy milk no more than a few hours ago.

Then there was the other thing. *Theo Abbott Wants Shannon Perry* was the title of some Chad's conspiracy theory cooked up from his parent's basement for clicks. It was a ludicrous idea.

"That's hilarious," she managed. The bartender wordlessly plopped a glass of water in front of her as she worked through her coughing fit. "But alas, the mystery still continues because that is not why Theo got involved."

"Well, I hope not because that would complicate things for me," he said, finally turning to face her.

All of Shannon's blurring thoughts focused in the blink of an eye, her heartbeat a steady rhythm in her chest as she fought against her immediate giddiness. This was where he apologized for ghosting her, admitted he had been miserable for the past six months and begged her forgiveness. In the fantasy version of this moment, she had been in black leather and heavy eyeliner. Her eyes glanced down in a quick once-over. The white blouse tucked into high waisted black jeans had a Peter Pan collar, and she was almost certain the rain had made her hair a little frizzy.

Close enough.

"How would that complicate things?" she asked, playing along.

His smile was lopsided, and completely effective. "Come on Shannon, it's obvious I came in today for a reason."

Her stomach fluttered as she took a small, steadying sip from her drink. She didn't want to seem overeager, but the grin that threatened her lips couldn't be held off for long.

"I know that…" he paused as if searching for the right words. "I know that things didn't end well between us. But you know I care about you, right? And I think you care about me."

She nodded. This wasn't the groveling of her fantasies, but it was doing it for her, nonetheless. Still, the grin didn't break to the surface as he went on, and she thought that deserved a little pat on the back.

"I knew something was wrong when you didn't reach out, and I swear, when I saw the listing, my heart just stopped. Things were rocky, but I thought we were still friends, Shan. I knew there had to be a reason why you didn't tell me first."

She cocked her head, brows drawing together. He lost her.

"Tell you what?" She asked, as her mind tried to catch up. So, things were going off the rails a bit, nothing she couldn't fix…

"That the café space is for sale," he said simply, that lopsided smile still in place.

She blinked, ignoring his grin and desperately trying to understand what he was talking about.

"What café?"

His smile dimmed. "Are you serious? You know that Cliff has been trying to secure that building and it would be huge for my career if I managed to help him. I asked you to tell me if Lulu showed you any sign of putting it on the market."

50

"Theo," she snapped, suddenly possessive over the nickname. It was fun when she said it. Hearing it from Ryan's mouth as he tried to take her café away was decidedly not cute. The minute he brought his overeager, real estate developing, dick of a boss into the conversation, she knew exactly what he was here for, and it had nothing to do with an apology.

Ryan had tried to convince her to nudge Theo into selling his building months ago. His pitiful attempts had been a huge waste of time of course, because Shannon would embrace the fires of hell as a new vibe before ever encouraging Lulu to get rid of the café. That space was her safe haven. The only place where she felt comfortable—confident. She hadn't been about to give that all up so fuckboy Ryan could turn it into a CVS or some shit.

Her brain zipped past irritation and hurt to focus on his earlier statement. "What listing? Did Theo put Bloem on the market?"

Ryan cocked his head, then took a slow sip from his beer that drove her absolutely insane. Twisting her mother's wedding band with stiff fingers, her knee bounced impatiently as all of her previous desires melted into a distant dream. It was so funny how quickly obsession could evolve into vexation. If "I want you" had spilled from Soymilk's mouth rather than "you owe me," this would be a completely different scenario. But that was hardly an important topic as the café's future sat hanging in the balance. Theo's future.

Her future.

"He didn't tell you? The listing was sent to us by his real estate agent this morning. The price is outrageous, but we're willing to work with him. I was hoping you could help me with that." He rested his hand on her bouncing knee and gave it a little squeeze. A heartbeat ago, the contact would have thrilled her. Now, as Shannon grappled with the very real possibility that Bloem could soon belong to him, Ryan's touch felt cold and wholly unwanted.

She slowly turned in her stool, breaking the connection and nodding to the bartender, wanting—no needing—to get out of there. Hopefully, she could catch Theo before he left for the day and confront his brooding face. Things were slow, she knew that, but giving up was not an option. Maybe he simply needed to hear it from her. Maybe he needed someone in his corner.

Maybe he needed a swift kick in the ass.

The bartender hit her with a total and she reached for her bag, snagging the cash in three seconds and setting it on the bar in an organized stack.

"Wait, where are you going?" Ryan demanded as she stood. He made to reach for her arm and Shannon danced from his hand, unwilling to feel that touch again. The man should have known that even after all that he did, after a full year of dates that focused solely on him, after finally having intimate, albeit mediocre sex just to be left vulnerable and broken, the one thing she would not tolerate was someone fucking with her café.

"Did any of this mean anything to you? Of course not," she answered without waiting for a response. "You never cared about me. And you know what? I deeply regret wasting time in your sheets, faking orgasms and giving you everything. You didn't deserve it, even if it was some of my best acting."

Shannon whirled and bolted from the bar; a sputtering Ryan left in her wake. Forgetting the umbrella, she launched herself into a steady sheet of rain, ignoring the way it dampened her clothes in seconds. Instead, she allowed the cold moisture to zip her thoughts into focus, feet splashing through puddle after puddle as she readied herself to confront Lucifer.

CHaPTer SIX

Shannon's chest heaved as she thrust her key into the front door of Bloem and entered the empty space. Classical music and gentle light spilled from the roasting room, and muscle memory alone provided Shannon with enough brain power to lock the door behind her before marching straight to the viewing window, glare firmly in place. She didn't care how crazed she looked, soaking wet and absolutely fuming. That giant, bullheaded Brit was going to get an earful before the day was done.

He wasn't there.

Shannon took in the motionless machine and empty space before deciding to try the kitchen. Light spilled into the café from the roasting room, casting the space in shades of gray as she navigated around the counter and through the curtains into the large kitchen. She was met with clean stainless steal countertops; the morning buns she had helped mix were shaped and rising in the floor to ceiling proofer. Theo was a mad man, baking late into the night just to show up bright and early the next morning to bake off the more delicate items and decorate before submitting to the roasting room for hours. But the man himself was not in the kitchen.

Not losing a second of momentum, Shannon swept from the kitchen, barely managing not to stomp her feet. "Theo," she called, her voice echoing in the empty space. There was no response as she cruised past the bathroom and rounded the corner for the stairs, ascending to her least favorite place in the café. The flash of lightning could not have been timed any better as she clogged up the steps reaching the small office space just as thunder clapped.

Hair clinging to her skin, eyes wild with anger, she must have looked truly terrifying. Good, that's exactly what she was going for…

Empty. The office was empty, a small lamp providing the only light in the cramped room.

If you could even call it a room. The office was a small, loft-like shoebox that barely housed a tiny desk, two filing cabinets and a compact set of lockers for the staff. You could see the entire café through the rafters. A measly two-foot-high wall was all that kept you from walking over the edge and falling directly on top of the espresso machine.

She hated heights and avoided the office when possible, but that thought had been the last on her mind in her determination to yell at her boss. She backed up a couple of steps, her back finding the wall. He was probably at the shop around the corner picking up supplies. Well, that was just fine, she would sit there and spiral until he came back.

Why would he sell the café? She knew business wasn't exactly great, but he had enough wholesale accounts to keep him roasting day and night, surely there was another solution. Her anger was momentarily redirected to the god-awful chain up the street. Why had they chosen a location two fucking buildings up from them? They had the entirety of San Francisco to house their terrible coffee, why directly compete with a small business?

Shannon took a daring two steps forward, gazing down at the dark café through the ceiling beams. She knew each table like her own face, knew each chair and where they wouldn't wobble on the concrete floors. She knew every loyal patron. The folks that contributed to the bookshelf with unwavering dedication and would never ask her to make hazelnut raspberry macchiatos if their lives depended on it. Her eyes began to burn as she thought about all of the selfies she had taken with Lulu glaring in the background. All of her dick jokes as he showed her how to roll cinnamon buns. Helping Bast with his homework at the window table or buying something obnoxious to add to the décor.

Eyes brimming with moisture, she lifted her gaze to the storage space across the rafters. Maybe if she spruced the place up a bit, ratcheted up the social media and announced a fall drink special, it would bring in more guests. Perking up at the prospect of having a task, she took another step, bringing shaky legs in contact with the small barrier that separated her from a miserable death. Okay, so it may just break a couple of bones, but still! A shiver coursed down her spine as she peeked over the edge.

"Come on Shannon," she whispered to herself, shaking her hands out as if her nerves would simply fling from her limbs. This was a promising idea. She'd snag the fall decorations and have this place covered in burnt orange and chocolate brown by the time Theo got back. Yelling at him for keeping her in the dark would be exponentially better if she were surrounded by candles and glitter.

Then, she would hit him with a grocery list of reasons not to sell.

Puffing her chest with a deep breath, Shannon gave herself zero time to think before swinging nervous legs over the wall and easing into a sitting position, her feet dangling over the edge. Slower than she would ever admit to, she lowered herself onto a plank, bouncing a little to test its strength.

The storage space wasn't too far, she would have to cross the length of the café which looked to be about eight beams away. The box she needed was in the very front, staring at her amongst the extra cups and gift bags as if taunting her to cross. She knew an easier route would be waiting until Theo grabbed a ladder, but time was of the essence.

With one last deep breath, she pushed from the wall and stood on the first joist, her gaze never leaving the small beam of wood in front of her.

"Okay, okay," she breathed, not looking down for even a second. "Just focus on the next step."

She did focus on the next step, and the next, and the next until her feet landed safely on the other side of the café. Her hands shook as she plucked the box from the ground in triumph. Okay, that had been easier than she thought. Confidence soaring, she balanced the box in her arms and stepped onto the first beam for her trek back to the office. Rain continued to smack against the windows as she took one, then two careful steps.

A timer sounded from the kitchen, and Shannon was vaguely aware of someone turning it off. Of the sound of the proofer door opening and distant whistling keeping time with whatever orchestral phenomenon was sailing from the roasting room speakers. She simply didn't have time to think about it. Four steps from the office's blissfully solid ground, lightning lit the café in a silver flash, three full seconds of brilliant light shone on the next joist until, to her horror, the café went dark. Shannon froze as the power went out and she was met with an unforgiving darkness. The small whimper that left her lips was drowned out by the following thunder and a curse sounding from the kitchen below.

"Theo," she called, or at least tried to. His name left her lips as barely more than a whisper while she balanced on the joist, her imagination providing sounds of creaking wood to go along with the rain.

For some reason, rapidly blinking her eyes did nothing in the way of adjusting to the pitch black. It was no use. The next step was impossible to see.

Below her, Theo appeared from the kitchen, a small circle of light moving with him. Hope flared in her stomach at the sight of him, grumbling something incoherent under his breath. Barely daring to breathe, she tried again. "Lulu."

Gaze still locked on the alleged next step, she missed his jump, then the frantic swing of his phone as he searched for her. "Lil? Jesus, you scared the life out of me. I thought you left."

The swing of his light was barely visible as her eyes began to fill with tears. The box shook in her arms as she desperately tried not to panic, or sob, or make any sudden movements that would lead to her untimely demise.

"Where are you?" Theo's light had moved from behind the counter and into the café, causing Shannon's anxiety to lift off as he moved further away from her.

"I'm up," she managed as a sob escaped her lips.

"Shannon," he sounded strange, almost pained as her crying became harder to hide. "Are you alright?" His light followed her crying until, after what felt like a lifetime, beams of dull illumination lit the step before her.

"Jesus fuck," he exclaimed. "Stay where you are."

"Obviously," she said through her tears, her body trembling uncontrollably. She was going to die. Her stubborn desire for Autumn leaves and pumpkin spice was going to be her downfall. Literally.

Relief flooded her body when Theo's light mounted the stairs, and he ran directly towards her. His phone illuminated a laughable radius, but it was arguably more than she had before. Gaze immediately seeking out his, she searched for the familiar tawny irises but saw nothing, his face completely blocked by the light of his phone. Probably for the best as she missed the pained expression and utter panic in his features as he took in her circumstances.

"Okay, let's get you over here, and then I'll yell at you," he said, throwing one leg over the wall.

She nodded, tears streaming silently down her cheeks.

"Step one is to ditch the box; it's not doing you any favors."

Her eyes went round in her head as she clutched tighter to the dreaded cardboard. How were they certain it wasn't what was keeping her balanced?

"Shannon," Theo tried gently. "It's not worth the risk. Toss that bloody thing into the café and focus on the steps. I'll light your way."

She shook her head, every muscle pulled way too tight. She couldn't move. It was as if all of her earlier momentum had vanished with the lights. Her blood had been completely replaced by an icy cold fear, pumping through her veins and freezing her to the spot. Another tear slid silently down her cheek, and she squeezed her eyes shut, willing the lights to return when she dared open them again.

"Open your eyes, love," Theo said softly. She did, and relief washed over her after realizing he had shifted the light, her gaze finding his and holding on for dear life. "Keep them on me. I'm coming to get you." He made to throw his other leg over the wall, but Shannon squeaked her protest. What if the joists couldn't manage both of their weight? He was a complete bull of a human, there was no way she was sharing a dusty old beam with him. To his credit, Theo didn't move an inch. He held the phone aloft, the dim glow barely reaching her as she steadied herself for another step.

Every single inch of her trembled as she managed to look down at the next plank. Slowly, she stepped onto it, wobbling slightly as the contents of the box shifted in her arms.

"Christ," Theo whispered, panic lacing his tone. "That's good. You're doing great. Two more steps, love."

It was three, but nobody needed that kind of discouragement. Eyes glued to her next destination, she stepped forward, legs shaking as they fought their desire to collapse.

"Good girl. Keep going, just like that." Theo's voice was getting more and more frantic as she zeroed in on her next step. The box was rattling as if a living animal had been awoken amongst the garland and candles. Without thinking—without even breathing—she launched herself straight at the wall.

Theo snagged her under the arms, the box flying along with his phone over one shoulder where they landed with a dull thud. The relief that flooded her body was biblical as Theo snagged her from the plank and pulled her against his chest. She clung to him, arms and legs circling his body to gain the most security. For a few seconds they stumbled back from the momentum, but she didn't care. Somehow, even before his back met the wall and they stilled, she knew he had her. She was safe.

"Jesus." Chest heaving, Theo's arms clung to her just as hard, one hand cradling her head while the other wrapped around her waist. "It's alright. You're alright. Breathe, love."

It was then that she realized the broken gasps for air that cut through the darkness were coming from her. She frantically tried and to take a full breath—an impossible feat as her body emptied of its adrenaline.

He turned them, pressing Shannon's back against the wall and pinning her in place with his hips, bracketing her face with both hands and gently stroking his thumbs under her eyes, catching her steady stream of tears. "Breathe, Shannon."

She couldn't. Her body had officially given up and insisted on hyperventilating until she passed out and removed herself from the stress. He held her face in his hands as if she were precious, and she knew that if she could see him, his eyes would be soft caramel. They would be concerned, but the familiarity of those irises would make her feel safe.

But she couldn't see him, and her heaving chest and racking sobs were her body's way of telling her she very much was *not* safe.

Her legs still firmly wrapped around him, Theo pressed his hips in tighter, holding her up as he found her hands and brought them to his broad chest.

"Match my pace," he instructed, her hands lifting with his chest as he took a slow, deliberate deep breath.

She nodded, unsure if he could even see the motion and focused on the rise and fall of his torso. Her breath hitched, and she grabbed his hand and brought it between her breasts, desperate for her heart to stop racing.

Theo's forehead found hers as he took another exaggerated breath.

"Breathe," he murmured, his exhalation mingling with hers.

She squeezed his hand as her chest slowly matched his. Inhale, exhale. Inhale, exhale.

They sucked in air together, their bodies a tangled mass as he pulled his hand from the one on his chest and cradled her face again.

A shuddering, deep breath finally left her, providing some relief to her lungs as she calmed down.

"Good girl. You're alright."

"That was so scary," she whispered, finally managing to form sentences.

"I have about a thousand different descriptors for what that was, and scary doesn't quite do it justice."

A stray tear escaped and didn't last long as his thumb brushed it from her cheek. His touches were softer than she expected the devil's to be, and she leaned into his palm until that thumb brushed her lips.

"Thank you," she murmured against his skin. The feel of her lips grazing his flesh sent a shiver through her body, stirring something in her gut.

He was silent, his breathing steady and calm as he slowly ran that thumb across her bottom lip.

"I didn't do anything that requires your thanks, Lily."

She sighed, another caress making its way across her lips. "We're back to Lily? And here I thought we had turned over a new leaf when you called me love. It was very British of you, by the way."

His steady caress stumbled a bit, the pad of his thumb catching on her lip and applying a bit more pressure. All of her focus zeroed in on that point of contact. Not on their connected foreheads, hands, or the feel of him between her legs. But on that steady brush against her mouth. The urge to wet her lips was strong as she fought to remember how they got there, wrapped up in each other.

"I'll call you whatever you like if you promise to never do that to me again," he said, a little breathless.

Her own breathing became labored again for totally inappropriate reasons. Could it be that…yup—yes. She had in fact started focusing on the fact that he was between her legs.

He shifted his hips as if he too had just realized the delicate situation they found themselves in. Delicate, and yet she didn't stop herself from whispering, "In that case, tell me I'm a good girl again."

Theo went painfully still as her words landed in the dark, silent space between them.

What. The. Fuck? Her inner voice was raging at her, embarrassment fueling its rant. She knew there were a million reasons why she shouldn't be flirting with Theo—starting and ending with him being her boss—but she usually couldn't help herself. His buttons were too easily pushed. He was like an elevator with thirty floors, satisfying when you see all of the buttons light up, then painful as you waited through every stop. But this was not a situation she needed to flirt her way through. Not when she already felt vulnerable and mad.

You are mad, she reminded herself. Mad, and maybe a little turned on by the ease with which he had her pinned against the wall.

Mad, but also caustically aware of the hardness now pressed against her middle and making her want to shift her hips, just a little, to see what that friction would be like.

"Did..." Theo trailed off, voice gravelly. "Did you like that?"

Holy shit. Shannon's cheeks burned as his seemingly innocent question lit a fire in her blood. Of all the reactions she had expected, that was the last on the list. She and Theo had always had an interesting working relationship. It was familiar. She joked; he scowled. She danced; he scoffed. She poked, nudged, and leaned into him for unwanted selfies— he avoided touching her at all costs and generally hit her with nothing but frown lines and narrowed eyes.

Their relationship didn't go beyond that; they were not considered *close*. But boy did she like the press of his body against hers. The feel of his hand between her breasts and his thumb on her lips.

"I..." *Yes*, was the answer she was looking for. *Yes, I liked it. Maybe a little too much. I would like to hear it again with the lights on and our eyes locked.*

Suddenly every point of contact was vibrating and alive. She still gripped his hand to her chest and the warmth it lent was quickly spreading lower. This had to be adrenaline mucking up her emotions. Breathing in his familiar scent after a near-death experience was proving to be a fatal combo, confusing her emotions until they resembled a giant ball of yarn. And maybe she was part feline, because against her better judgement, Shannon really wanted to bat that ball away and see where those emotions lead her.

"Lil," he murmured, his breath hot against her lips. All she needed to do was shift a measly inch and his mouth would be on hers. She curled her fingers into his hair, the others squeezing his hand tighter to her chest. It was

62

happening. She was about to kiss Theo in the dark, the rain splattering the windows and the familiar smell of coffee in the air.

Coffee, and old books, and freshly baked cookies, and Theo's absurdly masculine scent. It was Bloem. It was home.

And she remembered with stark clarity the events that had led them to that moment.

"Were you planning on telling me you were selling the café?" Her voice came out strong and steady as she fought to align her thoughts.

Theo stiffened in her arms, but before he could formulate a response, the lights flickered once, twice, before winning out and soft lamplight illuminated bright, amber irises.

***

Theo's mind still whirled as his gaze connected with an icy blue. His feelings were in an all-out bidding war—fear, relief, anger, and surprise all throwing down to take up residence in his chest. Unfortunately, as his eyes adjusted to the sudden brilliance of Shannon's too-close face, the one thing he shouldn't be feeling decided to swiftly take out the competition and inject itself directly into his bloodstream. Desire, so strong he almost collapsed under its weight. It left his head to course through every vein before settling in a very unfortunate place. Unfortunate, as five seconds prior he had been certain that Shannon felt that desire just as strongly, and damnit, he had wanted that. From the moment she asked him to praise her good behavior his dick had been hard and his mouth practically salivating at the idea of her earning that praise.

Now, as her question still lingered in the very minimal space between them, the hard realization that he had misread the scene flicked him on the forehead with surprising force.

Pulling away, he leaned back so their eyes connected. He should have put her down altogether but that would involve stepping back and revealing his aforementioned erection. Not great.

"Who told you I was selling?"

To his dismay, Shannon released his hand and pressed him away. He really tried not to focus on the way her fingers scraped against his neck before pushing at his chest. Reluctantly, he set her back on her feet and turned away, adjusting himself and feeling about a thousand different forms of mortification. The lecture would come later, he promised himself. In the safety of his own home and after a long cold shower, he would give himself a stern talking to about inappropriate workplace relationships. Never mind that it was singular, as in one employee that had been testing him since the day he laid eyes on her.

"No denial then? Not a great start." Shannon huffed behind him. "How could you not tell me about this Theo? I had to find out from Ryan of all people, nothing but pity in his smug, soy-milky face."

Theo's blood cooled in record time. He turned to face her again, his cheeks heating with his anger and blazing as he realized her shirt was damp and revealed far too much. Snapping his eyes from her chest to the spot right between her eyes, he pulled his anger to the surface to hopefully smother his lust.

"What did Ryan tell you, exactly?"

Shannon winced at his tone before straightening her spine. "That your *real estate agent* sent him and his slimy boss your *listing.*"

The amount of emphasis Shannon was throwing into certain words should have been the first sign of her anger. Unfortunately, when it came to her, Theo never managed to back down. And at that moment, his anger was a living thing in his chest, fighting to beat louder than his pulse.

"Met up with him, did you?"

She blinked, crossing her arms. "That is none of your business. But you know what is very much *my* business? Knowing when you decide to sell Bloem to some asshole who is just going to turn it into an Urban Putt or some shit."

His gaze ran over her for a proper inspection, searching every inch of her face. She had left. Her hair was down and soaked from the rain. The blonde strands fell in messy waves past her shoulders and over crossed arms. She had just been with Potato before—before he got tangled up in her. Had she been wrapped around him too? Now that was an image that he didn't need, want, or have any right to summon. It truly was none of his business. That knowledge didn't stop an extremely foreign, unwanted feeling from draping over him like a cloak.

"I must be missing something, because that still doesn't explain why you decided it was a good idea to train for the circus during a power outage. Or was your date bad enough that you needed a little excitement?"

He didn't need to add that last bit, but he was feeling particularly sour. Maybe he was being a baby, but he didn't fucking care. The only way out of this argument was through it, and if there was one thing he loved about Shannon, it was her ability to go toe to toe with him.

Sure enough, her eyes lit with anger as she took a step toward him

"Maybe your lack of social interaction has stunted your cognitive growth, but I don't know how else to tell you to mind your own business without bringing the F word into it, so here we go." She uncrossed her arms only to fling her hair over one shoulder. "What I do with my free time is none of your *fucking* business. The only reason I decided to face the beams of death was because I thought it would help."

Her voice broke on the last word, lodging all of Theo's carefully curated taunts in his throat and just managing to keep them from spilling out to win the argument.

Shannon cleared her throat before continuing. "I want to help. I have plenty of ideas about how to drive traffic, and I've already been begging you to let me take on more. I can still apprentice in the kitchen *and* give your social media a glow up. I want to do those things, Theo." His name left her lips in a huff as she pulled an agitated hand through damp hair.

Those taunts from earlier? Yeah, they still rested somewhere in his throat, her words morphing them into something softer. Comforting.

She cared about the café. For whatever reason, this demonic ball of starlight held Bloem in her heart. There were a hundred places within a fifty-mile radius that Shannon could be lending her talents, but she chose here. She chose his place. He was proud of the café, more than anyone would ever learn. But for reasons unknown to him, Shannon's unwavering support had pride spilling from his ears. Her loyalty and trust mattered to him.

The hollow feeling in his guts told him it mattered a bit too much.

"What makes you think I'm not retiring?" he asked through his teeth, shoving his previous thoughts to the back of his mind.

Shannon blinked. "You're not retiring," she said on a laugh. "This place is your life. What the hell would you do next?"

Her words didn't sting because they weren't meant to. She knew him. And there was nowhere else he'd rather be than in this lofty space, roasting and kneading and baking and arguing, lord save him.

"I don't know, Lily, maybe I will embrace my true calling and flee to the underworld. Snuggle into my throne of bones and finally employ people who do what I ask of them."

She eyed him carefully, her gaze raking down the length of him in a lazy perusal before returning to his face. He fought the urge to shuffle his feet.

"Obedience is earned," she said, a smile twitching at the corner of her mouth. His jaw clenched as those words immediately roused the memory of Shannon wrapped around him, pressed against his cock and asking to be called a good girl. This fucking woman. If she were being held at gunpoint in the middle of a dark alley, she could probably flirt her way out of it. Charming her mugger until he was a puddle of adoration and subservience.

That was the thing that drove him mad about Shannon. He liked control and craved structure. There were too many things that had slipped through his fingers over the years, causing him to cling to his control in work and at home. The women in his life liked that. Almost too eager to be told what to do and hear his praise. With Shannon…

Theo snapped his brain off as if it were a breaker, giving in to his desire to shift on his feet. Where had his brain just gone?

The smirk on her face told him she knew exactly where it had gone. Jesus…

"I pay you for your obedience, or have you forgotten how a job works?" He watched her features light up, no doubt ready to make some sort of sex worker joke. He held up a hand before she could utter whatever devastating blow to his ego she was about to land. "Please refrain from whatever brought that much joy to your face. I'm actually terrified of it."

Her smile didn't quite make it to her eyes as she made a show of zipping her lips closed, reminding him of why they were flirt-fighting in the office to begin with.

"I'm not selling," he said on a sigh, snagging the office chair and collapsing into it, suddenly exhausted. "I asked Krista to put some feelers out there. See if anyone would be willing to actually pay what I think this space is worth. Which is a lot, by the way."

Shannon leaned back against the wall, her arms crossed once more. "Why are you considering that in the first place?"

He swallowed, ignoring how sky-blue eyes bobbed to his throat and back. He wanted to tell her it was none of her business. Bloem wasn't hers. If it all came crashing down around his ears, she would waltz right into the next café and charm a new round of idiots to do her bidding. The idea of her working for anyone but him made his eye twitch. Shannon was talented, but it was Theo who trained her. She didn't own this place on paper, but she was built into its foundations. Every time he smelled the fresh flowers in the bathrooms or sneakily tried one of those sugary syrups in his coffee he would think of her. Think of how she practically bullied him into "providing whimsy to the suits" whatever the hell that meant. He knew she was a part of the roastery now—a part of his space.

And for fuck's sake, had he just lost an argument with himself within his own head?

Rubbing the brim of his nose, Theo spoke with closed lids, ignoring the way her floral scent still clung to his skin. "The business isn't doing well. I have been managing with the money made from wholesale, but that's simply not sustainable. We need more people to find us. We need more loyal customers and—" He swallowed as if the words left a bitter taste in his mouth. "We need more press."

He opened his eyes, reluctantly accepting the look of triumph he would find across angelic features. She had been begging to take over social media, and he couldn't quite explain his reluctance to let her. His reluctance to all of it. There was a desire in him to keep his café humble and sweet—a space filled with regulars and family. Somehow, putting himself out there felt like he was accepting what happened all those years ago. It felt like he was moving on without someone who clearly had no problem leaving him behind…But when he locked on to her, still leaned against the office wall, the smugness he expected wasn't there. It was hard to read whatever expression rested on her sweet face. The look was completely foreign to him. It was shocking that there were still details about her that were new after all their time together. Amazing, really.

She spoke before he could ask what she was thinking. Shannon never had an issue speaking her mind, and he allowed her words to cover him like a warm weighted blanket.

"Something you need to understand about me is, I don't run. What we need, Lulu, is a plan," she said simply, eyes bright and beautiful.

cHapter seven

Shannon watched the woman out of the corner of her eye, following her every movement as she scoured the bookshelf. A gasp nearly released from her chest as the woman's finger glided over the right book, huffing out as her perusal swept over it without stopping.

She couldn't take it anymore. Shannon had been cleaning the same spot on the counter since the woman walked in, her silver-streaked hair in its usual bun at her nape, an extremely flattering moss-colored scarf wrapped around her shoulders and a soft smile touching her lips. She had fired up a cappuccino the minute she glimpsed her familiar frame, chatted with her for a few minutes, then began organizing the weird pumpkins Theo had finally relented to, all while watching the woman like a hawk.

The space looked amazing. All fall colors and fairy lights and gourds and candles. The gloom outside added to the coziness, just begging their guests to order something delicious and curl up with a book.

Their guests, as in her and Theo's. A week had gone by since her near-death experience. Seven days since she felt his skin on hers, felt his pulse skip beneath her fingers. One week of picking apart every single detail of their conversation then quickly ignoring the outcome she landed on every time. That she finally took it too far. He agreed to meet with her and at least listen to some ideas. Said "we" as if Shannon actually had ownership of anything other than the fall decorations and finally let her string lights around the space until it fucking sparkled.

But Theo was nowhere to be found. He was avoiding her, reminding Shannon that things had shifted between them. Her constant sunshiny, flirtatious nature had finally broken him. He was barely even scowling in her direction these days.

Whatever. Lucifer's cold shoulder would have to wait. There were more important matters to attend to…

"What kinda book are you looking for today, Miss Juliette?" she asked as casually as possible. Her three other guests all sat at one table, each on their own computers and typing manically. They paid no attention to the yelled question from her perch at the counter.

Juliette sighed, her eyes finding Shannon's and crinkling at the edges. "A good old-fashioned whodunit, I think. Do you know if there is a good one up here?"

"A murder mystery?" Shannon asked, feigning surprise. She knew exactly what Juliette's next read was going to be, because it was the same genre she had been reading since her husband left her.

She circled the concrete bar and padded toward the front of the café, snagging a fallen napkin from the floor as she skirted the tables. The café's library had been her idea. A leave a book, take a book business model that helped keep the inventory varied. When they first started, Shannon had donated nothing but romance novels to the shelves, while Theo's contributions seemed to come straight from a high school reading list. She had teased him relentlessly when she found *Pride and Prejudice* wedged between Steinbeck and Orwell as if he didn't want her to find it.

Not because he shouldn't be reading romance, she felt that everyone had something to gain from the genre— especially men. She just couldn't help comparing him to Mr. Darcy. A dark, broody sort of man, whose pride rivaled that of any peacock.

A sigh loomed in her chest as she fought to clear her mind of Theo. Her thoughts trailed to him way too often for someone with perfectly good fantasies waiting in the wings.

She saddled up next to her target, shoving the napkin in a belted apron at her waist.

Knowing exactly what book she was going for didn't stop her from sweeping pride-filled eyes over those well-stocked shelves. *Mine*, she thought as her eyes soaked in each colorful spine. That slice of the café had been entirely hers. Shannon's corner.

Pushing it all aside, she focused in on her task, running a finger along the spines until she reached the exact one she wanted.

"Oh, this one was good," she said innocently. "A murder mystery with a touch of drama and a little spice. I couldn't put it down." She left out the fact that it was first and foremost a romance. Juliette didn't need those details. All she needed was what was between its pages.

The woman didn't read the description, trusting Shannon like she had been for months. Her stomach did a little happy dance as she watched her tuck the book under an arm with a smile, no idea that Shannon's carefully organized plans had been set in motion. There was just one more seed to plant in this garden.

"You haven't steered me wrong yet," she chirped, her smile barely making it to her eyes.

"I can't take all the credit for this one. One of our regulars donated it a couple weeks back and I always insist on reading his donations. He likes to write notes and little poems in the margins. It adds a little personal touch to the story."

Shannon watched as Juliette flipped through the book, text flying by alongside occasional scribbles and written word.

"Oh, I think I've read one of his books before," Juliette murmured.

She had. Almost half a year ago when Shannon started this particular matchmaking conquest.

"Did you enjoy the chicken scratch? I know it's not everyone's cup of tea, but I like it." She paused before adding, "And Vincent writes such beautiful words."

"Vincent," Juliette said, rolling his name around her tongue for the first time. Shannon's heart practically melted in her chest at hearing it. "I'll give it a go. Thank you, love."

Love. Shannon refused, REFUSED to think about that term of endearment leaving someone else's lips. Rich, honeyed voice leaving his throat to collide with her stupid face. It didn't matter how luscious the devil's voice was, she would not be tempted.

Open your eyes, love. Keep them on me...

Her shoulders went rigid as she fought the urge to press her head between her palms and exercise those demons. The act wouldn't be dramatic at all. Not after Theo's voice somehow crept into her thoughts at the most inappropriate times, telling her she was a good girl as she worked herself to a very satisfying climax with one of her favorite toys.

That memory wasn't helpful. That memory, she thought as she said goodbye to Juliette and waded back to the coffee bar, was giving in to the devil's temptations.

Her eyes darted to the viewing window and froze. Lucifer was watching her. His eyes locked on hers, one eyebrow slightly quirked as if he knew what she was thinking. Shannon's cheeks heated and his eyebrow rose a little higher, those hawk-like irises trailing over her face before slowly making their way back to her eyes.

She pulled her focus away, choosing instead to mindlessly adjust the pastry case while the real organization was happening in her head. She would be meeting with Lulu today, and those unrelenting, inappropriate thoughts would have to be whisked from her mind. So yeah, maybe she never cared if she was inappropriate before. Flirting was her preferred method of communication, and that had never bothered her. She got used to warding off dinner invitations and misread interest. If she was honest with herself—which she rarely ever was—she could admit that her flirting had always been a bit of a defense mechanism. Pulling people's interest validated Shannon, and she honestly couldn't remember the last time someone blatantly disliked her.

Maybe that was why Ryan had been such a conquest. She needed his admiration so badly, she was willing to belittle herself to get it.

Her gaze danced to the roasting room and back, zeroing in on a pumpkin roll and holding on for dear life. She didn't need to be making parallels where they had no business being.

Shannon had a million other fantasies she could be spinning to pass the time.

And she did. Through the afternoon rush and solidly into her final hour, she managed to think of anything and everything that wasn't Theo Abbott.

The man himself sauntered out of the kitchen just as she flipped the open sign to *closed* and locked the door. Early evening sunlight spilled through the front window, casting everything in a warm, golden glow. Shannon left the blinds up, allowing the sunshine its well-deserved pageantry.

"Let's take the homework table," Theo said, reading her mind. The window seat was her favorite. A small table set next to a cushiony window bench and a couple of chairs. The perfect gathering place, or in Bloem's case, the perfect spot for Sebastian to pretend to do his homework.

"Want a latte?" Theo asked as he pulled his own shot. The steamer barely made a sound as he worked, no doubt producing the perfect textured milk.

"Just an espresso for me, please," she said before flopping on to the bench. She leaned into the cushions, snuggling in until her back fit between two pillows just right. Surveying Theo as he worked was always a guilty pleasure of hers, but especially today. His scowl was particularly crabby as his strong hands worked. She had been too nice in her request for an espresso and her mind raced to come up with something snarky to say, but she was distracted by the glimpse of a sunflower on his neck, disappearing beneath the collar of his black shirt.

"Are all of your tattoos inspired by nature?" She asked, forgetting the snark for a second.

He glanced up briefly from the espresso machine. "No," he said with absolutely no additional information.

She hummed in response because she knew it would drive him nuts. In reality, a million nosy questions burst to the forefront of her mind. What else do you have? Where do you have them? Any words? What do they say? Her restraint was worth it, however, when he glanced up again, brows furrowed.

She simply let her gaze wander over the café, casually playing with her hair. It was in a half up, half down style with a silk bow tied sweetly around her ponytail. The ribbon's ends blended with the rest of her wild mane, and she found the smooth fabric and ran her thumb along its length while fighting a smirk.

Theo heaved a sigh before grabbing their cups and joining her at the table.

"Do you have any tattoos?" he asked, falling into a chair and extending the small espresso cup to her.

"I do." She didn't.

His scowl deepened. "Where?"

"Nowhere safe for work," she responded sweetly before taking a sip of her espresso.

Theo's eyes narrowed before he called her bluff. "Liar."

She shrugged, giddy at the idea of him trying to wrap his head around a tattoo on her ass.

"Show me yours and I'll show you mine," she teased.

"I think we both know none of that is safe for work," he mumbled against his cup.

The smile that stretched across her face was almost painful. She loved when Theo spoke his mind.

"Behave," he warned before pulling the pencil from behind his ear and drawing a small notebook from a jean pocket. "Okay Lil, you wanted to kick some ideas into the net, I'm all ears."

"Wow, just when I thought you couldn't get anymore British. A soccer analogy?" She rolled her lips together as Theo just stared in that way of his. No humor, no patience.

"Nervous?"

Shannon huffed a laugh. Of course not. She was about to take the things she had been pestering Lulu with for years and regurgitate them into spoken word proper for a formal meeting. It was nothing he hadn't heard from her before.

She wasn't nervous.

"I'm not nervous. I—"

"Because you're doing that thing you do. Where you joke away your discomfort." He took a sip after the statement, as if he were talking about the weather or asking after her sisters. Not like he just called out a very real, very personal defensive trait of hers. As if he paid attention.

"No," she murmured, unable to admit that she may have been a touch nervous. "I'm sorry, I promise I'm taking this all seriously."

His eyes softened, a tiny shift in his angular features that would have been missed had she not been staring back at him. He said nothing as he tucked his chair in closer to her and crossed his legs ankle over knee.

Clearing her throat, she pulled her phone from under her thigh and opened her notes app. She had taken this task seriously, organizing all of her thoughts and suggestions into order of easiest to, well—more complicated. She started with the former.

"Obviously, I've put up the fall décor and added some fall inspired drinks to the menu. I'm happy to see you've added the pumpkin buns to the menu as well as cinnamon brown butter cookies and maple cake. I'm sure I'm not the only one who feels that way. Can you guess how many people have commented about the new additions?"

He cocked his head, interest in his solemn features.

"Nobody." Her eyes met his. "Absolutely no one cares that we have rolled out these arguably stunning items because you don't promote them. And before you suggest it, Harper and Evie don't count."

His mouth snapped shut as he pivoted away from that very suggestion.

"Your social media is atrocious," she said with little remorse.

"Why? Because I don't post about PSL season and paint nights?"

"Because you don't post at all. And I hate to tell you this Lulu, but a PSL season post will get people in the door."

He frowned at her, jotting down a note that she desperately wanted to see.

"Allow me to add some tasteful kitsch to the space and give your social media a zhuzh. It will at the very least, gain you more followers and potential new guests. As much as you hate it, it's free advertising."

A few words were scribbled on his notepad before Theo looked at her, nodded with a sigh, and ran a hand through his hair.

"Yes. Alright."

"Yes, alright? You sound like I asked for all of October off, not as if I just offered to work harder." If she sounded angry, it was absolutely his fault.

Sliding the pencil behind his ear again, he scratched the side of his neck, drawing her focus to the swirling stars and clean lines. Most of his ink was black, save for a few pops of color here and there. It was like a treasure hunt. Find the bright blues and yellows among a sea of grey.

"Yes, alright. Thank you for taking that on," he said in a tone that indicated he wasn't grateful at all. "What's number two on your list?" He gestured to her phone which was flat on the table, revealing her list of tasks. She snatched it from view before sitting up a little straighter. Unfortunately, task number one had been the easiest suggestion. Now, the real fun started.

"I'm wondering if you would allow me to take a look at your books?" Without looking, she knew Theo had stiffened before her. As she took a sip of espresso, he pulled the pencil from his ear and replaced it without writing anything down. A tic that he always did when trying to actually think through a response before simply handing out a hard no.

"No. What else ya' got?"

Apparently, a hard no was the outcome anyway. Shannon's teeth ached from grinding them together as she waited for her patience to arrive.

"Before we move on, can we at least talk about your financials?"

"It won't change the answer," he warned before taking a sip from his cooling latte.

This was her moment. "Did you know that I originally studied business management in college? Yeah," she said when he quirked an eyebrow. "I had dreams of running a restaurant with Evie and Ben. And since I was the more…we'll say *structured* of the group, I chose to pursue a less technical, more operational field. I did end up getting my associate's before we all moved here but continued online classes until I got my bachelor's."

This was all new information. She hadn't included any of it on her application and not even her best friends knew she had continued her studies. There was no particular reason why. Evie and Ben would never judge or set ridiculous expectations for her; she knew that. But in the back of her mind, she couldn't shake the feeling that they would take a look at her choices and ask "why?" Why didn't she pursue a career with her degree? Why didn't she take the internship at that startup a few years back? Why did she constantly try new hobbies and not commit to a single one? Why had she remained stagnant at the same café when she could have scaled the corporate ladder somewhere else? Why was Shannon Perry such a conundrum?

"I also recently took some accounting classes, remember?"

Theo's features went serious and dark. His eyes narrowed as he plucked the damn pencil from behind his ear again and began writing.

"You misunderstand me, Lily. There is absolutely no doubt in my mind that you have the qualifications to run my books. I just don't need it. That task has been mine alone since Bloem opened. I already have my work checked at the end of the year by my accountant and have a solid bookkeeping system. There is no reason for you to step in."

Shannon fought the urge to pout. Unconsciously finding the ribbon in her hair, she smoothed it between her fingers, the feel of the soft fabric soothing her nerves. This was good practice. Her therapist told her that situations like these were not failures or rejections, just challenges that would most likely evolve over time. Logic told her that Theo already had systems in place. Not that he didn't want *her* systems in place.

Logic wasn't something her brain liked to process very often.

"You're being stubborn," she accused, ignoring the whininess of her own voice.

Theo cocked his head, eyes piercing. "I am," he said slowly. "Because as much as you want to help, Shannon, that might be too much."

"Why? Is this all a front and you're actually laundering drug money?"

"Because my financials are a very personal thing, one that an employee should not have access to."

She leaned back, feeling hurt for unknown reasons. "I'm a manager," she said lamely. It didn't quite encompass how she felt about her role in the café.

His eyes softened in a way that infuriated her. She didn't need those pitying looks, not one bit.

"You are a manager as well as an extremely valued employee with a multitude of skills that I can't even attempt in my daydreams. And as such, you have access to all the daily sales and payroll costs. I'm sorry, but that's all the access I'm willing to give you." His voice was as soft as his eyes, and she couldn't have been more irritated by the sound of it.

Insecurity furled in her gut, morphing into flaming hot anger she had no business feeling. In fact, the ridiculousness of her own reaction was only contributing fuel to the fires of her disappointment and fury until they swirled with embarrassment. This was usually where Shannon let her self-doubt take control. She had been in a wash, rinse, repeat of this exact scenario her entire life. Rejection, letting people down, it was like a cold plunge that she would inevitably sputter her way out of.

And today was no exception.

"Let me invest," she spat out. No grace, no subtlety.

Theo nearly choked on his latte. Eyes watering, he pulled in enough air to croak, "What?"

"I have money." Again, not her most elegant delivery. "And I want to invest it in y—in Bloem."

Theo managed to cough the remaining latte from his lungs. Wide eyes watched her over the hand he held fisted over his mouth. A small chess piece ran along his hand just below the pinky, and she focused on it rather than on her wavering nerves. It was the tower. Rook? Whatever. It was nice. Clean lined save for one edge of the spire where the ink bled. No shading, just a crisp rendering of a small tower that looked worthy of an architectural mockup.

"No," Theo said, his voice strong and final.

Shannon stood from the bench, her temper finally getting the best of her. "Why not?"

"Because I don't want your charity, Shannon. I got myself into this mess, and I intend to get myself out of it. Now, do you have a fourth suggestion?"

She looked down at him, crossing her arms and giving in to the desire to pout.

"That was number four. Number three was getting a liquor license and capitalizing on alcohol markups. Host a boozy *paint night.*"

Theo's eyes burned with intensity as his face took on a contemplative look. "That's not a bad idea…"

"It's not charity," she cut in, unwilling to give up. "It's an investment. I would be getting something out of it. Getting something back." And gaining a substantial share in a business she felt attached to. She kept that last bit to herself, not wanting to inflate Lulu's ego.

"And what if Bloem can't be saved? What if you don't make your investment back?" Theo's posture remained unbothered, legs still crossed, back relaxed against the chair cushion. But the pencil in his hand was tap-tap-tapping a rapid beat against the tabletop. Uncrossing her arms, she placed both hands on top of his one, stopping the incessant rap of pen against oak. The sun was beginning to lose its battle with the surrounding apartments and storefronts, painting the café in muted browns and golds. The rays reflected from the striking amber of Theo's eyes as they wandered from her face to her hands on his skin.

"Let me take a look at the books, and we'll decide if the investment is worth the risk," she said softly, hope radiating from every word. The desire—the consuming need—to own a part of Bloem had replaced the very blood in her veins. She was entirely made up of determination and refused to give up.

Theo stared at her hands, laughably small compared to his, before lifting his focus to her.

"No, love."

Shannon snatched her hands back as if she had been burned.

"Shannon, I'm sorry, but I won't accept money from you," he said, slowly rising to his feet as well. He towered over her, and every muscle screamed at her to launch onto a chair and gain the higher ground again. She needed some control of the situation before it completely went off the rails.

"Okay, so I don't even have to give you the can't, or won't speech. Will you at least hear my pitch? I…"

"No," he said with a finality that had Shannon snapping her mouth shut. "And if there is nothing else, I need to pick up Sebastian from practice."

Shannon hated the heat that rose to her cheeks. Despised the sting she felt behind her eyes as she tried not to blink out a tear.

Is that how it usually happened? A quick fifteen-minute conversation and a two-letter word was all it took to stomp out a fully formed dream? She couldn't explain her connection to the café. It was small, cold, dark, and quiet—everything Shannon was not. Most people loathed their jobs. They didn't have completely indescribable attachments to it that bordered on obsession. But she loved the café. She loved her regulars and their weird book selections. The UPS man that almost always told her about his Tinder dates and their weird quirks. The quiet of the space when it was just her and Theo, flour coating her hands as he showed her how to shape potato rolls.

She didn't want to walk away without a fight.

But as Theo watched her, usual scowl painting his features and dark circles under his eyes, the fight slowly crept from the forefront of her mind to the dark recesses, smothered and contained. He looked tired. Through the grumpy exterior, she could tell he was stressing. Doing the devil's work got tiring she supposed. And even as her inner dialogue compared him to Satan, it didn't have its usual effect. There was no way for her to ignore the pressure bearing down on him.

So, she didn't fight. And after telling Theo she had nothing else, hearing one of the sincerest admissions of gratitude for her help leave his lips, and walking out the door as if it had been another day at the office, Shannon couldn't help but wonder if she would regret that choice.

CHaPTer EIGHT

Theo glowered at his empty wine glass, wishing it would magically refill itself. His terrible mood had only increased after Krista told him someone came back with an offer on the café space, a fact that should have thrilled him if it weren't for one pesky little problem: he didn't want to sell.

He had taken Shannon's advice and handed the social media over to her. Her selfies were even more relentless than ever, and Theo wasn't going to do a fucking thing about it. The hurt in her eyes as he ruthlessly rejected her pitch still made him want to vomit. *He* had put that look on her face. And now *he* would pose shirtless with a cinnamon cold brew and a jack-o'-lantern if it meant never seeing her deflate like that again.

Unfortunately, it had been a necessary sacrifice. There were expenses that would be difficult for him to explain, and quite frankly, he didn't owe anyone an explanation for how he spent his hard-earned money. Avoiding the conversation altogether had been his best option.

But that didn't keep him from running the conversation round his mind repeatedly, Shannon's tear-lined eyes and disappointed face consuming his thoughts. Self-inflicted torture for having been the cause. That, and a burning desire to know more. If things had been different and the sting of his brother's abandonment hadn't left a constant ache in his heart, maybe he would have heard her out. In another life, he knew he could trust Shannon, and he could admit that there was something oddly appealing about her having a share in the café.

But they weren't in another life. They were in the kind of life where people used and discarded you onto a pile of rubble, leaving you alone to pick up the pieces. That hard-learned knowledge was what kept him from asking the questions he was burning to voice. How did Shannon have enough money to invest? What kind of return would she want? Did she think the return would be worth it? And maybe the most pressing of all: why did she care?

"If looks could kill, that wine glass would be a pile of sand," Krista said as she sat next to him, filling his glass before attending to her own. "I take it you're not happy with the offer."

He sighed as he leaned his head back against the couch, completely comfortable in his sister-in-law's small apartment. Occasional outbursts and muffled curses sounded from Sebastian's room, his gaming in full swing.

"I'm sorry. I'm not great company at the moment," he said in lieu of an honest answer.

"That's okay, you're never really great company," she chirped before taking a long sip from her wine glass.

Theo snorted a laugh. That was probably true.

"I just never thought I would be considering this, you know?"

There was never a time when his future didn't include Bloem. He thought the café would be a constant in his life, a place where his children would grow up, even. He had plans.

Dreams of actually fixing up the apartment upstairs and living out the rest of his miserable days in that roasting room. Pretty vulnerable admission, especially for him.

Clearing his throat, he reached for his wine glass, more than ready to move on from the subject of selling what was precious to him. "Anyway, there is no way I am accepting that offer. That man is a certified prick, and his minion is even worse. So, we trudge on."

Krista stared at him as if she knew all the things he left unsaid. Pretty brown eyes patiently watched him over her wine glass.

"Have you even considered Shannon's proposal?"

Theo shook his head, suddenly not grateful for a subject change at all.

"There is nothing to consider. I won't take her money."

"It's not taking money. It's a transaction, Theo. And I know you don't want to talk about it, but she's not Simon." Her eyes softened even as she leaned forward and gripped his arm. "That woman would never do anything to hurt you."

Theo stiffened. His brother's name on her tongue made his entire body seize, his jaw clench. Krista shouldn't have to talk about Simon. She shouldn't have to think about him or worry, or dredge up any kind of memory from her rocky past. The asshole didn't deserve her attention, and he certainly didn't deserve to be compared to Shannon in any way. That still didn't dampen his resistance.

Dangerous. His mind screamed the warning anytime he looked in Shannon's direction. The woman was fiercely loyal to her friends and way too easily trusted. That was the kind of person that did the most damage when they walked away. The type of person to lower your defenses until you gave them all the power to destroy you. Dramatic, if he hadn't actually lived that exact experience.

So, Krista was wrong. Shannon could absolutely hurt him, and most likely would if he brought her any further into his life.

86

He gave her hand a little squeeze of reassurance. "I'll think about it," he lied. "I'd much rather talk about your son's latest obsession."

Krista gave him a knowing look before dropping the subject. She pulled her hand from his arm just to run fingers through short, cropped hair.

"I guess I should be grateful it's not a girl," she said with a soft smile.

As if on cue, Sebastian let out a wail of despair at whatever loss he had just suffered on screen. Krista rolled her eyes but couldn't stop a wide grin from plumping her cheeks.

"I'm not so sure," Theo said innocently. "I'm fairly certain someone on the other end of those headphones is named Melanie."

Her eyes widened before darting in the direction of Bast's room as if she could see through the wall with that accusatory gaze.

"He's never mentioned her to me."

"Yes, but I'm his cool uncle with infinite wisdom and whatever the fuck rizz is." Grabbing the wine bottle, it was his turn to top off his sister's glass. "He's not going to tell his *mother* about his gamer girl crush."

She stared into her wine glass looking a bit disappointed. "Why not? I can have rizz."

"Do you?" Theo asked in a rare moment of prodding. "How has the online dating world been treating you?"

"Okay, asking that question is just rude. We both know the answer is unsavory." She glanced to the hall then back to him when Bast's cry of outrage confirmed he was still in his room. "But…I did meet someone recently. And before you ask, his coffee order is a cappuccino with two sugars."

Theo narrowed his eyes. "Where have you been getting said coffee?"

"As if I would go anywhere else," she seethed, clearly offended by the suggestion. "I actually met him at Bloem, thank you very much."

Theo's eyes narrowed even further. A funny feeling tingling up his neck. "You strike up a conversation with him in line or something?" As if he ever really had lines these days.

"No." A smile tugged at the corners of her mouth as she told him, "He brought me my drink. I must have been distracted with my morning emails and didn't hear Shannon call my name. Apparently, she asked him to do her a favor and pass the cup to the most beautiful person in the room." She rolled her eyes even as a light blush crept over her plumped cheeks. "Cheesy, I know."

"But effective," Theo said, fighting his own smile. He knew Shannon's handiwork when he saw it, and that woman's matchmaking was smeared all over this scenario.

"Yes. We've chatted at the café a couple times and have a proper dinner date on Friday. Thank you for watching Bast by the way."

He raised his glass in a toast, waving away the gratitude. Watching his nephew had literally never been a chore for him, and if Krista was this happy just talking about this new man in her life, he would do anything he could to keep that smile on her face. She was family. And Theo knew without a doubt that she would do the same for him if the roles were reversed.

"How about you? Any Melanies out there for you?" He didn't miss the humor in her eyes as she asked. They both knew the answer to that question was a big fat no.

Still, that gleam in her eye sharpened as he paused, his thoughts immediately wandering to blonde hair and silk ribbons. To the feel of soft lips under his thumb and fingers sliding into his hair. He shifted in his seat as his mind attempted to steer him straight towards the memory of strong thighs wrapped around his hips and the feel of a rain-soaked body pressed against his…

"Oh my God." His eyes snapped back into focus, finding Krista's rounded gaze. "*Is* there a Melanie?"

"Don't be ridiculous. I don't have time to play video games."

"You took an awfully long time to answer," she said, excitement evident in her voice.

"I had to shuffle through the three dates I've been on in the past four months. Determine if any of them were worth mentioning."

"Uh huh. I'm not convinced. I need to know all the tea. Is it this woman Shannon keeps referring to as Lip Filler?"

A scowl returned comfortably to Theo's face. "Trying to decipher who her nicknames belong to is an impossible task. It's like she has a filing system only she can understand."

"Is it Flower Crown? MILF and Cookies? Sunshine? Tat Daddy? Oh wait," she said, shaking her head. "That's her nickname for you."

Theo choked on his own spit, barely managing to keep his wine from sloshing over the glass's rim. He sat up on the couch and pinned his sister with a serious look.

"Tat Daddy? Please tell me you're joking." He thought Lulu was as bad as it could get and truly should have known better.

Krista laughed a full, joyous laugh because she clearly didn't value his friendship.

"Joking about what?" Sebastian asked, shuffling past the living room and straight to the fridge.

"Nothing, mate. The last thing I need is you and Shannon teaming up against me." A mocking shiver ran down his spine at the thought, but Theo couldn't help the small lift at the corner of his mouth.

***

"He's impossible. Stubborn, defensive and…" Shannon pulled the hand from her hair to wave it in searching loops. "Bossy," she landed on before resuming her manic braiding.

"Okay, want to try that last one again? He is technically your boss, so that insult didn't exactly stick the landing," Ben said, his head resting on Evie's lap on the couch.

"Dogmatic," Evie suggested as she played with Ben's long red hair.

Shannon's gaze circled their living room, the ridiculous colors soothing her as she fought not to think about the black and gray swirls of Theo's skin. The man had been taking up too much space in her mind as it was. She sat cross-legged on the floor, still in the sweaty outfit she had worn to the gym. Since their usual Dolores Park session had been rained out, they collected their provisions after the gym and lugged it all back to the apartment she and Ben shared, none of them bothering with a shower afterwards. Between holding Ben's hair back as he vomited up mimosas in college and giving Evelyn's butt mole a thorough inspection when she thought it looked funny, they had all seen way worse from each other than sticky skin and frizzy hair.

"It doesn't matter what adjective I use for the man. They're all fitting. I just don't understand why he won't even hear me out."

She had filled them in on everything. Well, she hadn't told them about her degree, an odd truth that she just couldn't release into their circle of trust.

"He's too proud," Ben said, wincing when his hair was tugged too hard. "Sexy Brit doesn't want to relinquish any power. It's very Thomas Shelby of him."

Shannon snorted. If only. If she were in an episode of Peaky Blinders at least she could don a flapper dress and have amazing hate sex. As it was, her dry spell was somehow getting dryer, and all her fantasies had started to feature the same main character. Tatted, amber-eyed and crooning about how good she was being. A shiver raked down her spine as

90

she fought to suppress the image. Clearly sexual deprivation was not great for one's mental stability if she was having fantasies about Lucifer incarnate.

Although the one that involved caramel and whipped cream had been particularly…riveting.

Growing frustrated with her own weakness, she unraveled her braid, running her fingers through the plait just to immediately start braiding it back together.

Get it together.

"I don't think that's it," Evie chimed in. "Theo doesn't exactly give off ego-driven misogynist vibes."

"Agreed. And we all know Bloem is his life. He would do anything to save it."

"Except bring you into the mix, apparently," Ben said with a simple directness.

Hurt unfurled in her chest at a mortifying speed. Eyes stinging, she focused all her attention on the vibrant, obnoxious colors of the rug beneath her butt.

Ben cursed and sat up, rubbing his head where Evie had obviously pulled his hair.

"Be a little more sensitive, asshole," Evie scolded.

"No, he's right." Shannon sighed, falling back to lay flat on the floor. "I know that Theo and I have the whole love/hate relationship perfected, I just thought there was a little more love there. Enough for him to at least *consider* my investment in Bloem." His rejection irked her more than she let on.

"You care about that place and the people in it. Almost as much as Theo," Evie said simply. "In my opinion, he's being a Grade A douche canoe."

She shrugged, a nonchalant gesture that looked as synthetic as it felt. Not ready to admit exactly how much it stung to be cast aside; Shannon kept her sour thoughts to herself and focused her energies into something she *could* control.

"It doesn't matter. What matters now is that I take my new responsibilities seriously."

"The socials have been great lately," Ben sputtered out. An apology for his careless response earlier.

Shannon smiled reassuringly at the ceiling. "Thanks. I've got Lulu working on the liquor license as well. We should be able to rebrand and promote a happy hour within a month. I'm drawing up a contract so we can rent the space out for events, and I have a possible artist lined up for a month-long residency. People will show up for some live entertainment. I just hope it will be enough."

A flimsy word—hope. She didn't just *hope* it would be enough to keep Bloem in business, she wished for it with her entire being. Every new face that walked up to the bar set her body on edge. Like they were the make or break of her happiness. An insane thing to feel about a collection of concrete and stainless steel.

"Well, you could take my friend's place in Whisk Wars," Evie threw out, patting her lap at a distrusting Ben.

"The baking competition?" Shannon sat up, watching as Ben flipped her off before sipping from his mezcal soda, pinky in an upright position.

"Yup. She was supposed to be on the next season but got knocked up."

"Ew, don't use the phrase knocked up. It's a gross descriptor for the miracle of childbirth."

"Everyone stop talking about childbirth." Ben cringed. "It's killing my buzz."

Evelyn waved him away. "Buzz or no buzz, she's not doing it anymore which is crazy to me. Sure, she'd be kinda pregnant towards the end of filming, but the cash prize is two-hundred fifty k. That's some major baby money."

"Two hundred fifty thousand?" Shannon's eyes went impossibly round. "Dollars?"

Evie bit into a peanut butter cup, nodding her head.

"Not to mention the press. If you got on a show like that, you'd have a line out the door after the first episode aired. Especially with Sexy Brit in one of those tiny aprons of his."

Shannon smirked. Aprons *did* look tiny on Theo's hulking frame.

"Right. Then there are the promotional and sponsorship deals that present themselves if you win," Evie added. She flashed Shannon a sad smile when she caught the gleam in her eye. "But Tat Daddy will never go for it."

He wouldn't. Even picturing Theo faking smiles for the cameras had her fighting back a scowl. He could barely be nice to their guests for sugar's sake, and grumpiness probably made for terrible TV. There was absolutely no doubt in her mind that he would rather sell the building than ham it up on a baking competition.

"Where is it filmed again?" Shannon asked, ignoring Evie's gentle statement.

"England," Ben said through a mouthful of popcorn.

Evie's vision narrowed to slits. "It doesn't matter, because Theo will never agree to do it."

A funny feeling zipped through Shannon's nerve endings. "What if he didn't exactly have a choice?"

"Oh my God. Yes," Ben sang, sitting up straight and holding his drink aloft in toast. "She has that look in her eye Evie Jean."

"Can you connect me with your friend's agent?" Shannon asked, excitement coating every word.

"Shannon, you can't be serious. Theo will skip over firing you and go straight to murdering you slowly. Besides, he can't just take off for what could possibly be months. Are you expected to do all of his wholesale fulfillment? All of the baking, ordering, managing? You'll burn yourself out."

"I'll be going with him," she stated simply, ignoring Evie's gaping mouth. "It's a team competition. He needs a sous chef."

"And who's going to run the café?" Evie's voice was growing a bit frantic. "Who's going to be there to…help?"

Shannon gave her an exasperated look. "I'll figure it all out. I already have ideas about production, and I can get Theo to roast his little heart out until we leave so his wholesale accounts are fulfilled."

Shimmying on her knees, she positioned herself in between Evelyn's legs, desperately clinging to her forearms. "Please help me with this. A couple months is nothing when it could literally save a business. And there is nothing I want more than that."

Brown eyes met hers, soft and maybe a little sad. She couldn't quite place her friend's strange mood and didn't have the head space to dissect it. In fact, the remainder of her precious head space was overtaken the minute Evie nodded, a grin spreading on her beautiful face.

"Okay, let's Mission Impossible this baking competition," she said, flipping her arms so she could give Shannon's a little squeeze. Ben whooped and shifted on the couch, his hands joining theirs in a weird pretzel of friendship, trust, and purpose.

"Sexy Brit is going to crush it in those tiny aprons!"

Shannon's smile cracked like a whip because yeah, Sexy Brit was going to crush it. And she was going to help him do it.

CHAPTER NINE

Theo read over the email for what had to be the twelfth time, eyes running along the words yet not fully understanding any of it. Accepted, partner, Cotswold, cash prize. All of those things were words that held meaning in the English language, he just struggled to comprehend how they related to him.

The timer on his phone rang out, pulling him from the email and into motion. He descended the stairs, giving a brief nod to one of their regulars before passing by Shannon and into the kitchen. He barely looked at her as he passed while she openly stared. Her attention wasn't unwelcome so much as it was uncomfortable. As if she could see through his calm demeanor to the panicked man underneath. The one who met with a potential buyer that very morning and failed to tell her about it.

He had turned down the offer of course, but couldn't quite bring himself to tell her. *Not her business,* he reminded himself and those words settled in his bones like a betrayal, achy and persistent.

Snagging a couple of mitts from their designated hook, he circled the wood-topped workstation and opened the oven door. Warm spices and the smell of apples met him, caressing his senses with comfort. Apple tarts had always been his favorite fall treat. People went crazy for those damn pumpkin buns when he knew their minds would be blown with one bite of his flaky, buttery apple tarts.

Alas, his eyes grew a little wistful as he slid the tray onto a rack to cool. He would probably end up consuming half of the tray himself, a fact that still didn't keep him from making them. Stubborn in his attempt to get people to try something simple and delicious.

The curtain separating the kitchen from the espresso bar flung open as Shannon came back with a handful of dishes. Their eyes met for a brief pause before she walked past him towards the dishwasher. Her hair was tied back in a long braid, a dusty pink ribbon weaved into the plait. She wore a cream-colored shirt similar to the one she had on during her high beam performance, the collar a sweet little scallop at her throat.

She looked adorable, and Theo forgot for a second how fiery she could be. A hurricane stowed into the most delicate little package.

"Nice apron," she said, whipping him from his thoughts. He had been staring, and the smirk on her face told him she knew it.

A frown settled into his features. "It's the same style I've worn for years." He barely managed not to look down at himself for an assessment. Why was he so jumpy lately?

"Yeah, and they all appear to be toddler sized when you wear them. It's truly adorable."

His frown deepened. He had just thought the same thing about her, but the sentiment hit different when pointed back in his direction.

Shannon took a few steps closer to him, tucking a loose strand behind her ear.

96

"What's up? You've been avoiding me lately, is it the increased selfies?" She asked with absolutely no bullshit.

"I haven't been avoiding you," he lied. "I've been busy."

She hummed; her eyes darted to the tattoos on his neck for the briefest of seconds.

"Anything to report?" She raised her chin, lips in a thin line even as her eyes softened to an impossible blue. Even with that stoic demeanor he saw the vulnerability there. He hated it. Hated that it had such an effect on him. He wanted to run his thumb over that stubborn jaw, ease the tension and soothe her worried mind.

Inappropriate and not at all what she wanted from him.

"No," he said simply, hating himself for the lackluster answer when her eyes fell to the floor. "Unless I fancy a trip to the mother land apparently."

Shannon's head snapped up, her eyes pinning him to the spot. "What do you mean?"

He shook his head, brows pulling together. "Just some scam email about a baking competition. Apparently, I could win a large sum of money." Theo rolled his eyes. Another timer pinged, almost managing to pull his attention from the woman, open-mouthed and staring as if he had just claimed that he loved pumpkin spice.

"You alright?" He managed to keep one eye on her while pulling another tray filled with maple hazelnut biscotti from the oven. He racked the tray just below the apple tarts and turned to find Shannon clutching her phone in a death grip and poring over its contents. His lips fought a smile, instead pulling down as he took in the sweet little daisies peppering a light blue phone case. Matched perfectly to the human that wielded it.

"We were accepted," she whispered, her eyes running along lines he couldn't see.

He took a step closer, worrying at her tone. "Lil—"

"Whisk Wars."

Theo paused in a second step nearly tripping over his own feet. That name sounded familiar.

"You got that email too? Just delete it before you get hacked or something."

"It's not a scam, Lulu." Shannon's eyes were round and bright and searching, scanning his features as she continued. "Bloem has been accepted to compete in a team baking competition in the UK. This email literally has the full itinerary attached. Did you seriously not read it?"

Theo scoffed, stepping to Shannon's side and glancing over the email on her screen. There was a full itinerary. One that kicked off in an impossibly short month. Shannon practically vibrating with excited energy as he continued reading. Cotswold District. Okay, so it was close to his mum which was a plus. But there was no way in hellfire he would be able to zip off to England for, he looked again, *six weeks*. There was no one on the staff that he trusted with the bake aside from Shannon, and he wouldn't leave her with all the stress. It was too long of an absence. Not to mention the travel. He couldn't exactly spend frivolous money gallivanting across oceans.

"I can hear you thinking," Shannon breathed, their faces closer than before as he leaned in to read from the small screen. "And we can figure this out. I already have a few ideas, and travel expenses will be covered."

Slowly, Theo turned his attention to Shannon with narrowed eyes.

"*Thank you for your submission?*"

"Don't be mad," she cooed, her own eyes shooting daggers as she turned to face him. "An opportunity grew, and I decided to pluck it."

He searched her face for any sign of teasing. This had to be a joke, right? There was no way this woman, the one that knew him better than his own brother, actually signed him up for some cheesy, demoralizing bake off.

"You are perfectly serious, aren't you?"

She rolled her eyes before telling him everything. How she contacted the agent who passed along a submission video and application. How the agent said they were desperate to fill the spot but there was a waitlist, so her chances were a little slim. How, at the end of the day, it all depended on if they were the right fit for the show.

"I'm actually shocked," she said with a little smile. "I thought we were too late."

"No," Theo said, before walking to the curtain and glancing out to make sure there wasn't a line for the other barista. There wasn't, and his employee leaned against the counter with a useless rag in one hand and his phone in the other.

This only added to his anger. He barreled from the kitchen, scaring the life out of the barista and kicking him into action. The kid wiped at nothing so quickly, he ended up knocking over several syrup bottles then frantically setting them straight, avoiding Theo's eye.

Ignoring him, he turned instead to the office knowing Shannon wouldn't follow him there. She had refused ever since, well, since that day. And maybe he was a coward, and that was fine. There was no timeline in which he would dance off to England in the middle of a financial crisis so he could humiliate himself on television. And simply put, he would avoid Shannon for the rest of his life if it meant never seeing that sad look she would inevitably wear when he rejected another one of her ideas.

The minute he mounted the steps, he whipped off his apron, Shannon's taunting still ringing through his brain. He was a big man; it wasn't his fault they didn't make appropriately sized clothing for his bulky frame. He flung the apron aside, trying to rein in his scattered thoughts enough to read through the email once more. Giving it a more thorough look, he made it to the paragraph explaining the filming schedule when Shannon's voice cut through whatever indie station she had playing.

"That's not an answer I'm willing to accept." Her tone was ice cold. Freezer burn inducing. "*No*. You sound like a broken record. Only managing to produce hard rejections rather than any real solutions."

Theo spun his chair around slowly, noting the way Shannon stayed tucked into the corner near the stairs. She wouldn't be getting anywhere near the loft wall and reminder of her brush with injury. She certainly wouldn't have died, or at least that's what he had told himself only five hundred times in the past month. Still, he tracked her gaze as it shifted warily to the wall and back to his face, her chin lifting.

"This is hardly a real solution. Taking a vacation across the pond is not an effective use of my money right now."

"I told you, travel is covered—"

"I'm not taking your money," he cut in.

"It's a gift," she snapped. Taking a step forward, she stared him down in a way that said what she really wanted to gift him, was a swift kick to the balls.

"I appreciate your efforts here, I really do. But let's think about this logically. This is a team competition and the only person here who has the ability to bake is you. If you come with me, there is no one here to run the café and the fact remains that I don't have the kind of money it will take to float us."

Us. He said the word so easily these days. With the way Shannon was fighting tooth and nail for the café, it was almost easy to ignore it until unease and something like fear shrouded him. There had been an Us once before, and that had ended poorly to say the least. Devastating him, Krista, Bast, and his bank account. None of which truly ever recovered.

"I'll be going with you."

Theo laughed, a true laugh that practically started in his toes before being ejected from his body.

"And if you're with me, who's here? Who will do the baking and roast for all of my wholesale accounts?"

"If you would pump the breaks on this stand you seem to be taking, I would love to actually explain my plan."

Leaning back, Theo gestured for her to go ahead—waste her breath on something that would happen when the gates of hell were covered in Christmas lights and the underworld enjoyed a little snow day. She would have to take the floor in a big way if there was any hope of convincing him to carry out this insane plan.

And take the floor she did.

Theo didn't utter so much as a grunt as Shannon laid everything out, making points about the press and notoriety the show would bring before even touching the subject of prize money. Her plan for the staff wasn't his favorite, but it was one he hadn't even considered before she laid it out so crisply, it was clear she had given it hours of thought.

At some point in her speech, he stood to pace. His feet carried him back and forth in the tiny space, eyes constantly darting down to the empty chairs and silent espresso machine. His apprehension didn't come from insecurity. He knew what he had was special. Having truly started from the bottom, Theo had clawed his way through bakeries and Michelin kitchens across the world until Bloem stopped being simply a dream and became a hard-earned reality. One that he knew, in the deepest corners of his soul, was something special. People just needed to see that.

One already had.

His pacing slowed to a stop as he realized the only sound was that of Lord Huron playing from the café's speakers. Facing Shannon, his eyes swept across her face like they always did. Memorizing every line, dip, blush, and blink. Searching for signs of deception and coming up with nothing but trouble. Trouble because, try as he might to unmask the villain beneath her angelic features, he always came up empty. Instead finding things that made him want to run for his fucking life. He wanted to believe in those things so badly, it took all his energy not to whisk her up again, press her right back into that wall and demand she tell him the truth. Speak the words out loud with nothing separating them but the air they shared.

He'd find the lie then—hear it in the quiver of her voice and tremble of her lips. Although painful, that scenario was one he knew well and knew how to handle. As it was, he didn't know what to do with the fierce, unwavering faith he saw in her now. Faith in Bloem.

Faith in him.

Crossing her arms at the chest, Shannon lifted her chin impossibly higher, one brow quirking up in defiance. She was expecting a rejection and fuck if she wasn't the only one.

Taking a step forward, he frowned down at the woman, steeling himself. "I see one glaring flaw in your plan," he murmured. Shannon cocked her head but kept her chin up, daring him to present her with a challenge to crush. "Who is going to continue your matchmaking while we're gone? I'm not all that confident in Trent's abilities." He nodded his head in the direction of his barista downstairs before, shocking even himself, Theo extended his hand in a gesture that brought back carefully suppressed panic and doubt. An involuntary shiver sliding over his spine as Shannon jumped to take it in hers, eyes widened to rounds.

"I have a plan for that too," she squeaked, giving his hand a little shake to seal the deal. She stumbled closer, a blush rising to her cheeks as they plumped with excitement.

"Okay Lily, looks like we have some work to do."

Theo barely had time to properly appreciate the unfiltered glee that lit her eyes up like stars before he was stumbling back from the impact. A blonde bundle of sunshine held tight in his arms. Christ, but she squeezed him tight, her arms circled behind his head and her face nestled into his neck. Her breath heated the sensitive skin there, and Theo had to work really REALLY hard not to lean into the feeling. Let it make the tough decisions for him. Decisions that would have his arms lifting her further off her feet and forcing her face closer to his.

She smelled just as good as he remembered. Feminine. Floral. Not like those fucking lavender lattes he constantly had to make, more like walking past jasmine vines on a summer day. Like sun-warmed petals and earth. It irritated the shit out of him, and still his arms tightened ever so slightly around her waist. As if his body wasn't quite willing to do what his brain demanded.

That wouldn't do. He pulled away, and the way his skin felt without her pressed against it was admittedly awful. Like he would never feel warmth again for as long as he lived.

"We are going to win this thing," she murmured, her hands snaking down his arms as she pulled away. His fingers twitched, attempting to catch those wandering hands before they could disconnect from him in any way. She sounded so sure—so confident in their futures. And it was truly for the best when he allowed his hands to fall to his sides and took a large step back.

Shannon did a little happy dance, a small squeal released from her throat.

"We are going to win this thing," she said with more oomph, her happy dance turning into a little trot around the small office. Her enthusiasm didn't quite spread to him, however. As Theo watched his longest standing employee— and arguably Bloem's biggest fan—celebrate, a pressure crushed his lungs.

They had to win. This plan only worked if they got that prize money to make up for missing six weeks of work. Shannon's trotting turned back into a little dance as she began chanting "Whisk Wars! Whisk Wars!" her confidence practically emanating from her skin like sunlight. Again, with the fucking faith. Faith in Bloem, in Theo—in them.

He just stood there, rooted to the spot and having a mild panic attack when the door to the café opened, and a large group walked in from the fog. Shannon darted a glance at the door, then back to his face, an odd expression painting her features.

"How many of those apple tarts are included in my manager's salary?" She asked.

Theo let out a surprised huff. After a tilt-o-whirl morning, hearing Shannon voice a very Shannon question suddenly grounded him.

"One half. You have to split one with Trent so he knows what he's selling."

"How about I take a whole one, stage it up nicely for some content, eat the whole thing, then describe what it's like to Trent."

"How about you go help that group that just ordered six maple cinnamon lattes? God save us." Theo looked to the sky for strength just as someone below commented on how cute the café looked. "It's like the *Keebler cottage*?" he whisper-hissed.

Shannon simply turned on her heel, extended her hand, and snapped a photo of their faces before sauntering towards the stairs.

"I was going for the house from Practical Magic, but potato potahto I guess."

"I suppose you fancy yourself the level-headed sister," he blurted, the conversation distracting his troubled mind.

She paused at the top of the stairs, tossing a parting grin over her shoulder. "Don't be silly, Lulu. *We* are the wise Auntie's who have midnight margaritas and cast love spells." She descended the stairs, her steps fading into the throng of café guests and soft music.

He had no idea what that meant.

But as he watched her from the loft, a strange fondness wedged its way into his chest right next to the pressure from earlier. There were a thousand things to add to his to-do list now that he was to be absent from Bloem, but still he watched her. Tracked her efficient movements as she pulled espresso and steamed milk, the sound of the busy machines comforting him more than he cared to admit. Remaining focused on her task, she didn't look up. Didn't see him staring and thinking and feeling. Didn't notice his attention as he ran his gaze along her hands, the stubborn line of her jaw—that fucking ribbon in her golden hair.

Shannon didn't see his eyes fill with things he never allowed himself to feel. Dangerous, off-limits things that would make her smug and absolutely insufferable for weeks if expressed. No, she worked on, completely unaware of his warring emotions as her hands moved with quick, no-nonsense movements. But she was smiling, and shit—so was he.

CHAPTER TEN

Flying was a series of carefully tested procedures and practices for someone who feared heights. Evie and Shannon had always had that in common. Where Evelyn's fear rested in relinquishing control, Shannon's was a bit more visual with the point starting and ending with her preferring to be grounded. A sixteen-foot high-dive at the pool was just as bad as a thirty-one-thousand-foot cruising altitude in her humble opinion.

That said, after thirty-two years of traveling the skies, she had rules. Keep the window shut, always have a movie on, fly first class. That last one was not necessarily a requirement so much as an indulgence. She liked her space. Her day-to-day was to the brim with schmoozing and smiles and she genuinely loved that. She liked people. That was one of the greatest parts of hospitality—all those fresh faces and personalities and quirks and lessons. Sometimes, the thought of all those fleeting interactions congested her with sadness, making her wish for a sponge-brain to soak up the missed wisdom and funny jokes.

But it got tiring. Always being *on*. Her quiet, solitary moments were a gift. Precious minutes of blessed quiet where she focused in on her own well-being rather than caring for everyone else's. Unfortunately for her, Theo's death stare was louder than any chatty guest. The minute they called first class to begin boarding and Shannon popped up from her seat, his face had shifted into a flame-inducing glower, landing directly on her eyes, and roaming. He always did that, ran his gaze over every inch of her face as if seeking out her flaws. It unnerved her.

Too soon they had been seated next to one another in thick, bitter silence. She wasn't going to apologize for spending the money. The flight was ten hours, and she was traveling with the world's largest grimace. She wasn't about to share leg room with the ogre. Even then, the man glowered down at the extra space as if it were the most offensive part of the airport when they all knew that particular gold star went to the eighteen dollars you spend on one watered-down vodka soda.

But grumpy, lump of a boss aside, she was practically vibrating with excited energy, ignoring Theo's foul mood as she scrolled through the movie options and planned her marathon. They had spent the past month working tirelessly to prepare for their departure. The ache from making and freezing about a thousand cookies and cakes could still be felt in her fingers, bone deep. It was nothing compared to Theo roasting coffee until he looked about ready to chuck himself into the roaster. They needed to relax, keep their minds at ease knowing that the café was well cared for.

Having worked at the café for a few years when they first opened, Krista was given a full refresher course and took over as the official boss while they were away. They had also managed to bring Benjamin, Evie, and some of their regulars into the mix. The wholesale production had been packaged, labeled, and organized alphabetically by business. All but one of them willing to pick up their order rather than have it delivered for the next six weeks. After only a little bit of schmoozing, Shannon managed to convince two of their usual buyers to pay them in advance for their orders and she personally delivered them before leaving.

She didn't mention how one of them had asked for her number and a dinner date because why infuriate Theo any further? After their initial celebration, which admittedly was quite one sided, he had gone back to ignoring her when they were together and sharply looking away anytime she caught his eyes on her. Quite the conundrum seeing as they were supposed to be teammates for the next month and some change.

"Are you going to tell me?"

Theo's voice cut through her musing just as the last passengers were trickling onto the flight. His voice was downright hoarse from underuse, and she had to ask him to repeat himself to be sure he had actually spoken to her.

"I just—I don't understand all of this. Why?" He waved his hand around the first-class cabin. "Look at these seats. They're more comfortable than the couch at the café."

"Champagne?"

Shannon suppressed a wince as Theo zipped his gaze to the flight attendant carrying a tray of sparkling wine in mini stemless flutes. His hands appeared to be moving without his permission as he plucked two glasses from the tray, handing one to her, and a muffled "cheers" to the attendant.

God, he was kind of cute when he got extra broody. His brows looked primed to kiss and the wrinkle around his eyes formed sweet little designs that begged to be smoothed away. She valued her hands staying attached to her body so there was no chance of that happening, but a girl could appreciate a good face when she was inches away from it. Even if the owner of that face was a devilish old grump.

"You're wondering why I am able to blow money on boujee travel expenses and hospitality ventures?" she asked, getting straight to the point. He grunted, taking a sip of his bubbles and rolling his eyes when he clearly realized it was delicious.

It was none of his business. Shannon had always been tight lipped about her family, their Ivy League educations and mansion in The Hills. It was a difficult subject for her, which made her feel like a spoiled little brat. Poor little Shannon with her privileged upbringing. How difficult it must have been to go on ridiculously extravagant family vacations and never have to worry about money. She knew that was how people would see her if they knew. Hell, she would probably feel the same.

But as she watched Theo actively try not to word vomit every one of his questions, an odd feeling came over her. Like she could trust this man she had nicknamed Lucifer. Like the pressure on her chest was in fact eagerness to get it all out there between them and know for sure whether or not he would judge her for the things she did and the way she felt.

She began speaking before even registering her lips were moving. "My family has always been swimming in wealth, and I don't necessarily mean money although there was a good amount of that too. We had each other. Where too many family dynamics can be cold and distant, ours was rich and full and overflowing with love and affection. It was the type of family that you scoffed at for being so perfectly clichéd." Ring swiveling around and around on her finger, the words spilled out, plane slowly creeping forward. The simple band always adorned her finger, a constant accompaniment to her showier vintage pieces. Catching herself fiddling, she reached for the champagne, taking a sip before continuing on, lowering her voice to a whisper as the preflight announcement flashed on their screens.

"I was really young when my dad died. Heart attack. It was so sudden and so unexpected I think my mom would have completely fallen apart had it not been for us. My sisters and me. We kept her going when all she wanted to do was shatter to pieces." Theo shifted in his seat, his legs angling towards her. She crossed her own legs in his direction, finding the near connection comforting as she laid it all out. Her eyes remained locked on the dance of her champagne as she continued.

"We had a full, love-filled upbringing. My mom and grandma both cared for us until—well, until my mom passed when I was twenty."

"Lil," Theo murmured, his fingers flexing around the champagne flute. "You don't have to tell me all of this." His voice was hoarse and filled with something she couldn't quite place. Possibly regret for inviting her to hit him with this sob story.

"I want to." Her eyes finally lifted to his, finding them soft, his frown in perfect form. "You've opened up to me lately, it's only fair that I do the same." They both knew his opening up had been minimal at best, but he had let her in a little. And that had to count for something.

"That was a tough loss, one that I won't get into, or I will certainly end up ugly crying all over your shockingly black shirt." He grunted in agreement, the noise alarmingly close to a growl. "My sisters and I weren't totally alone. We had each other, our bonds only growing stronger through the grief. There was my grandmother, who had lost a son and daughter-in-law within a ten-year period. I still think about how lucky we were that she was able to take us in. She helped us *so much* through it all.

"But she also passed, right? Just after you started at Bloem?" Her wide eyes surveyed his serious features with surprise.

"Yes. How did you—"

110

"I remember," he said simply. His gaze running over her brows, cheeks, lips before settling on her eyes once more.

She swallowed, her emotions swarming every nook of her brain like angry hornets. Looking down at her bubbles once more, she fought the urge to cover her head with a blanket as the plane rumbled down the runway and lifted from the ground. Stomach hollowing out, her eyes squeezed shut for a few moments before deep breaths brought her out of it. She willed herself to stop focusing on how high they were climbing and instead thought about her sisters, her mother's smile, the dimple in her grandmother's left cheek and the ribbons she used to tie into her long, silver hair.

Taking a final deep breath, she allowed her stomach to even out just as the plane did and met Theo's narrowed gaze once more. He had an odd look, as if worry and impatience battled within him. Still, his furrowed brow and downturned lips comforted her in a way. She could always count on his surly demeanor and that settled her—grounded her.

"To answer your question, I'm a trust fund baby, I believe that's what they call people like me. My mother placed the inheritance from my father in a trust that dished out funds to us the minute we turned eighteen. When my mother passed, we—well she left us everything. The money from the trust was distributed as well as the inheritance from her. I'm sure you can see where this is going."

"Your gran passed away, and you inherited an even larger sum?"

Shannon raised her glass to him. "Bingo. My sisters and I had more money than we ever could have imagined, and you know what? I would give it all up just to have one more year with any one of them."

She took a bigger swig from the bubbles, hoping they would soothe her raspy throat. Thinking of her family always made her feel so terribly sad. Then she felt guilty for feeling sad because, compared to some, she was insanely lucky. She had experienced two amazing parents who loved and nurtured her. A grandparent that not only raised her, but raised her to be a strong, independent badass. Her sisters were the most amazing, hardworking, caring people on this rock of a planet. Shannon had loved and been loved. She had been given so very much.

She had just lost a lot too.

"What's with the face?" Theo asked. A teasing question asked in the softest of voices.

"Oh, I'm just wondering if you bought all of that," she teased back before grinning up at him. He merely shook his head, a small twitch at the corner of his lips.

"So, we have a couple of options for the movie marathon. We can do the Twilight franchise, or…"

"I still don't understand why," he cut in.

She blinked, looking over at him with furrowed brows. "I just told you. I inherited all of my money, made some amazing investments, saved my ass off and now we're here." She swept her hand over first class as if that was all the answer he needed.

"The money is not in question here." Shifting his bulk, Theo turned even more to face her in the still-tiny-for-him seats until their knees connected. "I have no doubt in your ability to earn, build, and obtain wealth. I just don't understand why you want to invest it in me."

Setting her champagne aside, she shifted in her seat and began fidgeting with the ring once more, her eyes trained on the shiny gold.

Why was she investing in Bloem? There was an extraordinarily long answer to that remarkably simple question. She could give in and tell him about her family's obsession with success and perfection. About her sisters' Ivy League educations and the expectations and pressure that put on her to strive for their level of success. Every single member of her family had made something cookie cutter of their lives. Her eldest sister lived with her wife in a sweet little rambler with a white picket fence and swollen belly.

She was also the Elle Woods of her law firm. A tiny, blonde, force of a woman with a reputation for winning. She could now add mother to that powerhouse list of descriptors. Then there was Dr. Middle Child. A respected surgeon who, aside from an epic career, also ran a non-profit to fund children's medical needs. She didn't just tend to people, she cared deeply, and it showed in her work every damn day.

Between a lawyer and a doctor, Shannon's own dreams had felt like they were constantly running from expectation. From that very first guest at her grandmother's diner, hands shaking as she poured coffee into ivory mugs, she had been in love with hospitality. The couple had been in a pretty intense fight which had relieved and annoyed her. They never noticed how nervous she was, but they also did not notice *her*.

It was love at first serve. At once fascinating and vexing. Such diverse people and humbling interactions. Every person, every bond built, it had always boosted her up rather than make her feel less-than. And even as she tried not to dredge up the memory, her grandmother's words came rushing over her like a waterfall.

"Do what you love, Banana. Follow the path that leads you to butterflies in the tummy and stars in your eyes. Don't let people tell you that success is money and status. Success is finding happiness in the mundane. It's about smiling in between customers or appreciating a well-baked pie. True prosperity is when you look around yourself—finding strangers and friends alike—and feel at home. Your true North."

Bloem.

Bloem was her true North. Her very own orienting point, keeping her grounded in this spinning pile of rubble. And even as her lips pressed together in the most stubborn line, Shannon's brain begged her to express those feelings to Lulu. To have out with it and give the man all the ammunition needed to take her down or at least be smug about it for the rest of his life.

But…

Soft fingers found her chin and it was a miracle she didn't jump out of her skin. Those fingers gave her a gentle nudge, guiding her face up until she was gazing into an amber stare. Her breath gave an embarrassing hitch as his thumb gently brushed her jaw before he broke the contact and dropped his hand.

"Why, Shannon?" he murmured, his voice softer than usual.

"Because," she breathed, swallowing the truth. "I will never be able to live without your pumpkin morning buns."

Theo's eyes lit as they narrowed, a barely there shake of his head indicating he didn't buy that answer for one second. She refused to break the eye contact, reveling in the way his frown intensified as a grin broke out on her face.

"How many times do I have to tell you to behave?" he rasped before draining the rest of his champagne.

Shannon made a show of snuggling into her seat before saying, "Every day for the rest of your unnaturally long, diabolical life, Lulu."

***

"Are you kidding me?" Theo asked, his eyes ready to pop from his head. "Have you seen a single good film in your life?"

"*Hook* is hardly the pinnacle of cinematic genius, Lulu. How is this making you so upset?"

Shannon ran fingers through her hair, breaking apart the braid she had just spent fifteen minutes constructing. As if he were stuck in a loop of jasmine scented strands and movie trivia, she began the braiding process anew as soon as the last plait was loosed.

It was fascinating to watch, but still didn't change the fact that, "*Hook* is one of the movies that molded my childhood. I was Rufio for Halloween three years in a row." Theo turned further to face her, holding three fingers up as if that would drive his point home. "We have to add that to the queue."

Shannon pouted, but he caught the corner of her mouth twitching.

They were a good five hours into their ten-hour flight and Theo would be kidding himself if he claimed it wasn't some of the most fun he'd had in a while. After getting over the initial awkwardness of sitting inches away from a person he had actively avoided for the past month, he and Shannon settled into a familiar camaraderie. One built of pushes and pulls and jokes and jabs. One he was more than happy to lean into after sadness set those blue eyes swimming as painful memories spilled from trembling lips. Just thinking about the sparkling burst of sunshine that was Shannon having to go through such devastation made his chest ache. It was a marvel to think that someone so sweet—so *good*—had endured such heartache.

Shannon had been all too willing to shift the conversation herself. She forced him to sit through two hours of *Whisk Wars* episodes to give him an idea of what they were heading into. Her exasperated laugh when he admitted he still hadn't seen a single episode still rang through his head like a song he couldn't get unstuck.

But he had suffered through three full episodes, each one more painful than the last. The idea was simple. Bakers and their sous chefs competed in two challenges before the lowest scoring teams battled it out in an elimination round. The first challenge was usually something foundational like crème patisserie or classic shortbread. This challenge went to the sous chefs alone, with the executive chefs only allowed to watch from the sidelines. The show's producers obviously leaned heavily on the drama of it all, filming the baker's reactions to their sous chefs working without them. It would seem every season had at least one douche with an inflated ego talking shit on the sidelines and getting a lot of screen time.

Shannon had fidgeted in those moments, twisting the ring on her finger anytime someone said something demeaning or rude. Nervous, when he knew damn well that she could out-bake any of the competition.

When it was clear neither of them was going to get any sleep, she chose the first movie. An allowance that would never be repeated seeing as it was *Twilight* and Theo fought not to gouge his eyes out within the first half hour. There had been no suggestions of watching their own movies or one of them reading. They were a team. A team that had ten plus hours of unrelenting flying time to get through. They were doing it together.

"Oooh, what about *Ten Things I Hate About You*? It's a classic."

"A classic? Lil, classics are considered to be the most outstanding of their kind. Judged over time to be exceptional works, worthy of at least one if not multiple viewings. You said the same thing about *Twilight*, and I will have to work tirelessly to get that terrible acting out of my brain."

"It's not about the acting; it's about the romance. Something you clearly know nothing about," she said, her words shifting to a whisper as another passenger turned out their light.

Theo spread his long legs, knowing in his heart of hearts that he would never admit it was fucking amazing. Being a man completely resigned to coach, he had never thought there would be a world in which flying didn't consist of cramped knees and knocking elbows. Now what was he going to do knowing this beautiful world of free bubbles and space to breathe was going to drastically change how he traveled to see his mum?

Eyes crinkling at the corners as he thought of the woman who raised him, he leaned over the armrest and whispered, "If romance was something I needed help with, I promise you I wouldn't be taking advice from teens with barely formed brains. These characters have less depth than a kiddy pool."

Not wanting to be annoying, they had turned their lights off so the rest of the passengers could rest easy. Shannon's profile was gently illuminated by the screens in front of them, however, so Theo was able to watch with almost obsessive attention as her neck popped with goosebumps. He knew to expect it. Her skin always reacted to his closeness like that. As if she could sense a ghost and was thoroughly spooked.

She glanced away from her scrolling and pointed a raised brow in his direction, snagged a cream sweatshirt from her lap and pulled it over her head. For reasons Theo would dissect later, he moved, reaching out and plucking the base of her braid, gently pulling her hair from where it had gotten trapped within her neckline.

Shannon paused in her movements, her hands stilling where they tugged the sweatshirt over broad hips. Feeling like an idiot, he dropped the braid over her shoulder but couldn't quite help himself from appreciating the feel of those silky strands between his fingers. She watched him, her lips slightly parted, eyes searching.

Clearing his throat, he turned to face the screen and continued to die a slow, painful death.

"Was that you being romantic?" she asked, her whisper closer than before.

"Don't be ridiculous. I was just helping you out."

A long hum was her only response, driving absolutely insane.

"The bar must be on the floor if a simple assist feels like a romantic gesture to you." His finger continued to shuffle through the movie selections though he saw none of it. His mind distracted with her response.

"Maybe it's the person behind the assist that makes it feel that way," she said quietly. "My big-bad-Brit doing nice, soft-spotty things is kinda romantic."

He scoffed, turning to face her again and regretting it immediately. Shannon's face was right there, inches from his as his words stuck in his throat. She looked up at him, a soft smile playing on her features and a small blush on her cheeks. His eyes moved of their own volition, soaking in long lashes and pink cheeks, soft lips, and blue eyes.

Maybe she was right. The way his gaze always somehow found hers from his perch in the roasting room. The way his stomach hollowed at the sound of her laugh, or his constant fight to ignore whatever pull she had over his body. It truly felt…different. Romantic wasn't the right word for it at all. It felt—catastrophic.

Not to mention completely inappropriate. He was her boss for Christ's sake. Romantic gestures, however small they might be, were not something bounced between coworkers. They weren't even bounced between friends, at least not where Theo was concerned.

This thing between them was simply inevitable. Shannon was the only person outside of Bast and Krista that he had allowed himself to trust. One was bound to feel something about that one person, right?

Deciding that was best kept in the deepest pits of his skull, he played one of her own tactics against her.

"Big-bad-Brit? What happened to Tat Daddy?"

Shannon gaped at him, a gleam in her eye that made him want to do things that were quite off limits. Like brush the loose hair from her face or cup her cheek—press his lips to her forehead.

Okay unhinged-highlight-reel, let's pump the breaks.

"Who told you that nickname?" she whispered.

"I'll never reveal my sources. Now, will you please release me from this plotless hell?"

Peeling his eyes from her delighted features was as much a chore as it was a necessary survival tactic. He quickly pulled up the Robin Williams actual classic *Hook*, getting the film primed and ready as he waited for Shannon to do the same. The cabin noise muffled as he slipped a pod into his right ear, she put in her left, and on the count of three, they each hit play and grinned at each other as the films began in perfect unison.

CHaPTer eLeven

The thing about Shannon's flying rituals was, they didn't end when the flight was over. Once the plane landed and they exited safely, she was required to find ice cream. Preferably soft serve, but really any aerated sweet cream would do. She had downed two scoops of pistachio gelato from the nearest shop, barely taking in any of the scenery before they were picked up by one of the show's drivers and began their almost two-hour drive to the Château.

Their drive to the Cotswolds was something out of a fairytale, and what Shannon missed as she crammed whipped dairy into her gullet, she more than made up for as they traveled. Her eyes took in every rolling hill, cobblestone road, and honey-colored village.

Having seen it all before, Theo passed out immediately after greeting the driver, his gentle snoring almost soothing in the near silent car. But Shannon's nerves were on high alert, her excitement a living, breathing thing within her chest. Her family had traveled well. Shannon remembered trips to Bali and Paris, that one wild year they went to Italy for Thanksgiving then spent Christmas in Prague. But for some reason, she never traveled to England, and she certainly had never seen anything like the picturesque villages and gardens that passed by her window now.

As they took turn after turn, the car slowing to a cruise, she knew her nervous energy wasn't coming from the sugar rush of traveling a new country. Her confidence in Theo was unwavering. The things that man did with butter and sugar were criminal. Nowhere in her mind was there an ounce of space provided for doubt in the ogre snoring gently at her side. He was brilliant, and the world was about to see it.

There was just a large chance they were going to see her crash and burn as well. Her fear was awake, stretching like a cat readying to quickly and efficiently pounce on the mouse of her self-confidence. Nerve was a hell of a thing, wasn't it? Unfortunately, hers truly was like a small rodent, skittering all over the place, unable to slow or catch or control. One minute she was boosting herself up with a movie-worthy pep talk, the next she was practicing her elimination speech in the mirror.

At least she had confidence in that elimination speech being an absolute slapper.

"We're about five minutes out, Miss," the driver said quietly with a glance at Theo through the rearview.

Not possessing nearly as much chill as the driver, she shook Theo's shoulder, waking him with a jolt. His hair was mussed on one side, a line from the jacket he had been using as a pillow streaked across his cheek. Panicked eyes darted around before he settled, cracking a yawn and snuggling back into his jacket-pillow.

"Don't go back to sleep, Lulu. We're almost there." Her voice shook slightly, the octave scary high.

"I'll wake up if you say it," he murmured, his voice rich with sleep.

"Don't start this again. You're going to miss our first view of the château."

"Why is this thing called a château? We're in the Cotswolds, not the French countryside."

"Well, it was built by a French man who had a genuine love of annoying his British neighbors.

"Not far off the mark, there," the driver murmured.

"Great, you still have to say it."

"Lulu, you're being unreasonable…"

"Say it, Lily, and you'll have my undivided attention."

"*Hook* is better than *Twilight*," she said in a rush, the words practically mushing together.

"Did you hear that, Samuel? She said the nineteen-ninety-one cult classic *Hook* is better than a steaming pile of dung."

Poor Samuel acknowledged the admission, his lips quirking.

Theo's eyes popped open, sitting up he stretched out as much as possible without touching her, leaning his head from side to side, his neck popping in response. Her eyes caught on that swirling constellation, the stars tiny and detailed as they cascaded under the neck of his long-sleeved shirt.

"Now, give me what I really want."

Shannon caught Samuel's eyebrow raise in the reflection, his idea of what that meant clear as his eyes stayed trained on the brick road ahead. Trees lined the road, hiding what lay beyond as they slowly made their way toward the mansion that was their temporary home for, hopefully, the next six weeks.

"I'm not sure you deserve it," she cooed. Her stomach did the little flip it did every time she decided to mess with Theo. Flirt, mess—whatever.

His sleepy eyes became alert, bright as they narrowed and his frown leveled.

A feathering kicked up at his jaw, drawing her gaze for a brief moment before it landed on those tawny eyes once more. She wondered what it was he was holding back from saying as they stared. Why he wouldn't just have out with it and lean in rather than push away.

Her lip quirked up, the twitch costing him as it pulled his attention away from their staring contest and down to her lips. Lips she had painted a rich, berry color as he slept. His gaze heated, and her upturned lips turned into a full-on smirk even as her own body reacted a little too eagerly to that look.

Shannon wasn't driven by vanity, but she knew her body. Knew that the cranberry combined with the soft lapis of her knit sweater would make her eyes painfully blue. Would pull the natural pink from her cheeks and hopefully make her look less tired than she felt. Pulling her hair in a high ponytail and sealing the deal with a soft, pink ribbon had been the cherry on top of her confidence boosting sundae. Who knew the actual cherry on top would end up being Theo's response.

Because it was doing it for her, and she watched every little reaction with laser focus.

His heated gaze disappeared for a brief moment as he squeezed his eyes shut, clenching his jaw as he fought some inner war. A decent person probably wouldn't enjoy Theo's control stumble, but she never claimed to be a decent person. And watching him grind his teeth as his eyes flicked open, landed directly on her lips before beginning that lazy journey to her eyes, gave her a thrill felt all the way down to her toes.

His gaze burned into her, the stubble on his face doing nothing to hide his still-tense jaw. Another little twitch near his ear, just under the cut line of his left cheek. Another thought gone unspoken.

"Here we are." Shannon jolted as the driver sang their arrival. His enthusiasm pulled her gaze from Theo's, frantically swirling around at the trees and the same old road before glancing at him once more. He was pulling his jacket on, eyes trained straight ahead.

She followed suit, unsure of when their flirting stopped feeling like a game and started feeling more *significant.* Even as the trees ended and the sky opened before them, a large courtyard and the most massive house she had ever seen stole the air from her lungs, the image of Theo's hungry gaze burned at the back of her mind.

She was vaguely aware of him shifting forward in his seat, a whistle of appreciation leaving his lips. They had made it, and it was time to push these wild feelings to the side and hustle.

Samuel pulled around a looping drive in front of the building that had Shannon gaping at its size. The building seemed to have several different sections, all honeyed brick covered in vines of orange and yellow leaves. The grass of the courtyard still thrived bright green although peppered with fall leaves, giving the property an air of enchantment.

Small, rounded balconies jutted from the building, giving depth to the architecture, and bringing some of the dark, rectangular windows into focus. So many windows. At least fifty on the front of the mansion that Shannon could tell. They surrounded the large front door, and lights flickered inside as the clouds thickened in the sky. Above the door, Château De Genevieve was scrawled in old, faded letters.

She didn't know where to look. Her eyes scanned the vines clinging to the brick, a gentle breeze stirring up the autumn leaves on the grounds and surrounding gardens. Seeing the warm brick and peak of each rooftop was a completely different experience in person. Her brain couldn't seem to reconcile the site with the one she had seen on television just a few hours ago.

"Well Lily, I'm afraid we can't go in there unless you say it," Theo murmured, his voice closer than she expected as he took in the château from over her shoulder. Her smile was slow and luscious and purely feminine. She opened her door, the fall breeze flinging her flyaways across warm cheeks and

124

giving her a much-needed slap of cold air. Throwing that smile over her shoulder, she gave Theo a wink.

"Bangarang," she said, before slamming the door in his face.

***

Just when he thought there couldn't possibly be anymore overly peppy, infernal blondes in his life, the show's Director of Operations landed on the scene like a fucking Marvel character. Maggie was her name. And he would never be fooled by a loose pant suit and large rimmed glasses again.

The way she had powered out of the château, greeting him and Shannon as if they were the best thing to happen to her in a long while. He wouldn't soon forget it.

"Good Lord, but the two of you are an even lovelier couple in person!" Theo barely had any time to bristle at the assumption that they were a couple before she grabbed his chin in a surprisingly strong grip. "Your bone structure is practically made for TV, dear. There's a razor in the room."

The glare he sent Shannon's burst of laughter had been some of his best work.

Now, after getting a full tour, hearing about the schedule (which blessedly allowed two days for jet lag recovery and one weekend off during filming) and meeting crew members whose names he would never remember, Maggie led them to their rooms. He intended to have a quick shower, maybe a little wank, dip into the covers and sleep like the dead for ten hours.

"Here we are, dears," Maggie chimed, her enthusiasm grating on his every nerve. Shocking absolutely no one, Shannon kept tempo with the woman the entire time they toured the château. He was equally as annoyed with her and those fucking lips. Berry red, lush, and begging for it.

125

Okay, maybe a wank was an essential part of the plan. He desperately needed to blow off some steam.

"So, I have keys for both of you." Maggie handed them each a small card, shattering the illusion a bit. Key cards for a manor in the Cotswolds? "Everything you need should be in there, just let me know if you have any special requests or questions."

She smiled and then, turning on her heel, made to walk away.

Shannon stared at the key card in her hand, then to the door, and finally up at him. Her wide eyes said she was as confused as him, which was a relief.

"Uhm, Miss Maggie," Theo stammered.

She turned immediately; her smile still locked in place.

"Is this my room, or Shannon's?"

Maggie cocked her head, her smile dimming slightly. "This room is for both of you," she said, her voice pitching up slightly. "I didn't think…you. You're our only couple, you see. So, all the other rooms are taken." Her eyes looked ready to bulge from her head.

Theo must have matched her expression, his mind racing. Couple? Why did she keep saying that? Shannon gripped his arm before he could voice the question.

"He's just joking," she said in a rush, tugging him toward the door. "This is lovely, Maggie, thank you."

Maggie smiled at her, frowned at Theo, then turned and strode away, her heels clacking as she rounded the corner.

Theo's brain was moving at a snail's pace, his jet lag getting the better of him as he silently watched Shannon swipe her key card and tug him into the room. His eyes swept over the sage green walls and lush floral couch, armchairs in the same florals bracketing a large fireplace already lit and gently heating the space. He registered the thick, cream-colored drapes, noted the round oak table in front of the windows, two chairs angled and ready for their occupants.

Gaze running over the surprisingly well-equipped kitchen, he collected the information of the room, the door to their right, the lavish four poster bed, the television that made absolutely no sense in this Jane Austen fever dream. Collected the information—yet only managed to cling to one glaring fact.

"There's only one bed."

"Yes," Shannon stated. Tossing her bag in the direction of the couch and flopping into an armchair by the fire. Legs swinging over the armrest, she said, "I can take the couch."

"You should be taking your own room, with your own bed and bathroom," he ground out. Dropping his bag, he stomped across the room and glared at Shannon's lounging form. "Why does she think we're a couple?"

A wince. "Well, I vaguely remember hearing that the contestants who dropped out were a couple. And, okay, I may have oversold our relationship just a tad in the application video." Ignoring Theo's exasperated "What video?" Shannon continued, her feet still swinging without a care in the world. "So, combined with the fact that I told the agent to try his damndest to get us here, it would appear we've gotten ourselves into a bit of a pickle."

"A bit of a pickle? Shannon, what are we going to do when we have to keep this up? If they think we're together and chose us based on that information, we will risk everything if they know the truth. And don't even think about telling me to *take a whisk* right now," he added, remembering the gross number of cheesy puns from the show on their flight.

"What's life without a little whisk? I'm going to be sleeping on the couch. You and I are going to just continue to be our lovely little selves, and no one will be the wiser."

"You can't sleep on the couch for six weeks," he growled, his frustration mounting for a handful of reasons he didn't care to pick apart.

Shannon swung her legs over and sat up, those fucking stained lips quirking up at the corners. "I appreciate your confidence in our chances, and let's say you're spot on and we win this whole thing, what's the alternative? You want to share the bed with me, Lulu? I'm not sure that's a great idea."

Hands on his hips, he looked to the heavens for strength, jaw clenching and unclenching with teeth-shattering force. "Behave," he ground out.

She popped up, placed her hands on his shoulders and gave him a gentle shake. "It's all going to be fine. I got us into this mess, so I'll take the couch. Lord knows your behemoth frame won't fit anyway."

Dropping her hands, she made to walk past him, but Theo shot out an arm circling it over her abdomen and holding her in place, his hand gently curling around her waist. She stopped mid-step; their bodies close and warm and suddenly charged with a strange sort of energy. Fire alarms sounded in his head, warning him to seek shelter under the icy cold stream of his shower. Sirens shrieked at him to keep his mouth shut and run, accept this fresh hell and try to move on without issue. Ignore the weird energy, ignore the pull. Ignore this thing between them that had been gnawing at him for too damn long.

Her head tilted down, taking in his arm wrapped around her front before her eyes darted up to his. He did his sweep, seeing parted lips and for the first time in a while, a serious expression. Some sort of mix of curiosity and reluctance. A strange expression he happened to know well for he felt that particular cocktail of emotions all the damn time.

"I don't think this is a good idea," he croaked, throat suddenly dry.

She cocked her head. "Why?"

"Because." He swallowed, almost managing not to watch her eyes travel down to his throat and back. "This feels like a lot."

It felt like too much. Too much of something that was very much off limits. He wouldn't be telling her that. Wouldn't be admitting that maybe their game of push and pull, of shoving aside unwelcome feelings and ignoring whatever attraction existed between them, was a huge mistake. And now that the buffer of the café didn't exist between them, his fight for control was extremely shaky. He couldn't share a space with her. The plane had been fine because the plane had been full. Seats filled with strangers, keeping him in line and out of trouble. There was no one in this room to referee their relationship.

Not even five minutes in and he was already touching her. Already fighting whatever brilliant inner voice was telling him to dip under her sweater and palm the smooth skin beneath.

"We just need to adjust," she breathed. The usual mischief that lit her eyes like fireworks was gone, replaced by something he couldn't quite name. Theo felt a pressure against his arm and realized that she leaned into him, just a little. Somehow pressing them closer and clearly testing the strength of this tether keeping sanity attached to his body.

"Adjust?" he murmured, his eyes trailing down to her lips. She nodded before wetting those painted lips with a swipe of her tongue causing his hand to tighten its grip around her middle in response. It was a desperate move when he dragged his focus back to her eyes. Looking at that mouth was going to get him into heaping piles of trouble, so he went to the familiar blue pools like a thirsty man. But no, that wasn't safe either. Usually wide in her wrath for him, he didn't know what to do with the slightly hooded gaze, crisp blue pinning him to the spot. Waves crashing on the shore. Whirlpools sucking him into its depths.

Theo dropped his hand and turned, attempting to lose himself in the god-awful floral wallpaper lining one wall of their room. Not working. He shut his eyes, squeezing until the image of those whirlpool eyes was washed from his mind, until unrelenting darkness was the only thing filling his vision.

This felt like too much because it was—because *she* was.

"Theo? Look, I'm sorry. I know you value your personal space, and this is probably the last thing you wanted. I can ask if there are any available rooms, okay?"

He smiled humorlessly up at the ceiling, more of a baring of teeth at whatever inner voice now wanted him to wipe that thought from her head completely. Yeah, he valued his personal space. Shannon knew this because she had been a permanent fixture in said space for years. He wanted to flip around, grab her by the shoulders and tell her that had nothing to do with it. She scared him. This power she lorded over him was downright terrifying.

Could she not feel it?

"Do you need to use the washroom?" he asked through gritted teeth, ignoring every instinct that told him to tell her the truth. Of course she couldn't feel it. Theo watched Shannon seamlessly wrap people around her finger with barely a word at the café day in and out. She could charm her way through customs, nothing but vodka and aerosol in her carry on. After his brother, he had been confident that no one would be able to pull one over on him again. It was a very humbling experience to find that he was wrong.

He focused on a splotch of fuchsia in the wallpaper. A wild rose without any thorns? Not very realistic, but it lent something to obsess over that wasn't the woman behind him. The one taking a step toward him and…

"I am going to go find Maggie…"

"You're not going anywhere," he said, his eyes watering as they stayed trained on that thornless rose. "As far as anyone here is concerned, we are the happiest couple on the fucking planet. You're staying in here with me, and when we win this thing, we're going to go back to the café and pretend this never happened." His head raced with things unsaid. He needed to go back to keeping a comfortable distance, back

130

to the buffer of their regulars and the glaring truth that he was her boss keeping them in line. When this was over, he was going to put as much distance between them as humanly possible.

"Do you need to use the washroom before I take a shower and sleep like the dead for the next eight hours?"

A long, painful silence stretched between them before she finally answered. "Give me five minutes."

Still staring at the wallpaper, Theo waited until the bathroom door snicked shut before bringing his hands to his face and rubbing at tired eyes.

This was a simple thing. He and his employee would be teaming up and could certainly stomach sharing a space with one another. He needed to pull his head out of his ass, focus on winning and getting back to the café where he belonged. It was simple. It had to be simple.

Deciding to pull his head from his ass immediately, he got moving. Snagging his bag from the—you guessed it—floral area rug, he strode to the bedroom and chucked it in the direction of an armchair by the windows. He would be taking the bed. Shannon was right about that. This was her fault and although he agreed to enter into this circus, he never agreed to subject his frame to the confines of the sofa. Moving to the left of the bed, he snagged extra sheets from an ornate armoire, managing to find a quilt as well. He plucked two pillows from his own pile and lugged it all from the bedroom and into the living space.

The last wrinkle was being smoothed from the makeshift bed when Shannon emerged. Gone was the makeup including the berry red lipstick, thank Christ. She had tied her hair in a loose bun on top of her head, and that's where his gratitude for the mercy of a higher being ended. He tried—he really *really* tried not to let his eyes roam. But as if drawn to the extra skin, his gaze wandered to her collarbone, still glistening with a little moisture from the shower, over the swell of her breasts barely covered in a flimsy cami with the smallest shorts on the fucking planet to match. They were covered in sweet little yellow daisies, and maybe Theo liked florals after all. Those little flowers practically made a trail down to her thighs. Thick, smooth, and downright *edible*. That was the only explanation for the way his mouth watered and he took an involuntary step in her direction.

He wanted to scrape his teeth along that smooth skin. Watch the goosebumps ripple across her thighs and figure out once and for all if she tasted as good as she smelled.

His foggy brain connected, realizing she slowly set her phone on a table near the couch and was staring at him, the smirk disappearing from her mouth.

She just said something, asshole. Stop gawking and get to the icy hell of a cold shower.

"What?" he managed gracefully.

"I said, you didn't need to make up the bed for me," she repeated slowly. As if speaking to a child.

Regaining a fraction of his brain cells necessary for conversation, he said, "You might not feel that way after sleeping on this thing. It has actual springs in it." Pressing his hand deep into a cushion, a determined squeak sounded from the whirling florals.

Actively avoiding looking directly at her, he caught the wince out of the corner of his eye.

"I'll be fine," she singsonged, and then did the last thing he needed and touched him. A simple thing. One soft hand wrapped around his forearm, one crushing blue-eyed gaze connecting with his, and one soft brush of her thumb over his shirt. Close enough to smell that ridiculously feminine scent and see the dark blue ring around her irises. Close enough for him to obsess over the fact that they were alone with an ungodly amount of exposed skin and metric tons of tension.

"Thanks," she said with a soft smile. Ignoring or oblivious to his frantic thoughts.

"Don't thank me yet." He had no idea why he said that.

She angled her head. "You agreed to do this and you're managing to roll with the punches even after my super small and almost insignificant single room blunder." He raised his brow, holding still and fighting every muscle as they begged to touch her back. "Combine that with your love of teenage vampire romance, and I'd say there's a lot to be thankful for."

He snorted a laugh and watched in fascination as her eyes lit up. He caught the tug of a smile just before she flopped back on the couch, the springs groaning as she pulled the covers over herself and snuggled in.

"Day one," she said lazily before grabbing a book from the table and settling into her pillow.

"Day one," Theo grumbled, forcing himself to move toward the bedroom and away from the temptress.

The shower was a cold one, and no, he didn't dare touch himself for fear of it doing absolutely nothing but fuel his already heated blood. He simply allowed the cold spray to wash over him, wiping away the grime of travel and hopefully his filthy thoughts along with it. Impossible. Was he utterly insane for actually being excited about their circumstances? Because his circumstances were as follows: he was about to be spending hours upon days with a woman he was so attracted to, it physically hurt. A woman that wore adorable, barely-there pajamas—on his payroll and off limits. But as he watched the water circle the drain at his feet, three hard truths pounded his skull on repeat, one louder than all the rest. He was massively, horribly, irrevocably fucked.

CHaPTer TWeLVe

Shannon's back felt like the camel's. One measly, dust covered strand of wheat away from breaking and taking them out of the competition. The couch was...less than comfortable. She would have preferred the hard cushions of first class thirteen-thousand feet in the air over the squeaky bounce house that was her current resting place. A *permanent* resting place would have been an improvement. A velvet lined coffin was starting to sound like a relaxing vacation stay at the Four Seasons.

At least Theo hadn't noticed. After two days of catching up on sleep and barely leaving their room, he had managed to somehow speak to her less than when they were in separate rooms at Bloem.

Probably for the best. They needed to focus, and unfortunately, the only thing she seemed able to focus on was the memory of his heated gaze as it burned into every inch of her body. Who knew a cute little sleep set would be Lucifer's kryptonite? And who the hell knew it would have such an effect on her? Theo had broken, a small little rift in his usually stoic mask had exposed something unexpected. The way he looked at her, all of her, searching every angle and dip—it had always felt like an inspection.

Until that first day and one daisy sleep set. There was a big possibility he had been conducting an inspection, but one thing had been clear as water, he *really* liked what he saw. It made her feel powerful. Sexy. Turned on and woefully distracted. Not a great combo when trying to win a competitive bake-off.

Theo's hand brushed against the back of hers and she jolted, twinging her back with the sudden movement. She winced, unable to hold it in, then fought back another wince as Theo's eyes narrowed from where he walked at her side. Maggie had called all the contestants to the main dining room for the meet and greet, and Shannon would be blaming every jolt, jerk and jump on her nerves. She was excited to meet everyone, to get the ball rolling and hopefully kick some ass. That was all it was.

"Are you okay?" Theo asked, raking that narrowed gaze over her.

"Yes, stop…" *Unraveling me with that strange look. Touching me with your eyes. Stop making me feel things I shouldn't feel and want things that I really REALLY shouldn't want.* "Looking at me," she settled on.

Nailed it.

"Stop looking at you? That doesn't seem suspicious at all. Tell me what's bothering you before we go in there."

Shannon snorted a laugh. "And maybe while we're at it, I can tell you how stressed I am about making Evie's wedding perfect, or how I don't know what to get my sister for her birthday. Come on, Lulu."

He frowned down at her, his brows drawn and face looking like it had every day since she waltzed into Bloem and demanded a job. It was the same exact face, she told herself vehemently, so stop pining.

"We tell each other things," he said quietly.

She paused a few feet from a table lined with name tags and the familiar blonde bob of Maggie's dome.

"One of us does," she shot back.

They didn't tell each other anything. She told Theo far too much about herself and he sailed through without uttering a question, comment, or sliver of detail about his own life. Shannon hadn't known he was selling, didn't know anything about his family. And okay, not the biggest thing in the world, but she had to share a bathroom with the man to know he wore contact lenses for sugar's sake. Maybe she was grouchy from jet lag, or it could be the incessant throbbing under her left shoulder blade, but Shannon was not interested in sharing any more of herself with a brick wall. She watched the familiar fluttering of his jaw muscles and turned before they inevitably drew her gaze to his tattooed neck. That would only make her more irritable on a day where she needed to be socially relaxed.

The smile she handed Maggie was big, bright, and fake. Not great for television.

"Hello dear," the woman sang. "Here is your name tag, just head in and familiarize yourself with everyone. We'll be filming a bit today, but I just want you to act natural—get used to the cameras."

Her eyes flicked over her shoulder, informing Shannon that Theo had stepped up behind her. Maggie handed him a card as well, nodding in approval at his shaved face.

Shannon strategically placed her name tag on over a lavender knit sweater. Paired with faded ivory jeans and her tan work clogs, she was hoping it offset the black hole that was Theo's frame. Black short sleeved shirt, dark blue denim, and faded black boots. Black ink to offset the black.

She sighed, watching him struggle to apply a sticker with so much blinding color. They had used red marker—whatever was he going to do?

"Here," she snapped, snagging the tag from his hands and peeling away the back sheet.

136

"I don't need to wear it," he rushed, angling his body away from her.

"Lulu, I promise no one is going to care that it doesn't match your outfit," she stammered. Still attempting to slap the tag to his chest.

"There are fourteen of us in there, how hard can it be to remember a name?"

"Just put the damn thing on."

"You're causing a scene," he said between his teeth, now attempting to grasp her forearms and keep them from his body.

Unfortunately for him, she was wriggly. Shannon slipped her hand from his grasp and reared up, slapping the name tag to his chest and pressing her palm flat. She would have noted the hard cut of muscle beneath her fingers, the rapid beat of his heart against her palm and the tingly sensation that radiated from her wrist where it rested in his firm grasp had her eyes not landed on the most fantastical sight she had ever been gifted.

"Theodore?" she whispered, her body filling with delight.

"Thanks Maggie, we'll just head in," he said before dragging Shannon into the conference room. She caught the woman's gaping expression just as her laughter bubbled to her throat.

"Theodore?" she asked again.

"Stop," he whispered back, sweeping his gaze around the room full of contestants and crew members, a few cameras already filming in the corners.

"Like the chipmunks?" she whispered, her delight radiating from every pore.

"Knock it off, Lil."

His scowl was amazing. Ten out of ten, a work of art.

"Your mother is an angel. Please, tell me your father's name is Alvin."

His frown deepened, but he leaned in, his lips a breath from her ear and whispered, "Alfie."

She shuddered, goosebumps running along her neck as they started walking towards the seated group.

"That's Theo-dorable," she teased, the quip a tad raspy.

"Quit it," he managed before they reached the other contestants and introductions began.

There was no time to dwell on her body's reactions to Theo, no time to add to her frustration at having yet another thing kept from her. As she grasped hands and tried to remember names, Shannon shuffled all of her confusing emotions aside and did what she did best. Schmoozed. Theo a stoic blob of muscle at her side, she made her way around the room, smiling brightly at the competition.

People came from every corner of the world for *Whisk Wars*. Her head spun as she laughed and joked with people from Canada, India, Belgium and of course, Britain. There was one other team from the US that she interacted with for all of five seconds before Theo's palm had pressed into her back, steering her toward an older team with soft French accents and an obvious love of patterns. She was all too happy to be swept away after their smug features had looked her up and down for the fifth time.

The room bustled with nervous energy as two men strode through the doors and applause erupted, surprisingly loud for the small crowd inside.

She recognized Charles Darlington, the show's host and as his surname suggested, an absolute darling. His brown hair was styled to withstand a small hurricane while his too-white teeth sparkled with a wide smile. She wasn't fooled for a second by that perfect smile. The man was a professional baker with years under his belt and a reputation for being a hard ass. He would be the one to rip her bakes apart if she had one misstep. Next to him stood the show's producer. A gangly fellow with kind eyes and a ball cap that appeared to have seen better days glued to his head. He clapped his hands, and the room hushed to a low murmur.

"Hello everyone, and welcome to your first day of *Whisk Wars*!" Cheers erupted in a ruckus of applause and shouts of joy. Theo was having none of it, his eyes straight ahead and his frown in rare form.

She nudged him in the side as the producer continued talking, half listening while he chatted about filming.

Theo grunted, sparing her a glance.

"You could at least try to look happy to be here," she whispered, leaning in close.

He turned his head, bringing his lips to her ear again and causing a zip of electricity to run along her spine. "This *is* me trying."

She huffed a laugh, rolling her lips together to keep quiet. He pulled away, his eyes finding those lips and a small twitch lifted his own. It was there and gone in a flash before he faced forward once more.

There was no way she could allow this power struggle to take her down. Leaning closer, she brought her mouth right up to his ear, her bottom lip grazing his earlobe as she said, "Try harder."

Theo's entire body went taught as she moved away, and she had to hold back another laugh at his reaction. Eyes closed; his jaw looked ready to shatter. She caught a small blush of red on his neck and her eyes darted to the spot below his cheekbone where—there! A muscle twinged as he surely fought back whatever words wanted to escape his tongue.

Instead, he shook his head mouthing *pay attention* and actively avoiding her gaze.

Satisfied with her small win, she faced forward, crossing her legs away from him and zeroing in on, what was his name? Paul? "Maggie is coming around now to pass out your mics, but don't panic. You only have to have them on during the competition or when we film confessionals. Please, for the love of everything holy, turn them off before you take that trip to the loo," he teased with an heir of someone who has heard way more than he bargained for.

Charles stepped forward, taking over the introduction flawlessly, his British lilt stronger and a touch more elegant than Theo's. "Now I know you all went through the literature we sent you with a fine-tooth comb." The smile he let soar through the room belonged in a Sensodyne commercial, eliciting a heavy sigh from the man to her right. She nudged him again. "But just as a refresher, lets go over the weekly schedule."

Producer Paul took over again. He explained how three potential baking challenges were given to the contestants at the start of each week. They were allowed to practice any or all of the three bakes in the days leading up to the technical challenge on Friday. That's when the filming would take place. Technical on Friday, competition bake on Saturday, and the elimination bake on Sunday.

Shannon's shoulders stiffened as the producer droned on. She had read through every single line of the provided literature about fifty times, it still hadn't prepared her for the nerves she felt now that they were there. Now that she had names, faces, and qualifications grossly exceeding her own to contend with. She regretted housing that blueberry muffin at breakfast as her stomach churned with nervous energy.

Leg bouncing in agitation, she half-listened to the producer as Maggie handed her a mic. Inconvenient is the word she would use to describe her sudden insecurities. What if she convinced Theo to do this, just to be the cause of their failure? It would absolutely crush her. And now that she was looking around at a room full of already nicknamed professional bakers, the repercussions of her pushing slapped her in the face.

What if she couldn't do it?

A hand landed on her knee, stilling its frantic bob and squeezing gently. She knew that touch. Not from years of receiving it, as if she had felt that grip every morning, evening, and night. The recognition came from her body, from the heat that burned off her panic fog and yearned for more. More contact. Pressure. Her body knew with stark clarity that this was the fourth time Theo had touched her with such *intention* before even dragging her eyes down to that tattooed hand, and she wanted more.

His palm stayed on her thigh just above the knee and she fucking felt it. Heat radiated through her jeans straight to her skin where it absorbed the warmth, sweeping through her bloodstream and lighting her entire body on fire. Theo leaned in close. "You alright?"

She nodded, finding his eyes and raising a brow in question. Why was he touching her again? That hand on her knee felt more intimate than any caress from Soymilk.

He said nothing, his eyes flicking past her and darkening before it was announced that they would finally get a tour of the kitchens. His hand stayed put as she glanced over a shoulder and caught one of the men from the American team openly staring at their connection.

Realization dawned, pulling the earlier heat from her body and replacing it with a strange sort of iciness. Something achingly close to disappointment that her fake boyfriend was touching her simply to play the part. It was a ridiculous feeling to have, seeing as they needed everyone to believe they were together. Still, she couldn't quite bring herself to return the intimacy. Keeping her hands very much to herself, she barely registered the congratulatory speech from Darlington, those damn whisk puns hitting every minute on the minute.

Focus, focus, focus.

"Now, as promised, Paul and I are going to give you three potential challenges for week one. It is up to you how you prepare for the unveiling at Saturday's competition bake." Shannon sat up in her seat, her attention finally leaving Theo's hand and landing where it belonged. "As you know, week one is biscuit week. You will be expected to have the foundations down, and also wow us with your stunning bakes. Your competition challenge is one of the following," he crooned, pausing for effect. "A three-dimensional biscuit sculpture of your choosing, a biscuit board game, or a three-dimensional biscuit jack-o-lantern."

Theo's hand drifted from her leg as he noted the challenges on his phone. Maybe she would have missed the connection if her head wasn't full to the brim with ideas and nervous energy.

Producer Paul clapped his hands, a single clap that signified the start of something much bigger than anyone in that room knew. They had to win this thing. She wouldn't let go of Bloem, not without a fight. And if she had to spend every single second of the next four days rolling out dough and documenting bake times, so be it. Point her in the direction of the aprons.

CHAPTER THIRTEEN

His head was spinning with ideas and recipes, ingredients, and techniques. They may as well just replace his brain with softened butter because Theo was going to be thinking about cookies for the next ninety-six hours at the very least.

All fourteen contestants made their way through the château, bustling with excited, nervous energy. None more than the woman beside him. He didn't know how, but Theo pinned the exact moment her nerves had gotten the better of her. He could feel the vibrations from her tapping foot through his own chair. Telling himself that the small gesture of comfort had been strictly to keep up their relationship charade was spectacularly easy, a lie that felt better than the searing truth. He knew her—better than even he thought possible. And lending her a comforting hand had felt like the most natural thing in the world.

Shannon was the last person in this floral nightmare who should be experiencing nerves. He had been training her for years and she never ceased to impress him. A fast learner—admittedly faster than Evie who went on to become a Michelin-recognized chef for God's sake. She had more patience too. He had seen her painstakingly frost hundreds of sugar cookies in ridiculous little designs over the years—not his idea, of course, but he could admit that her work was beautiful. Even the elf hats she insists need edible glitter and an unholy release date of Black Friday.

They passed a room filled with old sculptures and artwork before cutting left down a window-lined hallway that led to the kitchens. It was then that he realized he had almost been grinning as he thought of Shannon's paintbrushes and cookie cutters. As if the image he held brought on a strange bout of joy.

Insane. Elf hats and Easter egg cookies were just another gimmick for the influencers. Not something he found endearing.

Had he documented every single cookie design she had ever done? Yes. Would she ever know that information? Not in this lifetime. He frowned as the direction of his thoughts brought him full circle to her earlier accusations. Things had certainly been left unsaid over the years, but Theo wouldn't apologize for it. Too many times had he watched his misfortunes negatively affect the people he cared about. Had she not proved that when he spilled the tea about the café failing? Those blue eyes filling with moisture and frustration and sadness. It was his burden to carry and yet, here he was, walking side by side with Shannon into a cavernous space, seven workstations positioned in a semicircle around the room.

Thankfully, no floral wallpaper assaulted his vision. In fact, the space seemed out of place compared to the rest of the château. Almost industrial with its white walls and bright lights, the hum of refrigerators a constant drone and the glint from polished stainless near blinding.

144

At the front of the room was the judging table. A long, wooden slab where Charles—along with two other judges— would pick apart their bakes and for Theo, his entire future. Breezing past that thought, he brought his attention back to their stations, each outfitted with a stand mixer, crocks of rubber spatulas and whisks, a tiny sink, oven, and proofing drawer. Micro versions of his kitchen back home, and more than enough to win the entire thing.

Stepping up beside the producer, Maggie took over the tour. "Here are your workstations," she called out in a clipped, no-nonsense sort of way. "Find your name and familiarize yourself with the space. You will be practicing your bakes in your private kitchens to avoid wandering eyes, but the pantry and refrigerators are at your complete disposal and grocery lists are on the clipboards at the end of each section."

Aw yes, the grocery list. Theo could admit that the personal shoppers and large budget sent a bit of a thrill coursing through him. The recipes they could test for their return to Bloem were countless with that sort of freedom. He just needed to ensure they were good enough to impress the judges so he actually had a Bloem to go home to.

"So, bakers," Charles called to the group, his hands ringing in anticipation. "You have four days to prepare your bakes and ready your sous chefs for their technical challenge. The kitchens are all yours now, so preheat those ovens and make those bakes un*beat*able."

The room erupted in cheers and applause and Shannon's sunshiny laughter, hiding the groan that had no chance of staying contained within his body. The amount of baking puns he was about to be subjected to was criminal.

"Come on Theodore, let's go find our station," Shannon sang, a bounce in her step as she made her way into the kitchens.

Another groan rumbled his chest. "Please don't call me that. I'd genuinely prefer Tat Daddy."

Regret spread through each limb when she looked back at him with that wicked gleam in her eye.

"I bet you would, Daddy," she purred, walking backwards and pinning him with a mischievous grin.

A vision flashed into his brain so fast, he had no chance of blocking it. Some might call it a fantasy; others may call it a desire. He would call it a dangerous, entirely impossible scenario his brain concocted from the mass amounts of sexual tension he'd survived over the past few days. Either way, when that look of wicked delight covered her features and the word Daddy hummed from her lips, he saw himself closing the distance between them. Gripping the back of her neck and tugging her close, brushing his lips against the shell of her ear as he begged her to behave. Not demand, but *beg*. It wasn't beneath him, and the way she had him out of his mind—under some sort of spell of lust and longing—was something he would fall to his knees for.

To make it stop, of course.

Christ, but his thoughts must have been painted on his face with clarity, for Shannon slowed her walking, her grin slowly falling. Self-preservation had his jaw locking, a muscle ticking just below his cheek as he fought the impulse to say every indecent thought aloud.

Her eyes snapped to his jaw and a strange look passed over her features, but before he could pick it apart, she took a step directly into the bulky frame of some guy she called Meatball. Shannon flung around, steadying herself and the man before they toppled over, laughing an apology.

"It's alright. There are definitely worse things to get run over by than a beautiful woman," he cooed. Theo's glare was focused directly on the man's hands at Shannon's shoulders, a shock of possessive rage pulsing at his fingertips. This Meatball had been staring at her during the introductions, so much so, that Theo knew he had seen their little public display of affection. The prick was hitting on his fake girlfriend and damned if Theo didn't want to punch him in his smug, meatball-y face for it.

Insane. Insane, crazy, and uncharacteristic seeing as he wasn't even violent towards the spiders taking up residence in his apartment.

Shannon let out a little chuckle. "Right, you could be run over by this sack of tattooed muscle behind me," she teased, backing up until she was pressed against him.

Sticking his hands safely into the pockets of his jeans, he smiled at the man whose name tag surprisingly read Brad instead of Ground Beef. It was a smile for all intents and purposes, but for some reason, Brad quickly spun on his heel and walked away. Rude.

"Am I going to have to keep an eye on you this entire time?" he said, pointing to the station that read *Bloem*.

"Only if you want to." That smug tone was going to be the death of him.

Telling her to behave was a bad idea. One that only seconds before he had been—okay—*fantasizing* about with his lips against her skin and her chest pressed tight to his. A change of subject was vital.

"Let's just check out the station and beeline to the pantry. I want to head back to the room so we can get started."

"The station seems pretty self-explanatory. Mixer, oven, all the essentials in one tidy place." Pointing to three large hutches at the back of the kitchen, she continued. "Backup and specialty equipment all lives back there." She turned to a standalone Smeg refrigerator in a sweet yellow color and opened the door. "This is our personal fridge, and the walk-ins are all along that wall." Theo followed her gaze to the large walk-in doors built into the wall of the kitchen, the dry storage a large, organized room to their right.

"What do you two think?"

They both turned to the dark hair and round frame that belonged to that musical voice. He knew they were both actively trying not to call her Flora, Shannon's nickname that was somehow related to the delicate rose scent she caught when they hugged upon meeting.

"Is it even real, Samira?" Shannon asked with a soft smile. Pleasure eased his tense muscles as he noted the smile, a thousand times more genuine than the one directed at Brad.

"I'm sure it will feel real on Friday when I have to watch Chanda patiently work her way through the cookie method." She nodded to her sous chef who was actively fixing the fit of her hijab rather than inspecting the kitchen. The woman sighed before turning her smile on them once more. "At least we have the welcome party to look forward to."

"Do we?" Theo asked, earning him an elbow to his side.

"Don't be such a sourpuss," Shannon said with an impressive eye roll. "You won't burst into flames after two hours of socializing. Besides, I heard that last year, they served little cucumber sandwiches and provided Jane Austen themed props for photos."

"Well, there's some nightmare fuel for you, Samira," Theo said as he gathered the clipboard and pulled his phone from his pocket. He would snap a photo of the workstation and study it until the space was like a second home.

After wishing Samira good luck, they took stock of the dry storage and contents of the walk-in, brains already abuzz with ideas as they practically ran back to their room to get started.

"The challenges are all structural, so it would be smart to plan the same flavors and cookies for each one, then adjust the designs accordingly."

"Don't you mean biscuits? What kind of Brit are you?"

"The kind that has lived in America for fifteen years," he responded dryly. Sitting across from one another had been a good move, a smart move. He didn't need anymore opportunities to touch the woman and inevitably have to fight whatever trance she held him in.

"Boo," she said without any real enthusiasm. "What are you thinking? Gingerbread? It would be structurally sound."

"But everyone will be doing it," he mused, running a hand through his hair. "At the same time, we would risk the design by using a *biscuit* that spreads too much."

A grin flashed for the briefest of seconds before her brows drew together. "Shortbread could work if we mixed in something fatty, right?"

Theo nodded, pleased and maybe a little proud of her knowledge. "Cocoa nibs would do the trick, but we would still run the risk of them losing their shape." He paused, giving Shannon a proper span of time to think it out. Management through opportunity, that had always been his style. He needed her to know that his faith in her abilities was steadfast, that he wouldn't steamroll this competition like he was certain people like Meatball were doing to their apprentices.

"What if we stuck with the cocoa nibs but added them to gingerbread? It would add a nuttiness that would play well with the sweetened ginger."

That could work. Tapping his pen against the pad of paper before him, he closed his eyes. Thinking about the sharpness of cocoa nibs and the snappy texture of gingerbread. The texture would be great, but the flavors would be too disconnected. They would try the combo because he valued her ideas enough to see them all through, but a thought struck him and, eyes still closed, a smile stretched his lips.

"What's going on in that mad scientist brain of yours?" Shannon murmured. Snapping his eyes open he found her beaming too, nothing but patient confidence in that sweet smile.

"Grab the shopping list." The words were barely out of his mouth before she launched into action, snagging the clipboard and a pen to jot down his scattered thoughts. "I have an idea."

CHapter Fourteen

Theo gazed down at himself in the only type of formalwear he was willing to sport. His hand ran down the green cashmere sweater, thin but soft against the pads of his fingers and a swooping crew neck that would ensure his windpipe wasn't immediately crushed like a tie would. His slacks were lighter for once, their camel color fitted to his legs before the cuffs gave way to dark, warn leather dress shoes. The appropriate name tag now sporting Theo rather than the name gifted to him by a woman with the softest heart on the planet, stuck right over his left pec.

A welcome party. He paced before the fireplace, his eyes darting between the bedroom door and the sofa that had been made up with clean lines and not a wrinkle in sight. Shannon was in there, using the bathroom and readying herself for a party they had no business attending. After painstakingly creating the stencils for each of the challenges, they had only managed to successfully pull off one of them, and that was without the decorations and full assembly. He had no idea how long they would have for the challenge, but if it was anything less than four hours…

With the technical challenge a mere thirteen hours away, the last thing he wanted to do was make awkward conversation with people standing in his way. His energy was better spent offering Shannon support, seeing as tomorrow would be all about her.

Sitting on the sidelines while she did all the work sounded like a waking nightmare. He knew the cameras would be focused on him and the other contestants, waiting for one of them to talk shit about their own teammates. They wouldn't be getting that from Theo, that he knew with one hundred percent certainty. For one, there was nothing to critique because the woman was an absolute soldier. Everything she did was executed with militant precision and attention to detail. Time management wasn't her strong suit, but the fact remained that he often carried more praise than criticism when it came to Shannon.

And they were a team. There was a litany of things that teammates generally didn't do to one another, shit talking at the peak alongside insulting their mum and fucking. That last one was thrown in to simply cover the spectrum. Theo didn't have any sort of personal connection to it or anything. In fact, as he threw himself into one of the armchairs and rested his head in his hands, his detachment from that last option couldn't have been broader.

A muscle twitched just below his eyes, reminding him of how tired he was and the cause of that weariness. Every turn and roll and fucking sigh from Shannon could be heard through the squeak of those sofa springs. Theo was jolted awake at least twelve times per night, a fact that pressed on his temples, forcing him to recognize how terrible it had to be for the woman sleeping on the racket. The guilt of making her brave the sofa kept him awake, but it was the bone deep awareness of her presence that kept him wide eyed and aching.

Survival instincts finally kicked in, forcing him to rub one out in the shower. The stress of the competition had his nerves electrified with zero outlet. He was wound so tight; it had barely taken a few tight pumps of his lubed-up fist before his climax tore through him, doing absolutely fuck-all to settle him.

Footsteps padded along the rug, announcing Shannon's presence before she spoke. "Don't look so excited, Lulu. Your loyal servants in the underworld will begin to question your street cred."

Despite himself, his lips quirked, head still cradled in his hands. "I'm not sure how much street cred will be left after donning whatever prop is associated with *Pride and Prejudice*, God save me," he responded to settle himself. His thoughts had been far too salacious to confidently face the woman he had tried not to think about while fisting his cock. Tried, and failed.

Tossing his misdeeds aside, he rubbed his eyes before standing and facing the she-devil head on. A mistake, as it were, for his eyes at once found legs. Sure, they were held at bay with sheer tights and a short, plaid skirt, but his eyes were drawn, nonetheless. Her thick thighs on display for once, he soaked in the image. Attempting to lie to his own damn self about storing it for later so it could be properly appreciated. Properly praised.

No words were exchanged as Theo's eyes ran from those thighs, past the black and tan checkers of her deliciously short skirt to the black knit sweater that appeared to be painted on for Christ's sake. His gaze almost froze there, at the swell of her breasts and the silver pendant necklace that hung between them. But there was no way his focus wasn't being pulled towards that face. Those baby blue eyes, soft and gentle while her berry lips screamed at him. Called to him. Taunted him.

You look stunning. The words stuck in his throat where they rested uncomfortably, remaining unsaid. He felt the familiar twitch of his jaw muscle as he ground his teeth together to hold in the inappropriate words. That wank in the shower did exactly what he thought, fuck-all in terms of staving off this debilitating lust.

They weren't saying anything—neither one moving as the fire crackled at his back and their eyes remained locked.

"You look…" Shannon's eyes dipped, roving over his full frame before darting back to his face in an almost panicked snap. "You're wearing green." It sounded awfully close to an accusation, and was he losing his mind? Because he couldn't quite decipher if he felt smug or annoyed by her reaction.

"You're wearing black," he croaked.

Breaking eye contact, he launched into the small kitchen where they had been practicing all week, filled a glass and downed it in one manic move. "Shall we get this over with?" It came out a little breathless after his water guzzling, but he was happy about the tone. The grittiness gone.

Her silence had him whipping around, catching her wandering eyes on his ass before they snapped shut and she turned her back to him. No chill. In fact, absolutely boiling hot compared to the effortless cool she usually dealt out in spades.

Warning bells clanged in his head as he realized that maybe she was just as affected by the sight of him. Not good. A fucking catastrophic realization, actually.

"Yep," she chimed, answering the question he had forgotten he'd asked four seconds ago. "This will be fun."

***

It wasn't fun.

Much to her disappointment, there wasn't a silk ribbon or mini cucumber sandwich in sight. The champagne wasn't even served in an adorable vintage coupe glass! After over an hour of attempting to charm the pants off every contestant, crew member, and marble bust, Shannon was bone tired and still actively thinking about Theo's ass in those tan slacks. Snug. Those pants were perfectly snug and should be illegal in all fifty states, extending across international borders. That ass was a weapon, and one that had been used to render her speechless as she fought the urge to groan when muscles flexed as he walked.

After emailing a florist, caterer, and event coordinator about Evie's rehearsal dinner, Shannon had two minutes to fling her body into the shower and ready herself for the evening. Her idea to wear black had been smart, funny even seeing as she never wore it. But matching her fake boyfriend's outfit was just the sort of thing that would drive Lulu to those heavy sighs and tortured groans. It wasn't like she was reveling in his pain, she just loved to push. Loved to see his reactions play over those sharp features before the mask locked back into place.

She never anticipated having to stifle her own reactionary groans.

What an amazing thing to know someone better than most, but not really know them. Maybe she was overreacting, but she had never *ever* seen Theo Abbott wear green. She was sure of it. Her elephant brain would recall how the color made his eyes lighter, like a kaleidoscope of amber and mocha, almost more hypnotizing than his full muscular derrière. How his hair pulled even more red, and his skin looked creamy and soft. She would have remembered the contrast of dark, swirling constellations and bright yellow sunflowers against that mossy green.

Unhinged.

Lack of sleep combined with whatever intoxicating soap Lulu brought from the depths of Hell was clearly making her a little crazed. She had spent far too much of her time

154

obsessing over the color of her boss's shirt instead of actually listening to the two hosts they were finally meeting tonight.

Daisy Colley, and Jasper Pike, arguably the most valuable members of the show.

Daisy was an actor through most of the nineties before she tired of the cutthroat industry and focused on her true love. Cake. After leaving film, she released a series of baking books for people who barely knew how to hold a spatula. *Bake Someone Happy* had been her motto, a sunshiny intention to go along with her big personality. Shannon had always appreciated how her dark, tawny skin contrasted the bright almost frantic patterns she loved to adorn herself with.

Where Daisy was sunshine, Jasper was storm clouds. The man appeared to be gunning for the role of Captain Jack Sparrow with his heavy eyeliner and wild mane of black hair. His style could only be described as punk rock meets K-pop and Shannon was certain she had never seen him in anything but black, heavy boots. But the man was hilarious. A comedian and actor, he lent the show those much-needed laughs to break up the intensity. He was flirty, and goofy and at times a little crass—a personality cocktail she was familiar with.

Which was most likely why she found herself standing at the bar nestled between an alabaster sculpture of a naked woman and Jasper's heavily lined gaze.

"What are your signature bakes?" he asked, his Manchester English growing a touch stronger with each sip of the wine glass.

She cocked her head, considering. "Coincidentally, I enjoy baking cookies. Specifically, these pumpkin cookies that Theo hates. They have chunks of white chocolate in them that melt in your mouth." She smiled as Jasper let out an appreciative groan. "I haven't progressed in my training to laminated doughs just yet, but I do love assembling the morning buns for Theo."

"You'd be hard pressed not to enjoy those morning buns," he quipped with a nod towards Theo's backside just as the man himself let out a laugh she had never before heard.

Of course, after having full conversations with baroque oil paintings rather than face the temptation that was Theo, the moment her resolve collapsed he had to laugh like that? Booming and free, it threw his head back, soaring from his chest and pointed directly at someone that wasn't her. She hated it. Hated the fact that it was Chanda on the receiving end of that unicorn laugh while Shannon forcefully attempted not to think about those morning buns.

"You two seem very comfortable with one another," Jasper carried on, oblivious to the uncomfortable feeling of jealousy leaking from her brain. "You're in your own little worlds, making the rounds without a care. If that were my partner, I wouldn't let him out of my damn sight for fear of some twenty-something zipping him away."

Shannon crinkled her nose. "I'm not worried," she murmured as another insane laugh left his stupid face. Should she be worried? Without knowing it, Jasper had clued her in to the first mistake in their great act. What kind of couple avoided each other all night and flirted with other people? Because that's what he was doing, flirting with Chanda who appeared to be just the type of twenty something she should be worried about. And okay, it shocked absolutely no one that Shannon had done her fair share of teasing and winking this evening, but telling sixty-five-year-old Matis that the design on his shirt looked like well muscled abs was a far cry from—well, from whatever Theo was up to.

"Okay, so morning buns and cookies, what type of…"

Theo's laugh rumbled through the room again, drawing her attention away from Jasper's question and straight to the back of his head.

"Come to think of it, maybe I should be worried," she mumbled under her breath.

"What was that?" Captain Jack asked, distracted by a tray of puffed pastry and some sort of caramelized onion filling.

She turned back to him with what she hoped was a sheepish grin. "I'm sorry, I was distracted by Theo's biscuits."

"Amen," he said with a toast in her direction.

"What about you? Anyone waiting for you at home?" Shannon's matchmaking itch was a-itching and Jasper may just be the perfect back scratcher. "Are you finally going to meet your baking king this year?" It wasn't subtle, but she was a bit off her game with Theo mussing up her thoughts.

"If only." Own-leh. His accent was adorable. "There are strict rules about dating the contestants, darling. Hate to break your heart there," he added with a wink.

"Ugh, red tape? Boring." Shannon set aside her empty glass and snagged a water pitcher from the sleek bar top. Pouring herself a crisp one, her head swam with how she could possibly get past a rule like that. "What about after the show?"

"What about it?" Meatball cut in. Shannon suppressed a groan. Water in hand, she turned to face the now threesome of men.

Jasper chimed, "Oh, Shannon's just asking about the sad reality of my dating life."

Ignoring the lazy perusal from Brad, she reached out to give Jasper a playful little slap. "How on earth is your dating life sad? If Jasper Pike has trouble dating, then there is truly no hope for the rest of us."

"Says the woman in a happy relationship," Meatball crooned, a pointed look directed towards Theo's obviously chuckling back. Chanda picked that moment to place a hand against his chest and smile the most sickeningly beautiful smile. She was too short for him. Shannon had at least two inches on her, not to mention six years. Maybe Chanda was just the funniest model in the world, or maybe he was just—

Jesus Christ. There she went again, something rare and uncomfortable roiling in her gut alongside the envy already causing her heartburn.

None of her business. Not her man, and certainly not her right to go over there and break up whatever party for two he was sharing with another woman. Not even for show.

"Apologies, but I'm getting a bit tired. Think I might turn in," she said, her eyes finding Jasper's and a forced smile kissing her lips.

"Gotta be ready for tomorrow, don't ya?" he said with a nod.

She nodded in return, her frustration mounting as Meatball smirked at her goodbyes. Jealousy was not something Shannon Perry was unfamiliar with. Usually reserved for moments of unfortunate self doubt and questionable core feelings. Kinda like now. Theo was a grown man who she herself had encouraged to date. He was private to the point of fury, so she never really saw if her pressing went anywhere when it came to his love life. Another thing she wasn't privy to.

If you wanted to see him coupled so bad, then why didn't you try to set him up with anyone?

Ew, she hated her inner voice for that very nosy question. Still, as she silently swept from the room without saying goodbye, she searched through the multitude of answers to it, coming up with reason after reason. Those reasons began to spiral into excuses as she washed her face and pulled her hair into a long braid. Excuses for why she never even considered matches for Theo, for why he was off limits. She couldn't blame inappropriate work dynamics since that had truly never bothered her before.

Excuses slowly morphed into hard, difficult truths as she tossed and turned and tried her damndest not to look at the clock when Theo shuffled in from the party. The springs of the couch finally quieted when she stilled, her entire body taught with anticipation as the thud of steps on carpet neared

158

the couch. Goosebumps spread along her skin, and she imagined their journey was the same route taken by Theo's gaze, but he said nothing. Did nothing. He surely didn't laugh or smile or *give* because that wasn't their relationship. Boss and employee, she reminded herself as those hard truths fought for supremacy in her brain.

Shannon registered a sound similar to a sigh expel from the man watching her before his footsteps headed towards the bedroom and she was left alone with nothing but enthusiastic denial to keep her company as she lay wide awake. Sleep wouldn't be coming anytime soon.

CHaPTer FIFTeen

"Alright Theo, welcome to your first confessional."

Giving Jasper a half-hearted smile, he ran his eyes over the room where the party had taken place the night before. He sat on a couch, a large painting of a full picnic spread and two very plump individuals fanning themselves behind him.

Paul sat to Jasper's right, and between them was a camera pointed directly at Theo's tired face. He hadn't slept very well. After turning to find Meatball in the space where Shannon had been last night, his mind had raced with all sorts of accusations. He said something to make her upset, he probably chewed with his mouth open, his muscles were overwhelming the small conversation and forcing her out, and the most rage inducing—he hit on her again.

Trying not to allow his anger to come through on camera, he took a calming breath.

"We're just going to ask you a series of questions before and after each baking session. Occasionally, we'll bring you back in after editing to film some more in-depth confessionals, pulling questions from the bake that we want you to touch on for the audience, but nothing too intense I assure you.

Theo had a question of his own, what the hell were he and Shannon talking about at the party last night? She had one of those sweet smiles on her face, the kind that felt warm and genuine and held a touch of mischief within. It was a smile he had seen a handful of times, rare and beautiful and always pointed in the direction of someone she cared enough for to match. But the burning question that had kept him up all night was, is she finding a match for herself, or for Jasper?

Stop thinking about Shannon, and focus.

"Understood," he said with a nod.

"Great," he chimed, the camera tech gave them the go-ahead to begin. Suddenly sweaty, Theo rubbed his palms along black denim at his thighs, shifting for comfort on the deep cushions and noting how they didn't make a sound. "Tell us about yourself," Jasper said.

Great. Terrible first question.

"I am Theo. I own a bake shop and roastery in San Francisco California called Bloem. I am thirty-nine-years-old…"

"Hold up," Jasper held up a hand with a consoling smile. "This isn't an interrogation, mate."

"Then why is it called a confessional?" He countered, not in the mood to be nice.

"Great question, and one that I will lose sleep over, actually. Just try to relax. Where are you from originally?"

"Here actually. I grew up in the Cotswolds and my mum still lives here. She owns and operates a pub not far from the château, actually." And he couldn't wait to see her. That free weekend couldn't come soon enough, and they hadn't even started baking.

"Does she bake there? Is that where you would say you get your love of baking?" Paul chimed in.

Theo scoffed, a small smile grazing his lips. "She hates baking, always burned the dinner rolls at Christmas. So yeah,

I guess that is where I get my love for baking. Not being able to stomach another year of charred bread Christmas morning forced me into the kitchen with gusto."

Jasper let out a little chuckle. "Are you excited to be here?"

"Am I excited to be here? Absolutely not." He answered honestly, not giving a shit how it made him look. "I am here because Shannon asked me to be, period."

"Aw yes, our lovebird team." Theo blinked at the term which reminded him of their ruse. "Are you nervous for her first technical challenge?"

"Go ahead and answer this one as if we didn't ask," Paul added. "Answer for the audience."

He knew that had been coming after receiving a brief training on what would be needed on camera.

"I am not at all worried about Shannon's first technical challenge. She's a brilliant baker, quick on her feet and neat as a pin. She may not have as much experience as the other sous chefs in that kitchen, but there is no doubt in my mind that she can out-bake every single one of them. One thing you should know about Shannon is, once a goal is set in her mind, she is completely and devastatingly unstoppable."

Shannon shook off the fog in her mind just in time. It was go-time, and she couldn't afford to let a sleepless night get the best of her—not with an apron already fastened around her waist and her eyes wide as they locked on the table before her. She reached behind, flipping on the mic pack and joining the other contestants in the familiar motion. Her gaze flickered to the left, where Theo and the executive chefs sat to observe, all of them chatting quietly. Not Theo. His eyes were locked on her, following every movement as she tightened the camel-colored apron around her waist. The nod he gave her felt like a bear hug in its silent reassurance.

They hadn't exchanged more than a few words all morning—just a "Good morning" and "Do you need the bathroom?" acting as the only accompaniments to the coffee machine and incessant squeak of sofa springs. Shannon wasn't sure if her overwhelming nerves were clouding her already complicated feelings toward him, but in that moment, that single nod alongside unwavering eye contact steadied her. Grounded her.

Breaking their gaze, she focused on the table before her. It was a large station with a mixer and small sink to her right, an induction burner to her left. In the center was her challenge, covered in a checkered baby blue towel. Although she knew they were baking cookies, the style was a complete mystery to her until that towel was lifted to reveal the ingredients beneath.

Checking for the dozenth time that her mic was on, her spine stiffened as the judges filed into the room, Charles Darlington leading the way.

A round of applause clapped out from her hands alone, startling everyone and causing the judges to laugh. Eventually, the other contestants joined in, the clatter echoing through the cavernous kitchen.

"Hello bakers, and welcome to your first ever *Whisk Wars* challenge!" Charles held his hands up in triumph as the room celebrated once more.

"God, theres something so sexy about the first day, don't you think, Daisy?"

"Oh, absolutely Jasper. You think it's the flattering lines of those tan aprons?"

"I do, yeah," he said, looking dumbstruck by the truly terrible aprons.

A clap from Charles brought them all back with a laugh. "Bakers, today's technical challenge is for the sous chefs, so we've asked the big wigs to pop-off to the VIP section for a bit of a rest." A camera ran along the chefs who waved or smiled in greeting, soaking up the spotlight. All but one, of course. "Sous chefs, your challenge today will not only set the tone for the entire competition, it will also give you a bit of a leg up."

Time.

Whoever won the day's challenge was gifted extra time during the competition bake to assist their partner. Their competition, however, would be tagged in at halftime. Extra time was a huge advantage in a challenge with so many structural components. They needed the added time, and she and Theo both knew it. Every single one of their practice runs had failed with Shannon being the main problem. She was too meticulous and not nearly fast enough. Unfortunately, three days hadn't been enough to work that problem out.

Shaking out her arms as if it would discard the nerves, Shannon zeroed in on Daisy as she began to speak.

"Bakers, beneath these linens is your first ever challenge. None of you have seen beneath these scratchy samples of cloth, so you're all on an even playing field. You will find everything you need, from a carefully formatted recipe…"

"To the last granule of salt needed to construct the bake," Charles took over flawlessly. "Bakers, today we would like you to make a dozen, highly decorated sugar biscuits."

Shannon's shoulders jolted to attention, her eyes like saucers in her head. Sugar cookies? Highly decorated, annoyingly cute, perfect little discs of whimsy and glitter and all things that irritate Lulu to no end? The type of cookie that she had been making for every single holiday without fail for the past several years? Those cookies?

"The judges table is filled with biscuit cutters of all shapes and sizes, so choose wisely bakers. Oh, I almost forgot to mention," Charles said with a sly smile. "You have two hours. On your mark."

"Get set," Jasper said with a look of sheer joy on his face as he peered at Daisy.

"Bake!" she called, clapping her hands with one single slap.

Waisting no time, Shannon whipped the tablecloth from her table and surveyed the ingredients she knew with more intimacy than most of her lovers. Nerves fled her stomach and launched back to the depths from whence they came, a smile starting slowly at the corners of her mouth before it stretched her cheeks and reached her eyes. Eyes that eagerly shot up to where Theo sat with the other chefs.

He was already looking at her, his own smile lighting up his face in a way she had never experienced before. That smile continued through another small nod, and then Theo leaned back, his arms stretching to cradle the back of his head. He crossed one ankle over his knee, the picture of confidence in their success. In her.

She nodded back, registering that the other contestants were stress-reading their recipes as she just grinned at her teammate like an idiot. She could read the recipe later. Breaking her gaze from Theo, her attention refocused on a greater task at the judge's table. She had a plan.

***

Theo wasn't quite sure if it was sheer luck, or if Shannon had left the party early last night to cast a spell in a circle of salt and rosemary or whatever she-devils did to ascend. At that moment, he didn't really give a shit. Hell, if that's all it took for them to be handed easy challenges on a fluffy, silver-lined pillow, point him to the tourmaline and ritual candles.

He still leaned back, watching as Shannon absolutely annihilated the competition. She was the only one decorating, piping delicate outlines as almost every other contestant struggled to cool their cookies in time for the royal icing to go on without melting.

Theo couldn't see what she was doing, and he didn't have to. The force of that smile when she realized the challenge was her favorite way to taunt him was enough to relax his admittedly worried mind. And he did relax, after the sheer magnitude of that smile pierced through his chest and set his heart racing, he settled into a state of cool confidence and deep breaths.

"Not the fridge, dumbass," Meatball grumbled next to him as a camera focused on his face. "How long until we can go talk to them?"

Theo didn't spare him a single glance even as he listened for the answer to that question. The chefs were allowed to consult for five minutes halfway through the challenge. His consulting would consist of asking what sort of satanic ritual produced this challenge in such a pretty little bow for his sous chef.

"Ugh, did she just add more water to that icing?" Samira asked from his left. "It's going to be far too runny."

"You can fix that at halftime," Theo told her, unsure of why he was comforting the competition. He liked Samira. Having spent the majority of that awful welcome party with her and Chanda, the pair quickly became his two favorite people. Samira was born and raised in India where she worked in her family restaurant and learned the majority of her cooking skills. He had laughed along with her when she told him culinary school had nothing on her stern mother, who would knock a spatula against her back for bad posture as she sliced vegetables.

She met Chanda after moving to London and opening what is now a very popular Indian bakery. The younger girl was born and raised in England by her Indian grandmother. After she passed, she found herself stumbling into Samira's bakery in search of some comforts of home.

"I found her in the corner crying into a jalebi," Samira had said.

"It was love at first sight," Chanda had added. "I had mascara running down my face and staining this beautiful scarf my grandmother had given me, which made me cry even harder. Samira asked me if I knew how to make the sweet treat. No, *hello* or *are you okay?* Just a simple question about my favorite pastry and one where the answer was a resounding no. She took me to the kitchen and showed me how, step by step. I had to focus so hard, my mind completely whisked away from all the bad and focused on frying dough instead."

"And she just never left," Samira teased, but he had seen the love there. They were like family now. Brought together in a way he was convinced only food could accomplish with stubborn people. He saw it every day at Bloem—probably explained why Shannon's matchmaking business was so lucrative.

A flash of odd colors caught Theo's eye as Jasper walked by their little waiting area, his outfit completely insane. He wore a large black sweater with bright green blobs all over it, his signature eyeliner was pristine, and his black jeans appeared to be too tight for comfort. Theo didn't even attempt to hide his scowl, remembering how Shannon had stuck to the man's side for most of the night. Every trill of her laugh that had reached his ears had been a torture, knowing he would find her smiling at someone that wasn't him.

Territorial nonsense, but he didn't care as his glare cut through Jasper's back. Being angry with Jasper was deflecting the blame from his own damn self. That man had taken all of Shannon's attention last night, and Theo had done nothing but brood about it in the corner. He knew they were doing a shit job of keeping up the ruse, and a part of him knew it didn't matter. Nobody seemed concerned about their relationship, they were already sharing a room, and the competition was underway—maybe they didn't need to keep up appearances as much as they thought.

But that hadn't stopped him thinking about it. That he should walk across that party and slide his arms around her, feel if that black sweater was as soft as it looked. Run his fingers through her hair and kiss the corner of those fucking lips. Glue himself to her side until she pointed one of those bright smiles at him, and only him.

"Bakers, you are halfway through. Let's get your teammates in the mix for a whopping five minutes." Before the words had left Jasper's lips, everyone around Theo sprang into action, shooting up from their seats and racing to help their teammates, chased by cameras and boon mics.

Theo stood, slowly stretching his muscles which were probably sore from keeping his hands to himself last night. Idly making his way to Shannon's station, he ignored the cameras and stood opposite her, his hands landing flat on her workstation. She was smiling even before their eyes met, her lips closed but tugged up at the corners.

"Hey, Lulu," she said as she stood up straight, lifting the piping bag she had been hunched over.

"Hey, Lily girl." He was smiling as he said it, the space between them pulling taut as he fought all the same urges as the night before. He wanted to reach out and run his fingers over the blue ribbon weaved into her plait. He wanted to cup her neck and feel her heart pulse under his fingertips as he praised her work. It would skip under his touch at the admiration, he just knew it would. Excitement would send her heart racing as he told her she was being such a good fucking girl.

Her eyes were locked on his as he fought to keep…all *that* contained within his body. *You're her boss. Cool it with the fucking longing.*

Theo glanced down at the cookies, taking in the plain round shapes she had picked and the outlines barely taking shape within. The simplicity of the cookies didn't worry him

168

one bit. Shannon knew what she was doing, he was just over there for a little added support.

"Whatcha' bakin'?" he asked, his gaze leaving the cookies to travel over her features again.

"It's a surprise. I want you to be thoroughly awed by my genius, more so than the hat cookies."

Theo rolled his eyes at that, remembering those ridiculous cookies with a small chuckle. "Those monstrosities sold more than any other item in the pastry case that week. Did any of those assholes even know what the Kentucky Derby was?"

"You mean besides yet another excuse for rich white people to get shit-housed and dress like wannabe Dolly Partons? No, they had no idea. But I don't think you should be referring to our guests as assholes on television, Lulu."

He spared a glance toward the nearest camera.

"If the shoe fits…" he murmured.

"So, what do I get?"

Theo's eyes shot back to her. "What do you mean?"

"If I win this challenge," she clarified, going back to her piping. "What do I get?"

"You get to bake with me for the full challenge tomorrow. Weren't you listening?"

"I mean from you. A little side bet." She looked up from her work, eyes finding him from under her lashes, their wicked gleam blinding.

"What do you want?"

Yeah, that's what left his lips. Instead of noting that it was a losing bet because she was undoubtably going to win, instead of reminding her that more time with him was the real gift, instead of throwing something snarky and diverting in her direction, he asked what she wanted from him.

Shannon set her piping bag down gently, the tip landing close to where his palms still rested on the butcher block. Without hesitation, she brought her hand around his head, tugging him until her mouth pressed snuggly against his ear.

169

All reason said that she didn't want the mics to pick up what she was about to say, and that was all good and fine, but the message was not being received by his dick. Hot breath against his skin sent all of the blood south at an embarrassing speed. Worse were the words that landed against his skin in a whisper.

"I want the bed."

"Times up!" Daisy called from the judges table, causing Shannon to release him without another word and pick up her piping right where she left off.

A chill rushed over his body from the loss of her warmth, and it must have frozen him to the spot as well, hands still braced on the worktop.

"Do we have a deal?" she asked, the mics definitely picking it up and the innuendo hitting its mark.

"Deal," he heard himself say, a sliver of guilt creeping in on his good mood. What kind of an asshole made a woman sleep on the couch, knowing damn well she was tossing and turning all night? He could hear it, the squeaks from those fucking springs piercing him in the brain as he restlessly tried not to focus on Shannon's nearness. But how could he when they both knew he wasn't fitting on that sofa? If Shannon was in the bed, he would be right there with her.

Her eyes darted to his as he stepped away, a question expressed by one raised brow. *Are you sure?*

Theo just grinned as he backed away, his eyes sweeping over her features before he turned to walk back to his seat. Hell no, he wasn't sure. But he knew two things with crystalline clarity: Shannon was going to win this challenge, and he was about to have a very sleepless, very uncomfortable night.

chapter sixteen

"I feel incredible. I never thought I would be the winner of the first challenge. The sensation is intoxicating." Shannon smiled at the camera, pushing strands of escaped hair from her flushed face.

"Those cookies were genius," Charles laughed, his too-white teeth glinting as the camera stayed trained directly on her. "How did you come up with that design?"

She shrugged, her mind circling back to the moment she had solidified her tactic. Plain circle-shaped cookies with highly detailed images of each judge. Their little faces on each cookie were cartoon-like, all pink cheeks and smiles and winks. She had even given Jasper's character a swipe of pristine eyeliner. The judges had been completely charmed as the other contestants stared daggers at her creations.

Theo's presence at her side as the judges critiqued her work was somehow so charged, her arm hairs stood at attention. He hadn't been doing a damn thing out of the ordinary, just standing, arms crossed and a particularly broody expression darkening his features.

Deal. He had agreed to give her the bed if she won and, well, she freaking won. And maybe it was pride she felt rolling off of him in waves, lord knew she felt it when he looked at her, his eyes roaming her face and a small smile quirking his lips. Confidence in her abilities had been evident from that very first nod, before they even knew what the challenge was going to be.

Deal.

What was he playing at? Shannon had been confident, but her win had hardly been written in stone. Insecurities still smacked her in the back of the head periodically throughout the entire challenge, that familiar feeling of imposter syndrome making the most of a vulnerable situation. But not for Theo. His confidence had been unwavering, delivered in his usual Prince of Darkness style. Stoic, bored and surprisingly, with a small smile, just for her.

In his mind, agreeing to that bet guaranteed sleepless nights for him on that god awful couch, so why would he agree?

Brushing her unease aside, she focused on the confessional. "Honestly, I had this design in my back pocket. I originally wanted to decorate them to look like Theo, showcase his various frowns and scowls. It would have driven him nuts," she said on a laugh, still feeling that high only succeeding at something could provide.

"I thought I saw one of him after all," Charles replied, his features mischievous.

"I made a baker's dozen," she said with a wink. "And I think I captured his likeness pretty well."

He chuckled before asking, "Are you scared about the *Whisk Wars* curse?" Shannon raised a brow. "In previous years, the teams that won on the first challenge dropped to the bottom on the next. Are you worried that will happen to you and Theo tomorrow? He seems like a man who refuses to fail."

Shannon shook her head even as her stomach twisted at the thought.

"Answer that in a statement," Producer Paul added.

She took a moment to roll his words around in her head before she responded. "The *Whisk Wars* curse doesn't scare me at all. Aside from being one of the most talented pastry chefs out there, Theo is an amazing mentor. He's supportive and patient and knowledgeable—it's like working for a baking encyclopedia. All that aside, Theo puts others before himself. He knows what this means to me and will stop at nothing to see me succeed." She blinked; the room silent as her cheeks began to flush with heat. "See *us* succeed."

Shannon sat back in her chair; the weird, floral fabric scratchy against her sensitive skin. Heaven existed where floral prints no longer assaulted her every focal point, she was sure of it.

Didn't matter. Not even botanically incorrect patterns could ruin her good mood.

Taking another sip of her wine, she closed her eyes, allowing the fireplace's glow to wash over her, cheeks already red from the heat.

"Jesus, that smug face you're making comes so naturally, doesn't it?"

"I was just thinking about starfishing on that deliciously large bed."

Theo cleared his throat from the armchair opposite her. She heard him take a sip from his glass, his swallow audible alongside the crackling fire. She knew that if she snuck a peek, that muscle in his jaw would be frantic, working overtime to hold in whatever reply had zipped to the front of the line.

Her greatest accomplishment had always been when he just let those words fly. Loosing that steel grip on his control enough to forget he was her boss and show her little slivers of himself. She loved those little slivers. They were just as wild and inappropriate as she was. But lately he seemed to cling tighter to that control until his responses consisted of rough grunts and single words. It made her crave to know what he was thinking. What he felt the need to hide.

"What are you thinking?" A little direct but whatever. That was the question in her mind, wasn't it?

"Nothing safe for work."

The unmistakable sound of his teeth snapping together was the only indication of that little statement slipping past his guard. It was an act of God that she managed to keep her eyes closed and face neutral. It was immediate, the way those four little words heated her body.

"Good thing we're not at work."

A beat of silence as he rolled her words around. "Good thing," he finally landed on. A groan of frustration lodged in her throat, but she kept quiet, kept her eyes closed as she took another sip of wine.

Her nerves were shot. The stress of the competition combined with Tat Daddy's tiny aprons was a recipe for implosion. She needed a long, sloppy session with her vibrator to work it all out of her system.

"You were sensational today, Lily."

Her eyes flew open to find Theo staring at her over the rim of his glass. Was he serious? Did he not just hear her thoughts? Nerves, vibrator, implosion. Why the fuck was he giving her praise at such a time? Sensational—who even said that? Didn't matter who, she could tell you who hardly uttered so much as a "nice one" in her presence. Theo. Receiving compliments from him was a full lunar eclipse. It could happen two to three times a year and only when the sun, moon, and earth were all aligned. One year he held off on complimenting her until the Christmas party, where he gave her a bottle of champagne and a card that said, "thanks for all your hard work." Devoid of emotion and definitely didn't include big adjectives.

She watched his throat bob as he swallowed a sip of wine, eyes pinned to her face and roaming in that way of his.

"Wow. Is that all it takes to tame that smart mouth of yours? I would have complimented you sooner had I known." His voice sounded strange and coarse, like the tannic wine was rough on his throat. It was hot. He was hot. And she was actively getting hotter by the second.

Is that all it takes to tame that smart mouth of yours?

"There are other ways," she said, finally gathering herself and going for a kill shot. "To tame this smart mouth."

Theo's eyes widened, his irises swallowed by blown-out pupils. He adjusted in his seat, sitting up and setting his glass on the coffee table between them before resting his forearms on his thighs. Somehow closer, yet still too far away. His eyes bore into her, not roaming her face and searching for something unknown, but staring—that relentless muscle ticking in his jaw and his arousal crystal fucking clear.

"Should I count the ways?" she asked, setting her own glass down and slowly crossing her legs. His gaze snapped to her thighs and back before he licked his lips, all of it simple in the glow of the firelight, yet utterly pornographic. Heat pooled at her core as the tension grew charged and frantic between them.

Before she could start listing the ways he could *tame* her mouth, his eyes fluttered closed, breaking their connection and snapping her out of their little tease. Little tease? Her soaked panties would have to disagree with that description.

Eyes remaining closed, Theo ran his hands over his face to tangle in his auburn hair, mussing the locks. "For fuck's sake. Can you not behave for five minutes?"

Shannon's huff of a laugh sounded shaky as she rose from the couch with her glass. One more wouldn't hurt before she claimed that king-sized dream and tried to find some peace. The king-sized dream being the bed, of course.

The finding peace would be vehemently ignoring how turned on she was.

"I was going to say a large bowl of fettuccine Alfredo. Get your mind out of the gutter, Lulu."

His sigh was impressive as he rose to his feet and made his way to the bedroom. "I'm going to get ready for bed. We have a long day ahead of us, and your chaos tornado is not helping."

She snorted at his gall. He started all of that with his "Nothing safe for work" comment, yet she was the chaos tornado? That was Theo's problem. He would let loose for all of five seconds before reeling himself back in. He had to know by now that she wouldn't back down and yet he continued to push. Why? To make sure she was still playing the game? What would he do if she decided to end their game by stripping naked and slipping into that shower with him? She had a feeling his control had a breaking point, and she was finding it harder and harder to fight her own desires.

She wanted Theo, maybe she had for a while. Okay, she definitely had for a while but that was beside the point. It was clear he didn't want her back with how hard he fought against their attraction. Could that be the reason he constantly searched her features? Seeking out the reminders of her imperfection and clinging to them like a lifeline. His eyes trailing over the mole above her lip, to the lines forming around her eyes, over her large thighs and soft curve of her hip. He probably dated models in his free time. Twenty something's like Chanda with perfect skin and too-white smiles.

Ew. Ew, ew, ew. Jealousy, envy, insecurity, and body shaming all in one go? Gross. Out of character and completely unacceptable. Her life had been about facing challenge after challenge with so much unwavering optimism, it altered her own DNA to include a string of fucking sunshine. She didn't feel...feels. Her days were

176

fueled by the perfect balance of work ethic and daydreaming, and she didn't apologize for any of it.

If Theo wanted to deny himself the absolute pleasure of her intimate company. That was his loss.

***

Theo read the same line of his book for around the twentieth time. After the coldest shower of his life where he ran through thoughts of nursing homes, cleaning toilets, and those sad ASPCA commercials on a loop, he threw on a pair of sweatpants and settled into the left side of the bed. Even then, his mind supplied him with sad looking dogs in need of a good home, literally anything to calm his dick down and cool the embers of his lust.

Fettuccine Alfredo. The glassy-eyed look that accompanied that sweet little blush on her cheeks told him that boiled carbs and white sauce were not what occupied her thoughts.

She was going to be the death of him. Even before this trip he found it impossible to fight his attraction. He would watch her from the roasting room like a fucking psycho, completely obsessed with the way her ribbons twirled around her as she worked, and her small hands gripped the wands of the espresso machine. Certifiable. Arguably creeping closer and closer to stalker-like tendencies. Reining in that sort of attraction to your fucking *employee* was essential.

After all, a fling with Shannon would be just that, a fling. Getting close to people was not something Theo did anymore, right alongside having a relationship with coworkers, employees, or she-devils disguised as general managers of your most beloved possession.

Then what the shit are you doing in this bed right now, ya twat?

Shannon hadn't swung in to use the bathroom yet, she had no idea that he was there, warming his side of the bed with no intention of moving to the couch. Neither of them was getting any sleep with the earlier arrangement. Was he excited that Shannon won the technical? For so many reasons, chief among them finally being able to get some sleep.

"You sure are taking your sweet ass time—" All other sharp comments came to an abrupt halt as did the woman herself. She stood halfway through the door, her hand paused in the action of pulling a blue ribbon from her braid. The damn thing had been tied in her hair all day, brushing her cheek as she worked over those cookies.

Speaking of...Theo snagged the cookie with his face on it and took a big bite, filling his mouth before he had to answer for his crimes. Shannon's eyes narrowed and bulged, as if she couldn't decide what emotion his bare-chested frame elicited from her body. The ribbon was pulled from her hair in slow motion as she took in the sight of him under the covers, a book resting on his lap. Her eyes were covering so much fucking ground, sweeping along his bare chest like she couldn't soak it in fast enough. The covers were pulled up over his sweatpants, thank Christ. With the way she was looking at him, he wasn't fully confident in his dick behaving for the rest of the night.

"What are..." she trailed off, taking a step closer and narrowing eyes that were pointed somewhere near his left ribcage. He swallowed the bite of cookie, drawing her eyes up before they snapped back to his face and that cute little blush kissed her cheeks. "You wear glasses?"

"Oh, yeah," he said in his most casual voice. Then added "The bathroom's all yours."

"Yes," she said, her eyes taking on a sharpness. "I'm just wondering why the bed is only half mine."

178

Theo took another bite from his cookie before flashing her a closed mouthed grin.

Her eyes narrowed at him. "We had a deal, Lulu."

"Yes, and that deal said nothing about you having the bed to yourself."

She huffed a laugh, her eyes finding the heavens for strength. "We can't sleep in the same bed."

"We really can. We are adults who can stay on our own sides of a king bed. I can't listen to the springs of that sofa anymore and I'm sure you don't want to be tossing and turning on them, so this is the solution."

"Chivalry is alive and well everyone," she deadpanned.

"Look, if we are going to win this thing, we need to be well-rested. And the only way that's to happen, is if we are both enjoying the luxuries this rose-covered nightmare has to offer."

Silence stretched between them as he tried not to hold his breath. After lecturing himself about a hundred times about why this was a bad idea, his favorite inner voice of late had won out. Hitting him with the logic of how good it would be for the two of them to be in a comfortable sleep space throughout the competition. This would be fine.

"I don't know," she murmured. He didn't like that, the uncertainty in her voice. It was enough to make him want to try and squeeze himself into the confines of that tiny sofa.

"What don't you know?"

"I don't know if I can sleep next to someone who eats his own face as a bedtime snack. It's disturbing."

Theo watched her over the rim of his glasses as he took another bite of the biscuit. It was insanely good. Perfectly crisp on the outside, while the center remained soft and chewy. It was no surprise to him that they had won today.

With one last eye roll, she turned toward the bathroom. The door snicked shut, and he let out a heavy sigh, shoulders sagging as he finally relaxed. It felt as if five whole minutes had passed before the shower's spray cut off and Shannon's steps could be heard on the tiled floor. Pulse spiking, he scrambled to shove his book back into position, heart hammering in his fucking chest.

Glutton for punishment...

Shannon walked out of the bathroom as if everything were normal. As if she were in a flannel onesie instead of the very black, very familiar t-shirt. The thing swallowed her, its hem cutting off at just above her knee and the sleeves dwarfing her arms. Bloem's tulip was stamped just below the swell of her breast, with the larger logo spanning across the back. He couldn't see it, but knew it was there because that was his fucking shirt. The original design that he had been clinging to for the past ten years.

Busy shuffling dirty clothes into her basket in the corner, she turned to the bed and stumbled to a halt.

"What?"

"Why do you have my shirt on?" Fucking hell. That was awfully close to a groan, and it simply couldn't be helped. Seeing his shirt touching her skin did unholy things to his body. Reactionary, possessive things.

"You're clearly not using it, and I had to adjust to our new arrangement," she said with a shrug before turning the covers back and sliding in next to him. "What I was going to wear most definitely wasn't safe for work."

"Behave, for the love of everything holy," he laughed. "Are you—" Cutting himself off from asking, he averted his eyes. Theo didn't want to know if she was wearing anything underneath, already able to see that a bra had been left out of the ensemble. He wasn't sure his heart could take it if Shannon wore nothing but panties and his fucking shirt. Instead, he shook his head and removed his glasses in the hopes that his vision would be blurry enough to wipe that image from memory. It didn't work.

"Goodnight, Lulu" she singsonged without an ounce of remorse.

"Goodnight, Lily girl," he grumbled back.

180

Darkness filled the space around Theo's stiff body, cascading him into a miserable pit of horny thoughts and tense muscles. He didn't relax until Shannon's breaths evened out, becoming luxurious huffs of air breaking through the silence. The sound of her soft breathing filled his ears, surprisingly lulling him into one of the deepest sleeps since they arrived at Château Genevieve.

CHAPTER SEVENTEEN

"I'm not at all worried about some ridiculous curse. Shannon won the technical because that challenge was practically made for her. I ate my own face last night and can confirm that she had a perfect bake."

Daisy smiled at him, her almond eyes a little dreamy. "And how are you feeling about today's competition bake?"

"I feel confident, yeah. I have Shannon working by my side the entire time, and I think yesterday proved how much of an asset she is." His lips twitched up at the corner, a hint of a smile pulling at his usually downturned mouth. "I'm confident we'll have a good bake today."

Daisy let out an audible sigh as Theo received the go-ahead to exit the confessional. He rose, walking toward the kitchens and mentally prepared himself for one hell of a bake. It was his turn to pull out a win for the team, and he wouldn't let Shannon down.

"Nice one, you cack-handed prat," Theo cursed as another cookie refused to bend to his will.

"Lulu, darling, the more British you sound the more worried I become," Shannon said softly as she piped her little heart out. The creative bake was announced to be the three-dimensional jack-o'-lantern or more accurately, the only thing they had failed to practice. Assuming they wouldn't choose a Halloween theme because the show would be airing closer to Thanksgiving, they had made the decision to practice the other two options for most of the week. Only dedicating three hours of their precious time to making stencils and measurements for the giant cookie pumpkin. Insane.

When the judges filed in and the show kicked off, Shannon had been brimming with energy and chomping at the bit for that game board. They had created some seriously amazing designs throughout practice, convincing her that it was their shoe-in. Alas.

The rules of filming were simple, when the judges filed in and announced the day's challenge, all contestants were to look shocked and awed as if they hadn't been practicing for a full week. She had almost cried from laughing as Theo pretended to come up with a method for the bake, stumbling over his words and managing to work cocoa butter into the plan at least five times. She couldn't blame him. Using cocoa butter to harden the exterior of the cookie was the only solid part of their plan where the jack-o'-lantern was concerned.

That was why, instead of handing each other knowing, confident smiles and betting on the outcome, Shannon was sweating over intricate piping work while Theo became more British by the minute. It wasn't going terribly...it just wasn't a walk in the park either.

"Hello, you two."

Shannon made a really solid effort to hold back her sigh as Theo audibly groaned at Jasper's arrival. It was no surprise that chatting up the judges and pretending to be nice was his least favorite part of this ordeal. Unfortunately, the cameras were unrelenting in their love of his brooding face.

"Hi Jasper," she chimed, her brightest smile set firmly in place.

"Tell me about your competition bake today."

"Well," Theo said in a ridiculous tenor. "Today we are attempting to not lose our minds as these thin pieces of wafer crumble beneath my fat fingers."

"Wonderful," Jasper laughed.

"Or," she cut in before Theo could mumble any more damning information. "We are constructing our pumpkin using chocolate speculaas cookies. Using these molds," she paused, holding up a mold they had constructed from tin foil. "We are going to make seven rounded sections, which will make up the body of the pumpkin. See?" Snagging two of the already baked pieces, Shannon gently held them together, showing Jasper how the pumpkin would take shape.

"Wow, that will actually look like the grooves of a pumpkin. What will you use to bind it?"

"Dark chocolate royal icing. The handle of the pumpkin will be braided graham cracker flavored with chocolate and espresso."

"Handle? Don't you mean the stem?"

Shannon grinned over another round of muffled curses from Theo as he worked. "We are turning this jack-o'-lantern into a trick-or-treating basket. It will have a handle and will be filled with coconut shortbread decorated to look like candy bars."

Pride swelled through her chest as she saw the delight in Jasper's eyes. That last detail had been her idea. When the judges announced the challenge, they threw in a little curveball. The bakers had to include one element from the previous day's technical. If they knew anything about her at this point, it was that she loved decorating shortbread. Her cramped fingers and stiff neck said otherwise, but at least the cookies looked incredible.

Now if they could only construct the damn pumpkin…

"Wonderful," Jasper said with more enthusiasm. "Good luck."

Just as Jasper turned to the next workstation, Charles Darlington opened his stupid mouth.

"Bakers, you have one hour left."

"Jesus, feck," Theo grumbled.

Shannon glanced up from her work, watching as he struggled with holding a section of cookie in place while piping along another's edge.

"Here," she said, dropping her piping bag and moving around the butcher block to assist. He surprised her by making room, still holding his first two sections in place as she came up beside him.

"If you can just help me with the next two sections, it should be structurally sound enough for me to continue alone."

She nodded, snatching the royal icing and piping a thin, but solid line down the edge of their next piece. Bringing it to the structure, she attached it in the proper position, their pumpkin barely starting to take shape.

"Do you have the freeze spray?" Grabbing his hand, she repositioned so both of them held the structure steady.

"It's behind me," he said, his brows furrowing as he gently held the cookies.

Without letting go of the new addition, she reached around his waist, careful not to jostle him too much. Her hand reached blindly for the canister of freezing spray; nose buried in Theo's shoulder.

"God, why do you always smell so good? It's annoying." She hadn't meant to say that. But after sleeping in his shirt, his woodsy sent assaulting her nostrils as she dreamed highly inappropriate dreams, the thought just slipped from her tongue.

"Do I?"

Yes. He really did. Like cedar wood and something citrusy. Like the forest after a light rain. It was intoxicating.

Her fingers connected with the spray, saving her from answering his question and shoving her foot any further into her gullet.

"Hold steady Tat Daddy," she chose instead, bringing her face close to her work as she sprayed the fresh icing to freeze it in place.

"Jesus, please keep the nicknames to yourself. The last thing I need is Tat Daddy going viral after this airs."

Chuckling, she moved on to the next piece, repeating the process. They worked well together. Theo had baked off doubles of all their components, saving them as he indeed crumbled a couple beneath his large hands. But his bake was perfect, each cookie rolled to the exact same thickness, even and perfectly crisp. It was his idea to make chocolate speculaas dough which held up incredibly well and was easily shaped. Cocoa butter had been melted and brushed on every piece to keep them crisp and prevent sogginess.

It was genius. And truly a miracle that they were pulling it off with how little they practiced. But that was the thing with her and Theo. Sure they may be doing it while glaring at one another, but they always got the job done. This competition was going to prove that.

A timer sounded just as Shannon was freezing the second to last panel in place.

"That'll be the handle. Want to pull it from the oven and I can finish construction?"

And they did just that. Shannon pulling the braided cookie from the oven, its coloring perfectly browned, before setting it aside to cool. They were cutting it close, and she needed to finish piping the candy bars.

"Bakers, you have half an hour left!" Daisy called from Chanda and Samira's station. The latter of which found

186

Shannon's wide-eyed gaze with her own before quickly getting back to work. Yeah, the feeling was mutual.

The next half hour went by in a chaotic blur before she and Theo carefully set the handle on top of their jack-o'-lantern cookie structure—filled to the brim with candy and looking absolutely amazing.

How on earth had they pulled that off?

***

"Here we have a chocolate and cocoa nib speculaas biscuit, with a chocolate espresso handle, and shortbread candies," Theo rattled off as the judges broke apart the structure he had been building for the past three hours.

His palms were sweating as he watched them chew in silence, smiles touching Daisy and Jasper's faces while Charles remained stoically neutral. For all his bad cookie puns and cheesy grins, the man had turned into Gordon Ramsay real quick. His brows knitted together, eyes narrowing before he asked, "What is the flavor of the shortbread?"

"Coconut latte," he said feeling like a dick. If people thought he was going to throw a coconut cream latte on Bloem's menu after this, they were mistaken.

Still, Charles chewed on as Daisy spoke up. "This is really something, you two. The structure itself is solid and crisp, while also packing a chocolatey punch."

"Even the braided handle is the perfect texture, the flavors blending together nicely," Jasper added.

Charles glared down at the bake before meeting Theo's gaze. He felt Shannon stiffen beside him and instinctually brushed his hand against hers for comfort. She instantly interlocked their fingers squeezing gently in a show of solidarity. They were in it together, no matter what

187

happened. Eyes still locked on Darlington; he watched as the man broke into a grin.

"I agree,' he stated, brushing his fingers together to dust off the cookie crumbs. Theo felt his shoulders relax as he went on. "The shortbread are neat as a pin, and so beautifully seasoned. Your flavors and textures are spot on, and the overall look of the bake is quite effective. Well done, Bloem."

"Thank you," they replied in unison, a smile in Shannon's voice and a roughness in his own. After snagging the bake and bringing it back to their station, they watched the remaining contestants step up to the judging table. Although relief washed over him, he couldn't relax. The competition was fierce, and Theo wasn't blind to the fact that their bakes had been created with only one person for the first hour and a half.

A humbling thought as Meatball team's jack-o'-lantern was placed on the judge's table. It was a work of art, a thought that would only be escaping his brain when he started wearing orange and embracing baking puns. The thing looked almost real from the color work sprayed onto the frosting covering the structure. A candle was even lit, the flame glowing within the eyes and mouth with infuriating likeness. It reminded him that this was no amateur baking competition. These other contestants were some of the best out there, and they couldn't let their guard down for a second.

The majority of the competition had used gingerbread as anticipated, a small win as one by one the judges oohed and aahed over their works. At least Bloem had been creative.

After the judging, they gathered in the gallery where the confessionals usually took place, cameras capturing their nervous energy and chatter about what went wrong and who knocked it out of the park.

A small tremor had started in Theo's fingers when he saw Chanda crying over having to re-bake an item and sending

188

their team straight into the weeds. Her guilt-filled eyes as she looked to Samira for the hundredth time had caused his breath to quicken, anxiety coming from out of nowhere and knocking him down a peg.

His gaze found Shannon, comforting people who needed it, cracking jokes at her own expense and actively suppressing her own joy as they struggled. This was a competition, yes, but these were also real people with real problems. Any one of the contestants could be going through something similar to him—or worse. But he couldn't bring himself to console them. Not when everything he held dear was on the line.

The energy in the room was thick and tacky as they lined up to meet their fate. His palm sweated against Shannon's as somewhere along the line their fingers had interlaced without a word. He didn't care if his skin was clammy, he needed the connection. Needed the comfort.

The judges filed in, all of them happy and carefree—blissfully immune to the fear of going home.

"Alright everyone, I have the delight of announcing which of you won biscuit week and will receive our first ever *Whisk Wars* prize," Daisy said with a smile. "What is the prize this week, Charles?"

"The winner of this week's challenge." Theo gritted his teeth through the dramatic pause earning him a squeeze from Shannon's fingers. "Will receive a five-thousand-dollar credit from our sponsors over at KitchenAid."

Theo's stomach bottomed out. He had been hoping for immunity next week, but some new equipment wouldn't hurt, now would it? Five thousand dollars was enough to get him a new mixer, food processor, some new whisks, and spatulas. That would be a pretty sweet upgrade.

Getting ahead of yourself, mate. Shaking his head, he tried not to hold his breath as Daisy looked at each contestant. "The winner of biscuit week is…"

The events that followed Daisy's announcement blurred into a whirlwind of activity. Had she really just said his name? A few glares were pointed in his direction, but mostly smiles, nods—clapping. He was certain he heard clapping. His hands were gripping something soft, arms enveloped in warmth and squeezing gently. Theo couldn't make sense of his fingers tangled in soft strands of hair. In fact, his mind short-circuited completely as his gaze locked with bright blue eyes, palms cupped his face, and soft lips pressed against his.

Shannon jolted in his arms, seemingly shocked by her own actions before she sighed and relaxed into the kiss, pressing a bit closer. For five brief seconds, their bodies, skin, *lips* were connected before she pulled back, turned in his arms and faced the judges once more.

Theo dropped his hands to his sides, staring at her profile. Taking in the bright blush on her cheeks and the slow-motion rise of her hand that brushed a gentle caress to her lips, as if chasing the lingering kiss with the pads of her fingers.

"I think Theo is stunned," Jasper said, a clear smile in his voice. That brought him out of his stupor. Swinging his gaze from the woman beside him, he flashed the judges a rare smile and tried to ignore the gasps of shock that moved through the room.

Was his smile as dopey as it felt? Probably. The way his lips stretched and his cheeks plumped was extremely foreign to him. He tried and tried to focus his attention on Charles, who announced the second and third place—counting down to the bottom two teams. He couldn't focus. His hand brushed against the back of Shannon's, and she took a small step away from him at the contact. Probably for the best. The need to touch her—to request an explanation—coursed through his body, its port of entry his lips after that too-quick kiss. He needed to know if it was real for her. Demand answers.

190

Demand she do it again.

How was his brain so jumbled from a five second, close-mouthed kiss? This situation with Shannon had to be getting to him a bit more than he thought if he was this foggy after what felt like some of his worst work. He had barely even registered the press of her lips before she was pulling away and breaking their connection. A connection that he very much wanted to explore again.

Impossible. He knew sleeping next to her was the worst decision he'd ever made. Failure was never an option for Theo, but he sure wasn't winning whatever battle being waged where Shannon was concerned.

"…I'm sorry, but tomorrow, you will battle it out in the elimination round."

Theo snapped his thoughts into focus as the bottom two teams were announced. There was no time to think about that kiss, real or fake, when that could be them at the bottom at any moment. They had a good week. But if they were going to win this thing, he needed to get his thoughts away from Shannon's lips and focused on baking.

Charles clapped his hands before announcing the elimination challenge was to be macarons, explaining that it would be a solo bake for the executive chefs only, and required perfect macarons of three different flavors.

"Good thing that wasn't our challenge," Shannon murmured to him without meeting his gaze.

"I fucking hate macarons," he responded, his eyes burning holes into her profile. He just needed her to look at him. Meet his eyes once more and…he didn't know what he needed, really.

The outro was recorded as Theo tried to collect his thoughts. He would have to talk to Shannon about that kiss. They had the entire evening to get through, there was no way he was going to just pretend it never happened. And there he went again, thinking about the woman when he should have been focused on the show.

Paul took over as the cameras cut, his nasally voice rising over the excited murmurs from the contestants. "Alright, I am going to take the executive chefs in the gallery for confessionals, sous chefs, you'll stay in here. We'll get your joint confessionals afterward."

"Oh, for fuck's sake," he said under his breath. Shannon looked at him then, her eyes soft and a strange smile on her face.

"I'll see you at confessionals," she said before turning on her heel and walking away.

"For fuck's sake," he repeated to no one in particular.

CHAPTER EIGHTEEN

"State how you're feeling after that win," Paul instructed.

"I think I'm in shock," Shannon chimed, the smile she had worn since they won still lighting up her face. "This has been an insane week for us, but especially for me. I never thought I would win two challenges in the first round."

"How did you feel about your comp—oh shoot. Sorry Shannon, we're having a small issue with this camera."

Shannon waved it away. "No problem."

"It looks like we have to postpone this confessional. I'll send Maggie to fetch you once we get things up and running again."

Theo practically ran to his room. The first to give his confessional, he was gifted an hour of free time before his joint interview with Shannon and intended to use every second of it. The need was for a scalding hot shower, in which he would fuck his hand until his nerves settled and he had sufficiently worked whatever was happening out of his system. Then he would crank the shower to cold and let the icy stream calm the fire within him.

He needed to get his desires under control or there was no way he was going to make it through this competition, sleeping next to the most tempting woman on the planet and doing nothing about it.

The minute he entered their room, Theo kicked his shoes off, the door snicking shut as he unbuttoned his pants and let them fall to the floor. Time was of the essence if he wanted to perform his misdeeds before Shannon returned. Tugging on the back of his shirt, he pulled it up and over his head, the material obstructing his view as a strange sound reached his ears.

He paused his blind stumbling to the bedroom, straining his ears to make out the sound. Had he waltzed into someone else's room? No, Shannon's jasmine scent was all over the place and he had seen her raincoat hanging by the door. He listened, the sound becoming clearer as he stood still, his frantic journey to the shower paused. The buzzing noise continued, waxing and waning at a steady rhythm.

A new sound joined in as the beating of his own heart pounded in his ears. Slowly, Theo tugged the shirt from his head and blinked in the image before him.

Shannon lay on his side of the bed, eyes closed and cheeks a perfect shade of pink. The blankets were pulled to her waist, covering the hand that was busy while the other pressed against the oak headboard. That perfect little pout was parted, her breathing coming in sweet little jagged breaths that were so close to whimpers, it had Theo's dick hardening in record time.

Shouldn't be here, he thought frantically. But whatever sound advice his brain provided, his eyes refused to follow. They ran over her pleasure-filled face, down her neck and chest which was barely covered by a small, tight cami. He

194

soaked in the image of her heaving breasts, her gasps quickening and her movements beneath the blanket growing more frantic.

Managing a step back, then another, he hoped to hell that he could make it from the bedroom and out the door before she ever suspected a thing.

"I'm gonna come," she moaned. Theo bit down on his fist. Jesus Christ, he was harder than he'd ever been in his life, his cock tenting the fabric of his boxers and hiding nothing.

He wanted her to come. Was actively wondering if she had already and was working on another climax. But it was even more damning than that, because he wanted to be the one getting her there, taking his dick so well and deserving every little pang of pleasure.

"I'm, hmmm," She worked herself closer to climax, making Theo insane with lust. He needed to *get the fuck out of there*.

Daring another step as Shannon moaned, he rubbed a palm down his length, desperate for any kind of friction— any kind of pressure. By the sound of it, her impending orgasm was just around the corner and Theo could not be in the room when it happened. Even if walking away felt like the worst possible outcome.

His heel hit the doorframe just as Shannon's release clearly struck, the sound thumping through her breaths and making him want to die. Blue eyes flew open even as a moan escaped her lips, her legs trembling beneath the linens.

"Theo," she gasped, a mix of shock and pleasure thick in her tone, and fucking hell—he was a dead man. Hearing his name leave her mouth on an orgasm may have stopped his heart cold. "Oh my God."

Not better. He held his hands up, shaking his head to convey what? That it wasn't what it looked like? That he wasn't just watching her pleasure herself and getting rock hard in the process? That was, in fact, exactly what happened.

"I'm sorry," he blurted. "I didn't see you until it was…it was too late."

Recovering quickly, Shannon sat up, her cheeks growing ever hotter. "What are you doing here? Why are you naked?"

He looked down at himself, mortified at his erection still proudly jutting out, skin exposed and his fucking socks still on.

"Confessional was quick, I was trying to make it back in time to shower before you got here. I…I'm sorry. I'll just," he cut off, pointing out of the room awkwardly.

"Oh my God." To his horror, Shannon threw back the covers and jumped from the bed. Her ponytail was lopsided and messy, but that wasn't even the half of it. It wasn't a cami after all. All functioning brain cells left his head as he raked his gaze over the satin slip she had on, her peaked nipples visible and ass barely covered. She held a used toy in her hand as she stalked toward him with fire burning her gaze.

"How long were you watching me?"

"Not long," he promised, his hands raising to grip her shoulders for emphasis before he thought better of it and just held them in front of himself. "I only saw…the finale."

What the fuck is wrong with you, mate? The finale?

Shannon's eyes narrowed to terrifying slits. "Oh yeah? That ham sandwich in your panties is telling a different story."

Placing a palm over his bulge, he shook his head, anger rising in the face of embarrassment.

"Why are you pleasuring yourself in the middle of the fucking day?" It was an absurd question. One could argue that he was just about to do the same thing himself, the hour being the last thing on his mind.

"I don't know, Theo, maybe I just needed a bit of a release. Do you mean to tell me you haven't jerked off once since we've been here?"

196

"Yes, but I wank in the shower like an adult, where all my transgressions are rinsed down the drain. Not on my roommate's side of the bed."

Her cheeks somehow managed to grow redder. "How practical of you."

Dragging a hand through his hair, he let out a little laugh. "That's me, practical and controlled and responsible. A feat that should earn me an automatic spot in heaven seeing as I have you to contend with. Now, if you're finished in here, I believe it's my turn for *a little release*."

Shannon's lips parted, her eyes growing slightly softer. "Is that what you were coming in here to do?"

"Is that not the story my ham sandwich is telling you?" he bellowed, embarrassment making him a bit unhinged.

Blue eyes ran the length of him then, down to his dick and lower to the tattoos just above his knees. Goosebumps crawled along his back as that gaze raked itself back up in a slow perusal before colliding with his. Was he panting? His chest rose and fell at a pace too quick to be casual while he stared into those blue pools.

She crossed her arms, the vibrator still clutched in one hand.

"No," she said, cocking her head at him in challenge.

He took a step forward, keeping a foot of distance between them. "No, what?"

"I'm not finished. Usually, when I'm performing a little self-care, I make myself come three times." Theo's nostrils flared as he sucked in a breath, another involuntary step moving him closer to her warmth. "What you witnessed was only number one."

Breathing her in, his senses were overloaded with too much information. That tether on his control was fraying, every muscle screaming at him to reach out and touch her. To kiss her again and truly taste those pouty little lips.

"Is that right?" he asked, his voice low and rough. Goosebumps spread on her arms and Theo marveled at it.

Wondering what sort of reactions he would get with his hands if his voice alone managed to elicit that one. He watched in fascination as her skin rippled under his gaze, and then it struck him. That scent.

"Lily girl, why do you smell like me?"

Shannon's eyes widened, her lips parting on a gasp. She searched his face as he tried to control his reaction to his scent on her soft skin. Something primal was taking over his body. Some sort of demon from the caveman days, because as he breathed in his soap on her flushed body, his brain supplied one word to him without a second thought.

Mine.

He should have expected what came next. Should have known that when it came to Shannon, she would always push. Always shove. Without warning, she stepped forward, pausing as their bodies stood an inch away from one another before uttering the words that snapped his years-strong hold on his control.

"I use your soap before I fuck myself, Theo, so I can envision you more vividly when I make myself come."

Snap.

Theo's hand shot forward, fingers curling around her throat as he guided her back against the wall with a soft thud. His ragged breath came hard against her ear, her chest rising to meet his with each quick inhale. Six years of tension coiled tight between them, leaving no room for a slow takeoff.

His thumb brushed against a pulse point as his other arm leaned against the wall, boxing her in.

"Again with that smart mouth," he murmured, giving her neck a little squeeze. She whimpered, and his dick felt ready to fucking break in half. "A man can only take so much before his restraint crumbles to the ground. Is that what you need, Lily baby? Me, untethered and taking what I want?"

"Yes," she said without hesitation, the hand not clutching her toy shooting to grasp his wrist at her collarbone. "The thought of you losing control is my favorite fantasy."

He groaned, his lips pressing against the skin just below her ear. Humming her approval, she lifted her chin, exposing more of her neck to his greedy mouth. He couldn't help it, his tongue snaked out to taste her skin, a flavor profile he would compare to every other from that moment on. They would all fall flat compared to the taste of Shannon on his tongue.

Greedy was exactly what he was as he pinned her against the wall, his breath hot on her neck. Desire coursed through him, begging him to take more of her even as his common sense fought for control.

This couldn't work. It was his employee's neck he was tasting right now, hand wrapped around her throat, both of them near naked. There was no way this could end well for either of them.

Another groan escaped, this one charged with frustration and anger. His fingers loosened on her neck, shifting to rest on her shoulder.

"I can feel you spiraling," she huffed. Releasing his wrist, she brought her hand to his face, pressing until their eyes locked. It was a terrible sight, those lust-filled eyes. And one he would have a hell of a time not conjuring every hour, on the hour for the rest of his life. "Don't overthink it, Lulu."

"We shouldn't be doing this," he rasped. "There is no possible way this ends well."

"We can keep it casual," she said in a rush, her eagerness doing nothing to stabilize him. "There are no rules saying we have to turn this into anything more than hooking up and blowing off steam. And don't insult me by insinuating you're not into it."

Theo ran his gaze over every curve of her face, the dip of her shoulder—the look of his hand on her skin. His tattoos dark and chaotic against the smooth, flushed backdrop. That was another image he intended to return to. Commit it to memory so he could obsess over the contrast.

Her words were pretty, but they both knew casual wasn't realistic, not between them. Still, the notion that it didn't have to end sent a thrill down his spine. At once exhilarating and terrifying.

"I'm very clearly into it, Shannon," he said, pressing his hips into her and drawing a pretty little gasp from her lips. "My desire for you is not the problem here."

"What is, then? Afraid you'll catch feelings?"

Her focus zipped to his jaw before he clenched his mouth shut. Those fears would not be voiced because that was decidedly the opposite of casual. A muscle twitched in his cheek as he fought the urge to tell her the ruth, and a strange look passed over her features, a smile he did not trust in the least kissing her mouth. They were still tangled in each other. His rational brain not quite willing to tell his body to let her go and step back. She was warm in his arms, soft and so fucking sexy.

"Here's the deal, Theo, we are clearly wound up too tight to function and I don't know about you, but I won't be able to frost any cakes if I can't get this new image of us out of my head for five seconds." He muffled a curse as she held his head in place, forcing him to meet her gaze. "We need to get each other out of our systems. Squash this thing between us before I literally combust from the sexual tension."

"Been thinking about me a lot, have you?" he asked before his head could catch up to his tongue. He loved the idea of her being just as affected by his closeness as he was of hers. Was obsessed with it, actually.

Her smile cracked like a whip as she shifted and a buzzing sounded through the room.

His smile faltered as the vibration from Shannon's toy could be felt through his fingertips still grazing her collarbone.

"I like it when you speak your mind," she murmured, her eyes taking on a brightness as anticipation rocked through them both.

"Jesus, do you even have the capacity to behave?" His hand moved from the wall to the back of her neck, finally tangling in that mass of golden hair and proving that question had just been for show. "One day," he said, pretending to still be considering it when he knew damn well that his logic wouldn't be winning this war.

"Uh huh," she said, nodding as she brought the toy between them and pressed it between her legs. "Casual." The word left her lips on a gasp as he leaned his hips into her hand and the toy pressed tight against her core. "Just two consenting adults enjoying one another."

Their hands tangled in each other's hair as the toy began to move between them. Tightening his grip, he gave hers a gentle tug, bringing her lust-filled gaze up, her pout a breath away from his lips.

This feels like a lot. He wanted to voice it, tell her that what was about to happen felt like a hell of a lot more than just friends enjoying one another. That when he finally pressed his lips to hers for a taste, smelled his soap on her skin and touched her naked body, casual would be the last adjective he would use to describe it. Terrifying, magnificent—undeniable. All far more accurate for a night with Shannon.

Licking her lips, she gave him a lazy smile as the blush of her pleasure rose on her chest.

"You don't have some sort of boss kink, do you? Because I refuse to call you sir in the bedroom."

"Lily baby, when have you ever called me sir?"

She smiled, her eyes fluttering as her orgasm built by her own hand. She was already feeling good, and he fucking loved it. Loved that she was taking what she wanted, when she wanted it. But now it was his turn.

Theo watched her reaction as he finally, deliberately, trailed his hand down to her breast, his fingers barely a whisper against the silky fabric of the slip. Finding her hardened nipple, he allowed his fingers to hover, providing just enough pressure to be felt. The goosebumps that peppered her skin were some of the strongest he'd ever conjured, and he fucking loved the sight of them.

"No, I've been paying attention. And playing the submissive is not something I ever imagined for you." Her eyes fluttered shut as he hovered over her breast, fighting his desire to devour her in one fucking bite. "You are a temptress, Shannon. A woman who knows her power and wields it relentlessly. Women like you don't give and grovel, you take, don't you? Basking in the worship and praise of your utter perfection." When he softly grazed that peaked nipple again, she moaned, arching her back and pressing herself into his palm. He gave her what she wanted, groaning in approval as he caressed, circling her nipple with his thumb. Her hand paused between her legs, as if all of her attention was rerouted to his hand on her body.

"Worship *is* my favorite position," she said through shaky lips.

He chuckled, taking in every shift of her features. Part of him worried that his words were too much, too soon. Too many truths hung in the air between them. But the time for fear was long gone as he allowed himself this one moment. One day to say and do whatever he damn well felt like. "Open your eyes," he crooned as he journeyed lower, his hand grazing over the soft curves of her abdomen. "I want you to see exactly who is making you feel this good. Let my face be the last you see before I kiss the air from your lungs."

Another sweet little whimper left her lips as her eyes fluttered open. "Why don't you do it already?"

Great question.

"Because." His hand dipped lower, grazing her hip and causing her to jerk at the connection. Finding her hand, he nestled between her and the toy, taking control of the vibrator and easing her fingers off. "I'm exploring all the ways to tame that smart mouth before trying the most obvious."

Pressing gently, Theo worked the toy in, positioning it so the suction rested on her clit. He owed her two more orgasms, and there was no way he was lasting that long if he sunk into her himself. As it was, he was so achingly turned on, he wasn't at all confident in his ability not to explode the minute she tightened around him.

"This okay?"

She nodded, her eyes hooded and unfocused. Hand freed of the toy, she pressed it against the wall next to her head, a move he was starting to realize she enjoyed. His little she-devil liked to push into it, didn't she?

Turning the vibration up a click, he moved, keeping the suction pressed against her clit as he stroked the shaft in and out in a steady rhythm. Breathing intensifying with every thrust, her chest heaved with each rapid inhalation.

"Is this what you were thinking about, Lily baby? Me, using your own toys to get you off, obsessing over every sound you make? Christ, I thought your laugh was my favorite sound in the world until I heard you moan." Shannon rocked her hips, her breathing growing frantic as he reveled at the whimpers being pulled from her lips. "Or were you taking my cock when you dreamed about us?" Holding out and hovering over her mouth, her breath was hot against his lips, begging him to close the distance. His dirty words swallowed by her before being breathed out in a whimper.

The hand tangled in his hair tugged, attempting to connect their hungry lips. Her neediness made him week at the knees, unable to process that they were here. This woman wanted him.

Pulling his hand free of her soft hair, he thumbed her chin, their lips barely grazing as he worked the vibrator between them. *Too much.* Pleasure-filled eyes found his, their color reminding him of clearest skies, the still of the ocean. A tender gaze from across the café, a smile crinkling the corners over a mug of the exact same color.

He should snap his eyes shut. Block out that hypnotizing stare and focus on his job. Focus on her lips instead.

Something held him back from that kiss. A fear of what would follow once he finally allowed himself to break. But as a small gasp had her bottom lip connecting with his, his fear might as well have been a balloon in a hurricane for how quickly it simply blew away.

"Such sweet noises leaving your lips, but nothing to say? Looks like that mouth can be tamed after all."

She was close now, her lashes fluttering as her hand gripped roughly at his hair, the other pressing against the wall. He would never forget her that way. Free and pleasured and chasing exactly what she wanted. It would be burned into his brain for the rest of his natural born life.

"Theo," she gasped, a plea in the form of his name. "I need your lips on mine when I come. Nothing *tame* about it—"

Theo didn't allow her to finish that sentence before crushing his mouth against hers. His desire was feral, all-consuming as he launched into the kiss. All tongues and teeth and nipping and tasting. A pained groan vibrated against his lips, and it took him a minute to realize he had made the sound. An involuntary reaction to the taste of Shannon on his greedy tongue. Thumb pressing into her chin, he angled her head to take it deeper, his hand increasing the tempo between her legs.

Her whimpers broke their kiss as her orgasm built, getting louder and rumbling against his lips, their breath tangled.

"I'm…Theo, I'm—"

"Yes," he growled. "Come for me." A shudder rocked through Shannon's body as she arched into him, trapping his hand between their bodies. A long, rich moan spilled from her lips as he worked the toy, making sure she rode out the waves of her climax.

She was beautiful. Perfect. Her body bowed as she took her pleasure, hair messy and cheeks tinted pink. Her lips were swollen and glistened with his kiss, the sight bringing him down to claim them again. Capturing the moment through taste and touch. Smooth legs trembled as she settled against the wall and he clicked the vibrator off, ragged breaths and his beating heart the only sound reaching his ears.

She sighed against his lips, her hand leaving the wall to cling to him, and fuck if he didn't love the feel of it. Of bearing her weight knowing it was the only way she was able to stand upright.

Slowly, he eased back, leaving one more fluttering kiss on her lips before peppering them along her jaw and pulling his hand from between her legs. Insatiable. That wasn't nearly enough. He needed to be inside of her within seven seconds and prayed he could last longer than that.

His dick was throbbing against her thigh, precum spotting his boxers but he ignored it, bringing the toy up and into their focus. Raking his eyes over the shiny proof of her arousal, he groaned, more than ready to feel her slick heat against his own skin.

Focus still glued to the glistening shaft, his murmured appreciation was foreign to his own ears as he dug deep for control.

"Such a good girl."

Her eyes heated in record time and Theo decided that control was a distant memory as he tossed her toy aside and plunged his hand into blond silk, the other sliding around to cup her face.

"Are you going to take my cock just as well as you—"

His words were cut off by a sharp knock on the door.

They stiffened in unison, eyes going wide as they stared at each other in silence. The knock sounded again, accompanied by Maggie's clipped voice.

"Miss Perry, they're ready for your confessional now. And bring Mr. Abbott with you, they'll be interviewing you both right after."

CHAPTER NINETEEN

Shannon rolled her lips together to keep from giggling. After having one of the best orgasms ever achieved from Viggo (Her vibrator. She had been going through a major *Lord of the Rings* phase.) And hearing the most controlled man on the planet whisper delicious things in her ear, this was not how she anticipated things ending.

And she had been envisioning this scene a lot.

When her confessional was canceled, Shannon couldn't make it to the room fast enough, desperate to stifle whatever had possessed her to kiss her boss after their win. It had been decidedly the most unsexy kiss she had ever delivered, but boy had she liked it. Theo's lips had been soft and sweet from testing their bake's components all day. She had wanted to stay in that kiss. Lay in it and snuggle in until the entire room disappeared. She would blame it on the adrenaline of a good win, but she meant every word of what she said. The sexual tension between them needed to be taken out before it took them out. What had she said? Get it out of their systems?

He had certainly done his part. She and Viggo were about to have months of spank bank material from his dirty talk alone. Introduce his stupidly toned body and those tattoos on his thighs and she was a complete goner.

Tawny eyes ran the length of her face, dancing over where his own hand rested against her cheek before darting back to her eyes.

"Should we kill her?" Shannon asked on a whisper.

He laughed, a lopsided grin breaking through the dirty *dirty* look from seconds before.

"It seems like the only reasonable solution at the moment," he replied. She didn't move to disconnect their bodies, completely unwilling to let the moment end. They had been interrupted, not finished. She felt far from finished, actually.

"We don't have to stop," Shannon said, her hands tugging his face back towards her. "With what I'm feeling against my thigh, we could get it done in ten minutes flat."

Pupils swallowing up his eyes, he held her chin, angling her until her lips pressed against his and she was able to taste him again. Theo was a man who gripped and pulled and took charge. And it was doing it for her.

"I'm not even going to argue with that," he murmured against her lips.

The staccato wrapping of Maggie's knocks kicked off again, pulling a resigned sigh from both their lungs. Theo groaned, his forehead connecting with hers before he angled his face towards the door.

"Theo, no. We need…"

"Thanks Maggie," he yelled over her hissed whisper. "We'll be there in five."

Waiting until the click of her heels faded down the hall, she tugged his hair again, reluctant to admit that their moment was over.

"Okay, that timeline is a little trickier, but I have confidence in my abilities."

208

"Oh, I have no doubt in your abilities," he laughed, pulling away from her body and stealing her warmth. "But you should head to the confessional. I'll be right behind you."

Popping her bottom lip into a pout, she tried for her most adorable, disappointed face. "You're going to finish things without me? That's not closing the loop at all, that's…it's—that is not what I want."

"Trust me, there is nothing I want more than to ignore Maggie's existence on planet earth and drag you to that bed." Heat rushed to her cheeks at the image that provided her. Yes, that was very good. "But…"

"But nothing. I want that, Theo. Finish what we started." A pained expression moved across his features as he circled the room, gathering his discarded clothes. "Work each other out of our systems, remember?"

He paused, eyes roaming her face in that way of his, their intensity sending a shiver rippling over her skin.

"Is that how you feel, Shannon? As if I've been worked from your system?" It was a quiet question, a careful question. Delivered with a knowledge that they both knew the answer and it shouldn't be voiced.

"I…" No. At this point, it would take a horse tranquilizer to calm her desire for Theo. Nothing had been worked out, and everything felt changed.

He nodded, backing towards the bathroom. A doomed feeling settled in her gut at that nod. Why did he have sad eyes when mere seconds before, she was sure the fire would never leave those gold irises?

"You're running," she accused, her voice barely more than a whisper. She had been there before, knew the signs when they presented. This time she was face to face with the one leaving instead of watching his retreating back, but the feeling was all the same. Worse, even. She had been chasing after Ryan for a year and if she was honest with herself, his behavior hadn't surprised her.

Chasing after was not at all how she would describe her relationship with Theo. They tolerated one another, generally squabbled like an old married couple, and had managed to coexist in a professional setting for an ungodly amount of time. So, she had the gift of years to dissect every lingering look, every unspoken word. Weeks upon months of selfies and goosebumps and…tension. In the back of her mind, she knew this was something she wanted. To glimpse behind the curtain and see a side of Theo that made her blood heat.

But now that her blood was a rolling boil within her veins, was she expected to just walk away? Casual. Is that what she had said? A ridiculous concept when his touch still lingered on her skin, his words echoed through her head. Ridiculous when he had so easily unraveled her, a woman who had faked more orgasms than not as she generally focused on providing a great experience over receiving one. It was the overachiever in her, she supposed.

Lost in her own thoughts, she jolted when a soft hand palmed her cheek, lifting her face so their eyes met in a confusing whirl of emotions. Theo's face was set in his usual frown, brows furrowed, eyes anguished. She wanted to say something quippy, laugh off this awkward rejection and figure out how to move forward. Maybe she would quit her job, change her name and dye her hair brown. A whole new identity sounded just right for this nightmare scenario. And maybe she would have been able to lean into her usual defense if it hadn't been for the roiling sadness within her. Unwanted feelings of loss for a man she had never actually had.

She closed her eyes, unwilling to meet whatever was in his stare head on. She didn't need or want his pity, it was pathetic.

"I can feel you spiraling," he said, his voice soft and infuriating. That was her moment to make a joke and bail. Was there a dick joke that involved spiraling…

"Open your eyes, Lily baby."

Looking childish didn't stop her from shaking her head, refusing to open her eyes and reveal the tears burning her retinas.

"Shannon, look at me," he pushed, giving her chin a little squeeze. He should know better than to challenge her stubbornness. She would stand there with her eyes closed for the next hour if it meant not facing whatever rejection she was about to receive.

Soft lips met hers and had her eyes flying open. Theo smiled against her mouth, the feel of it sending a zip of awareness to her center.

"One thing about me is, I don't run." That smile still tipped his lips as he hurled her own words from what felt like years ago, right back at her. "You think that's all I have to give you?" Another soft kiss on her lips. "It's not even close."

Well, she didn't hate that. "Oh," Shannon gasped, steadying herself by grabbing his muscled arm just over the rose tattoo.

His smile grew wider before he turned from her and strode toward the bathroom.

"Yes sir," she managed, earning a rich laugh from Theo before he shut the bathroom door behind him.

The sound of the shower reached her shocked ears and forced her into action, quickly putting the same clothes on as before so she could film her confessional as if nothing happened. As if her entire world hadn't been turned on its axis in the short hour of time that had passed between winning, and whatever the hell was happening to her just then.

Her confessional was full of dumb questions that kept her from thinking about Theo's strong hands roaming her body. The feel of his calluses catching on satin and the pressure of his tongue on her neck. That thought brought up another, the grip he held around her throat when his control finally crumbled to ash was downright luscious. It was as if the man was a sexual medium, totally unaware of her feelings about proper café playlists, but practically writing the road map of her journey to orgasm. Well, she'd listen to a whole ass brass band as long as his hands were on her again. She had felt cared for and handled all at once. Praised and ravaged. An intoxicating combination that would insist upon playing on a loop until she experienced the conundrum all over again.

When Theo walked into the confessional, her entire body lit with anticipation. She should probably get that checked. That sort of reaction was reserved only for people open to becoming obsessed with her, not someone she had to fight tooth and nail to get a selfie with.

Basking in the worship and praise of your utter perfection. Had he said that? In *that* tone with THAT accent? Yeah, he really *really* had. Probably something he threw in there because for some reason he knew she'd like it. She wasn't lying when she said worship was her favorite position and Theo was the last person she ever expected to give that to her. Sure, she could admit to herself that she had thought about it quite a bit over the years, but those were just fantasies. There was no way Lulu actually felt that way. The man was constantly scrutinizing her every feature, looking for flaws and holding back whatever insults came to his mind.

But as his eyes met hers over the cameras and her sentence stopped dead in its tracks, she saw that look. The way his eyes went on a meandering path across her face, those narrowed slits providing a glimpse of something she hadn't recognized before. Heated appreciation, the likes of which she had seen minutes before and, she realized, many times prior.

"Oh balls," Shannon whispered into the silent room.

Theo's mouth twitched up at the corners, an eyebrow lifting as Darling Darlington laughed from his spot across from her.

"What was that?" he asked.

Peeling her gaze from Theo's, she almost winced at the discomfort painting Charles's features.

"Theo's here to steal my thunder," she rushed out, hoping it would cover her tangled mass of nerves.

"Aw, join us then, Theo," he called over his shoulder.

Was he...sauntering? The man moved like a cat in the grass toward her perch on the couch, sidling around the marble sculptures of the gallery and looking for all the world as if they had just fucked for the last hour instead of him coming alone into the hot spray of the shower. He looked smug as hell.

He sat, his thigh pressing against hers and the heat from his fresh shower radiated through her jeans. She crossed her legs away from him, managing to put a half inch between their thighs only to have his hand land on hers and give it a little squeeze. She met his gaze, his scent whirling up to assault her senses. Not his usual...

"You smell like me," she accused, completely forgetting where they were. Someone cleared their throat and she ignored it, watching in fascination as a glower she had seen a million times over revealed new depths. Heated eyes, parted lips. A tick in the jaw that sent her thoughts spinning, imagining what words were now going unsaid. The few that had been whispered in her ear earlier bounced around at the forefront.

"I had to use your soap," he said, his frown wavering a bit. "Mine just simply wasn't cutting it." The hand on her thigh tightened briefly and what the hell was happening? How was a conversation about soap this sexually charged. She felt ready to catch fire.

"Now now, before you two get *whisked* away on a random tangent, let's talk about the competition bake while it's fresh in your mind."

Theo winced as the pun was delivered, Shannon giggled, and they somehow managed to make it through the entire confessional without devouring one another on the spot.

It was early evening when they finished up, skipping dinner in the dining room, they practically ran to their suite, stumbling up the carpeted stairs and laughing like a couple of idiots. Well, she was laughing, Theo stalked after her with his scowl still firmly in place and it was confusing as hell to be so turned on by it.

"Give me five minutes," Shannon called over her shoulder as she entered the room before a hand closed over her bicep and tugged her back against a hard chest. Theo's shirt was already off and tossed at their feet, his warmth encompassing her deliciously.

Moving her hair aside, he brushed his lips along her neck as he tugged the ribbon from her pony. "Five minutes for what?"

Her breath was already embarrassingly labored even before his lips moved to below her ear, hands slid along her body. She gasped when they connected at the button of her jeans, working them open without waiting for a response.

A hum of approval caught in her throat as he slid his hand under the denim, playing with the hem of her panties and turning her legs to jello.

Okay, this was insane. Theo was sexy and clearly knew what he was doing, but she needed to regain the high ground.

Pulling away, she danced from his reach toward the bathroom, talking over her shoulder as she went. "Five minutes. Trust me, this is where I thrive." It truly was. Shannon had always been an attentive lover. See, Theo had been wrong about one thing, for all her flirting and joking, Shannon was a giver. She put others' needs before her own

214

because failing her partners, friends, family simply wasn't an option.

Finding what she was looking for, Shannon held up the lace negligee and admired it in the mirror. It was stunning. Oxblood lace swirled from tit to thigh where it cut off to reveal far too much of her ass. She hadn't exactly pictured hooking up with Theo on this trip, but she liked to be prepared for a little excitement. There was no doubt in her mind that he would provide that in spades.

Finishing the job he started, she unzipped her pants just as her phone began to ring on the counter. A glance told her it was a FaceTime from Ben which was ill-timed and definitely not happening. A whoosh of air sounded over the ringtone with the toss of her jeans, her focus moving to her socks as the phone cut out and immediately started ringing again.

She sighed, her worried mind unable to ignore a back-to-back call. Even if Ben was dramatic and probably calling to chat about an episode of The Real Housewives.

"Hi Benji," she trilled in what she hoped was a casual tone.

"Hi, wow, why do you have a postcoital glow?" he said without an ounce of think-before-you-speak energy. Before she could formulate a response, he gasped, pointing at her through the phone. "Are you hooking up with someone? Fucking the competition to get in their head? Genius. Ten out of ten for effectiveness although I'm afraid it's a little played out."

"Will you stop it? I do not have a postcoital glow," she whispered, thoroughly kicking herself for answering his call. "I'm in the bathroom; Theo is in the other room."

"Aw, okay. Rubbing one out while Sexy Brit is only a wall away. Classic."

"To what do I owe the pleasure, darling?" Her patience was growing brittle.

"Oh, right. Well, I know we're due for a chat, but I actually just need something really quick. Where did you put the napkins for Evie's bridal shower? I have everything else set up, but of course, your type-a, overachiever monogrammed napkins are nowhere to be found."

Shannon stilled in her attempt to flatten the negligee on the counter for easier access. Her focus snapped back to Ben, taking in his crisp shirt and perfectly coiffed man bun. His tattoos looked moisturized and stark against pale skin as he held his hands in front of him in a defensive position.

"I see that crazed look in your eyes. Everything is fine Shannon."

"The bridal shower..." she said, trailing off in disbelief. She had forgotten.

"Yes, and hear me when I say, Evie realized you forgot when you asked about *Whisk Wars*, but she didn't want you to change course when you clearly believe deeply in what you are doing."

Shannon could feel her heart beating through her fingertips as she struggled for air. How could she forget a thing like that? Evie was her best friend, someone who had been by her side for the better part of ten years. How could she have dropped the ball so massively? So effortlessly? Failing—missing the mark, even—was not something Shannon Perry did. It was in her blood to succeed, and her silly little barista job was already confusing to her family. The weight of success was unbearable, especially when broadcast on national television. But that didn't excuse this misstep.

She raked her gaze over the reflection in the mirror. Clad only in a long-sleeved shirt and satin panties, she looked the mess she felt. Her hair cascaded in messy waves around her face and her blue eyes shone with hot tears.

You're a failure to your friends. You can't do it. You will never live up to your potential.

"I can fly out tomorrow," she stammered, her voice thick with tears.

"Banana, don't be ridiculous. I am taking my role as Second Honorary Maiden very seriously. Lest we forget that fever dream of a vision board you sent me. I have essentially copied and pasted it right into the café, I promise."

"The café?" she asked, another of her mistakes shining through. She hadn't booked the venue. It was supposed to be at Evie and Max's favorite brunch spot, but she never booked it before she left. Because she forgot.

"It was Krista's idea, actually. I was working a shift at Bloem and was chatting about the party. She offered up the café…it's after hours so it seemed okay."

Shannon shook her head, blonde hair swaying with the motion. "That's great."

"'That's great,' she says while shaking her head," he deadpanned. "Look, I know you hate it when things don't go perfectly to plan, but we've got this. Harper's been helping me because, well, she has nothing better to do."

"Stop making fun of her burnout," Shannon scolded, her usual heat lacking as she grappled with all of this new information.

He waved her away in a classic Ben gesture. The familiarity of it calming her racing heart a bit. "Will you just tell me where the napkins are so I can put the cherry on top of this sundae?"

"They're still in the box, just to the left of my dresser." She knew this because she had shifted them aside as she packed for England. Another blunder to pick apart. She hadn't even removed them from the box to make sure they were perfect.

"Lovely, now go back to rubbing one out and forget we ever spoke. I promise, we have everything handled, so just have fun winning, and get back here so we can plan the most epic bachelorette party."

His eyes were round with worry as she muttered her agreement and hung up the phone. Setting it on the counter, the woman in the mirror stared back at her with hot disappointment.

This was not a new problem in her life. Shannon had always struggled with comparison. Her family was made up of powerhouses, but her sisters had been on another level. While their peers had been vomiting up jungle juice in the Sigma Chi pool house, they had been teaching their younger sister how to invest her money and apply for colleges. Her problems had always seemed so trivial compared to theirs. Boy problems tearfully recounted while her middle sister was on a nap break during her residency. Her frustration with a math professor who quizzed them right after Christmas break spilled to her eldest who had spent said break researching a huge case for her psycho boss.

Chasing after a life in hospitality had always felt like squandering the chances she had been given, and that guilt— that unwavering shame—ensured that Shannon would make up for it in other ways. She would excel at everything she did, stay fit, be charming, accrue wealth, work hard. Be the best possible friend anyone could have.

"Shannon?" Theo called with a small knock on the door. "Are you okay?"

Was she? Yes, absolutely. She had worked far too hard in therapy to allow one little mistake to send her into a complete break.

"Sorry," she called, moving her limbs and stripping off her clothes.

"I just answered a call from Ben, but I assure you, I won't be making that mistake again."

Pulling the slip on, she eyed herself in the mirror once more and smiled a watery smile. This was where she thrived, damnit. The rich maroon lace against her pale skin looked hot as hell, and she was finally about to gift Theo with an orgasm that rivaled the one pulled from her earlier.

Stepping from the bathroom and through the adjoined closet, her gaze immediately landed on him. Shirtless, gray sweatpants pulled over his hips as he sat on the edge of the bed. It was a bit odd that he had put clothes back on, but she forgave it the minute his eyes landed on her and darkened, pupils blowing wide. She basked in the response for three seconds before his eyes softened, finding hers, a question in his gentle features.

"Are you alright?" he asked, rising from the bed. "I heard…that is, I wasn't eavesdropping. But I heard your conversation with Ben."

Shannon twisted the gold band on her finger as her traitorous eyes burned once more. This wasn't happening. How was she going to seduce Theo with watery eyes? Crying wasn't a thing that she did and yet here she was, eyes filling in front of Theo—again.

"It was nothing. I mean, he obviously doesn't know how to live without me, but it's nothing." It was meant as a tease. Would have hit the mark too had the last word not exited her mouth on a sob.

Theo's face broke, his features tormented at that little crack in her composure. He was probably terrified, unsure of how to handle the crying naked lady in his room.

"Come here," he said gently, holding his arms open in a gesture that she had no hope of surviving.

The dam almost burst, almost released the flood of tears threatening to spill over and turn her into a snotty, teary mess. That was not the kind of mess she wanted to make right now. She bit down on her cheek to keep anymore embarrassing sounds from leaving her mouth and turned her back to him. Looking to the sky as if it would hold in the moisture, she took a deep breath and tugged the hem of her slip down, growing more and more unsure of herself by the minute.

"I'm sorry," she murmured, her voice thick with emotion. "Just give me a moment." The feel of Theo's warmth hit her before his hands landed on her shoulders. For someone who had spent a sizable amount of time avoiding her touch, his skin had been a constant companion of hers for the day. One day. That's what they agreed to, wasn't it? That thought brought another confusing wave of sadness with it, her eyes stinging for release.

"Take a couple of deep breaths and talk to me," he said softly, making no attempt to turn her around. He reminded her of her breathing, her chest ached from holding in gasps as she tried to control the wicked emotions swirling in her gut. Blinking back the tears as she took a deep breath, then another, she shook her head. She felt silly and childish and useless. Somehow, in a barely there, fuck-me red slip, she had still managed to botch a seduction. Looked like another swing and a miss for her. "I don't need to talk about it. I don't need to breathe," she said even as she took another steadying breath. "This is silly. I didn't just almost fall from the rafters and break my neck, I messed up. This shouldn't feel like the end of the world."

He raked his hands down her arms, and there was no chance of her goosebumps remaining contained. Unfortunately for her, the body and mind connection was a little too flummoxed at that moment. Reactions to his touch begged her to ignore her ill-timed breakdown, while her brain was a snowstorm, thousands of berating thoughts descending like angry little ice crystals.

"No, it's not the end of the world," Theo said quietly, a strange quality to his tone. "But I know it upsets you." Gently, he turned her to face him, and her flummox careened into full-on bamboozlement. Aside from the frown that she knew like the back of her hand and the jawline that admittedly distracted her all day, this version of Theo's face was foreign to her. Worry laced his brows; his brown eyes were soft and probing. Like he wanted her to admit all of her crazy, unhinged thoughts. As if he actually cared.

No, thank you.

220

"I'm fine," she lied, her stomach turning over as she rejected whatever this was. It was too much. Too much transparency and far too much vulnerability. A bone-deep weariness came to the forefront of her mind as she realized she couldn't come up with a joke to remove her from this scenario. Her exhaustion wouldn't be defeating the disappointment she felt towards her own failures, however. There was no way she'd be sleeping tonight. But continuing this seduction with Theo looking at her like that felt...

Transformative.

Like all of these new, strange feelings between them would rewire her brain chemistry in a way she wasn't sure she wanted. Wasn't sure she could come back from.

Theo's frown grew heavier, the corners of his mouth twitching down before he pulled them into a hard line. That meandering gaze journeyed over the bridge of her nose, her cheek bones, along her jaw and back to her eyes. "Why don't you go to the party?"

Shannon stacked her hands on her hips, relief running over her as a joke popped into her mind. "In this getup? I'm not sure it's proper."

Theo's eyes heated, his hands tightening at her shoulders as his gaze dipped over her body and back in an instant. As if it hurt to look at her scantily clad body. "Well, you're right about that. There is nothing proper about the way you look right now. It's absolutely..." Shaking his head, he trailed off, his hands leaving her shoulders. She instantly missed that touch. Hadn't realized how comforting it had been until his warmth left her skin.

"It's absolutely what?"

"Go to the party." He said, ignoring her question and settling into his usual scowl. "Change into something comfortable, post up in the floral haven of our room with a bottle of wine, and join them digitally. You'll have a front row seat to all the things Ben did wrong."

She stared at the gorgeous, shirtless stranger in front of her. His usual frown comforting, but not entirely convincing her he hadn't been body snatched. Shannon backtracked through the day, starting with his embarrassment when she caught his little voyeur act, to his control snapping, the dirty words that spilled from those stupid lips, to his complete dedication to finishing what they started. The way his eyes filled with concern as her voice broke, and now, this suggestion that was growing on her by the second.

It wasn't as if they weren't friends—they just weren't necessarily *friendly*. This was...too easy. She realized how insane that was, that she was questioning the ease with which they had gone from hurricane force winds to a well-placed ceiling fan. A little chaos had always been Bloem's weather system. Theo's raging, icy gale colliding with the scorching heat of Shannon's sunshine. Two extremes that balanced each other out. It just worked. But today felt like new, like a gentle breeze on a sunny day. Like the ocean kicked up your hair at the beach, too-hot skin slowly cooled by a gentle wind. It worked too. It had certainly worked for her earlier.

"Go to the party?" she asked, the idea already taking shape in her mind.

He waited patiently, his jaw flexing while his mouth remained shut and Shannon felt a wave of sadness roll through her at the sight. That, she was familiar with.

One day. That's what they had said. And instead of closing the loop, he was suggesting she shoot the shit with her friends, fully clothed and blue balled? That tic in his jaw told her he wouldn't say a damn thing to the contrary, so she wouldn't either. As it was, she'd had enough of Theo "Lulu" Abbott knowing her crazy without reciprocating. Sure, he had whispered gloriously sexy things in her ear earlier, but that didn't count. This wasn't the heat of the moment, and they both knew what would happen if they walked away.

Still, that muscle fluttered at his cheek bone. She could almost hear the grinding of his teeth.

222

"Okay," she said with a forced smile. "That's actually a really good idea."

His own returning smile looked painful to produce. Resigned, she turned, her movements sluggish and odd. Like she was walking through mud. Or like she didn't want to walk away.

"Allow me one more kiss."

Shannon froze. Her breath whooshing to a stop as she rolled his frantic plea around in her mashed potato brain. "Is that a good idea?"

"Yes," he said immediately, forcing her lips to twitch up at the corners. "No. I don't know."

This admission had her turning around to face him again. Her eyes couldn't help but wander down the length of his torso, over mass amounts of ink. Snagging on a bouquet of lilies before snapping back to his face. He had one hand snagged in his hair and a look of dismay etched into his features. He really hadn't meant to say that, had he?

"Why?" She asked, even as her brain begged her to shut the fuck up.

His hand finished its journey through auburn hair before he took a step forward. "You know why, Lil."

"Yes, but I want to hear it from you."

Stepping until a foot of distance separated them, he didn't clamp his jaw shut or grind his teeth. Instead, he opened his mouth and set her heart racing in her chest. "Because, we said one night, and although sending you to that party is the right thing to do, I don't want to regret not taking every chance I can get to put my hands on you. To taste you. To feel what it's like to have you in my arms before it's gone." The word gone was said on a puff of air that struck Shannon to the marrow of her bones. Okay, maybe this wasn't what she wanted. Maybe these truths pouring freely from Theo's mouth were truthing a little too hard and she didn't want to face how that made her feel. How his silence would make her feel after this night was over.

One night. Were they really going to be able to sleep next to each other for the rest of *Whisk Wars* without giving in to this temptation again? Fuck if she didn't already know the answer to that. Hers was a resounding no that would echo through the floral halls of this mansion until the end of days. But Theo? The man was a Wikipedia page on control. And the way he was looking at her now said that he knew that too. He wouldn't break again.

"Okay," she whispered, closing the distance between them and wrapping her arms around his bare waist. "Kiss me."

Without so much as a breath released, gasped, or held, Theo dove his tattooed hands into her hair and tugged their lips together. God, he knew how to kiss, tongue darting out to coax her lips apart and caress her bottom lip before licking into her mouth. A low moan crept from his throat to her lips, vibrating against her skin and causing her limbs to go slack. They had kissed before, and it had been passionate and full of surprised desire. This kiss was menacing. The kind that would pester her for the rest of her life.

His masculine scent mixed with her jasmine soap in a heady dose of aromatherapy as she clung to his back, her nails digging into the muscle in a desperate grip. He pressed her back until she stood flush against the wall and tugged at her hair, forcing her chin up so he could dip in and taste the heated flesh of her neck. Every lick had her skin electrified, every breath against her damp skin sent it tingling with goosebumps. Her body was feverish with desire as her chest heaved with her gasped pleasure. *More. More. More.*

Theo chuckled against her ear, his mouth making its way back to hers. "I'll give you more, Lily baby. We don't have to stop just yet."

Oops, she hadn't meant to say that out loud. Still, her heart raced as she focused on one word from his response. Stop. She didn't want to stop. This was Evie's first marriage anyway; she would do this again right? What was one little bridal shower to one unicorn of a night with her Tat Daddy boss?

"Behave," he said before she could entertain the idea any further. "Let's just enjoy this last little bit, okay?"

Okay, but he sounded tortured. As if the idea of stopping was just as miserable sounding to him as it was to her.

"Obedience is earned," she murmured, refusing to behave like she always did and taking his bottom lip between her teeth. Licking into his mouth as he let out another rumbling groan, she moaned against it, their lips reconnecting in a frantic mess. He angled her face, taking the kiss deeper, alternating between hungry caresses and gently sucking on her bottom lip. When one hand left the tangle of her hair to trail down her lace clad body, she swore the heavens opened and gospel music rained from the sky. There was zero subtlety in his touch this time. Theo cupped her breast, running his thumb around the peak of her nipple through the thin material.

She let out a whimper of longing, her leg sliding up to hook around his body. At the feel of it, he gripped her thigh, giving a little tug that pressed her center against his erection, turning her whimper into a tortured moan. Her senses overflowed with the pleasure of having Theo between her thighs. He took what he wanted and gave in equal measure, all as he continued to suck, lick, and tease her mouth.

His lips moved to her neck again, right to the pulse point beneath her ear as he slid his hand along her thigh. "You were sent to torture me, weren't you? These thighs were a torment before I ever had my hands on them, and now what? How am I going to recover now that I know how fucking smooth your skin is? How," he paused as his hand found the dip of her ass cheek, stilling just shy of giving her what she wanted and cupping her cheek. "How the groove of this perfect ass feels against my palm?"

"That's a problem for future Theo," she panted. Every jittering little nerve ending in her body begging him to grip her ass until bruises blossomed on her skin.

"I can't. I can't know what it's like. I'll never recuperate."

"Theo," she begged, her heart pounding as he slid his hand away from her ass, his tongue darting out to caress the sensitive skin below her ear.

He didn't listen to the plea in her voice. Didn't acknowledge the desperation in her heaving chest as he dropped her thigh and cupped her face bringing their lips together for the softest kiss on the planet.

No no no. He was pulling away. Not running like she had suspected before but ending this dizzying lust-filled evening. Ending it with his soft lips and intimate swipe of his tongue along hers. She sighed; know it was coming to a close and refusing not to enjoy the last of it. Angling her head, she twirled her tongue as his own sigh puffed air against her swollen mouth.

He laid an open-mouthed kiss to her lips.

She slowly tasted his tongue.

His mouth softly drew on her top lip.

She pouted a kiss onto his bottom.

One last kiss was landed, gentle as a soft breeze against sun-warmed skin before he pulled back. Shannon's lids fluttered open as she fought through her daze, expecting to find the familiar caramel swirl of Theo's stare. Instead, she watched in fascination as Theo stood frozen, his eyes still closed and his mouth soft as if stuck in the shape of their last shared kiss.

Open your eyes, love. He had said that to her once, in a moment of fear and desperation. Before either of them thought this flame between them could burn brighter than the fucking sun. She wanted to return the sentiment. *Open your eyes, love. Show me what I already know.* But she didn't have to. His lashes flitted up; the intensity she knew would be there connecting with her gaze with as much force as a freighter carving through water. She clung to his wrists, unsure of when she had done that. Unsure of so much more than that. He still held her face in the palms of his hands, his thumbs brushing small movements along her cheeks.

"Theo." His name was pulled from her in a whisper as she leaned into his palm.

"I know," he said, his voice brimming with words unspoken before he pulled away completely, reaching beside her to open the door that led to their huge bathroom. "Get changed, I'll get the fire going and find you that bottle of wine."

Without a second glance, he turned and fled the room, giving her a glimpse of the tattoos that littered his back as he went. Her gaze zigzagged across them, soaking in as much as possible before it was gone from her view forever. There weren't many of them. Four lines of script too small for her to read. A teacup with a chip resting on a saucer, the spent tea bag at its side.

Shannon brought the tips of her fingers to her parted lips. They felt swollen and damp beneath her touch. Used and utterly longing to be kissed again. Funny that Theo was so worried about his own recovery when hers was just as uncertain. How was she supposed to move forward knowing he kissed like that? As if his entire being was invested in the feel of another's lips against his own, taking and tasting like a man dying of thirst.

I can't know what that's like. I'll never recuperate.

"Shit," she said before reluctantly turning toward the bathroom. "Why can't I just behave?"

CHAPTER TWENTY

Theo's gaze ran over his bland breakfast with one of his favorite glares. Didn't he call it? Yes, he distinctly remembered thinking, "The taste of Shannon is going to ruin me for other flavor profiles for the rest of my miserable life. Nothing else will come close to the taste of her…blah blah blah." Sure enough, he pushed his eggs around on his plate as if they weren't deliciously seasoned and full of parmesan. Nothing tasted as good as her on his tongue.

She sat across from him, happily shoveling eggs and toast into her mouth with abandon. Completely unaware of his agony. This was not happening. This was not some sappy love story where the loss of her touch stripped his life of color. The absence of her kiss made food bland and ruined the sunset for him or whatever the fuck. He refused to sap around like a fool, dragging his feet and wishing to high heaven that he had never made that deal with her.

It was a great show of will, encouraging her to attend that party and setting aside his selfish need and crippling desire.

Kissing Shannon had been everything he thought it would be. Catastrophic, and completely electrifying. When she slipped into bed after her phone call, it had taken every ounce of those acting courses his mum had paid for in his pre-teens to pretend to be fast asleep. Even in sleep, he would have felt her presence. Clad then in a baggy shirt and sleep shorts, he had still vibrated with his effort not to touch her.

"Where were you two last night?" Samira asked, interrupting his bland breakfast. "I thought I would have seen you at dinner, gloating about that win and shamelessly accepting praise."

"Obviously they were celebrating in other ways," Chanda said, her eyes sliding to Samira from across the table. "Be cool."

Samira waved a hand before winking at Shannon and shoving a potato into her mouth.

His she-devil smiled a wicked grin although he thought the usual mischief didn't glint from her eyes. He spoke before she could confirm or deny how they "celebrated," keeping whatever tempting scenario from spilling from her tongue. "Shannon went to her friend's bridal shower, and I was just too zonked to celebrate."

Scooping his eggs up, he took a bite, avoiding the gaze he felt locked onto him.

"How are you two planning on spending your break? We get a few days off after filming week three."

Theo could have kissed Chanda for the change of subject. "I'm going to visit my mum," he said without thinking. Starving for a subject that didn't involve salacious content. "She doesn't live too far from here."

"Uh, oh. The in-laws," Samira said with a smirk in Shannon's direction. "By the look on your face, I'm guessing this will be your first time meeting her?"

Theo's gaze snapped to Shannon. She was staring at him with a strange look of shock and something slightly worrying. Was it anger? Probably should have been, because like a complete prat, he had forgotten to mention these plans to her. His alleged girlfriend.

"This will be the first time," she said, recovering quickly. "But Theo has assured me that it will be painless. And he'll buy me dinner after." She stared at him, her eyes sparking with intensity. "And a massage."

Theo's snort was mortifying but it couldn't be helped. He chuckled into his coffee, shaking his head at the idea that he would owe her after meeting the softest woman in existence. "Five minutes with Pearl Abbott and you'll forget all about fancy dinners and massages. The woman is almost as disgustingly charming as you."

A flicker of surprise cast over Shannon's features in a blink before disappearing. He hadn't meant to say that. Hadn't meant to snort-laugh—hadn't meant to get himself into a nightmare scenario of longing that was so bad, it loosened the navy-strength knot of his control.

"I'm looking forward to it," she said with a small smile.

After breakfast, the judges filed into the room, mouths stretched in big smiles that contrasted the sour mood in the château. It was elimination day. Two people who needed this probably as much as Theo did were about to be sent home in their first week. All of that money and time wasted before they could even build hope of success.

After a brief greeting and congratulations to him and Shannon, they detailed how the elimination round would work. Like the technical, this challenge was given to one chef only, with the other checking in at halftime to coach or awkwardly mutter words of encouragement. The only difference was, it was the executive chefs' turn in the hot seat.

The nervous energy that charged the kitchen was particularly voltaic. Hairs on the back of his neck tingled, lifting from his skin as the competition started. It was truly brutal, watching people bake like their lives depended on it while egg puns soared and idiots in anime sweatshirts asked questions that only succeeded in distracting. Jasper weaved back and forth between the contestants, nervous giggles and self-deprecating jokes thrown into his waiting arms as Theo stared daggers into his pirate face. Having circled around to flirt with Shannon on more than one occasion, his patience with the man was on quick decline.

Shannon, for reasons he would never be able to decipher, didn't seem to mind at all. She would quietly chuckle and answer his questions, at one point even going as far as to grip the man's bicep on a laugh. The fucking prat. Mere hours before, she had been gripping his arms like that, lust and pulsing need lighting up her eyes.

"Daisy. *Daisy*," Jasper said in a mock whisper, his camera operator following his frame like a lost puppy. "What's a cat's favorite biscuit?"

His cohost looked at him with a delighted smile. "What?"

"A meow-caron. Get it?"

Theo shut his eyes, his teeth grinding to keep from barking his utter misery at having heard that joke. But Jasper's next words had his lids snapping open in a panic.

"Bakers, you have five minutes left!"

Out of the corner of his eye, Shannon's fidgeting catapulted to Olympic speeds, the gold ring twisting around more feverishly as the five minutes counted down. He knew this was hard for her, failure. Hell, even tripping over a loose floorboard sent her so far into her own head, the jaws of life were required to rescue her from toxic thought. He found it completely maddening that such a selfless woman could have such fear of imperfection. He knew that was why she hadn't mentioned graduating college to her friends. It had confused him at first, but after reconciling the woman he knew with all of this newfound information of the past week, it struck him. She didn't want to build up their expectations on the chance she would let them down. His Lily, a woman who had been putting the needs of others over her own since he'd known her.

Now, don't go thinking foolish thoughts, he scolded himself, her taking what she needed popping directly into his brain receptors where they happily projected it in IMAX 3D. That line of thinking wasn't helpful to either of them.

Still, it was a sad thought, that the success of Shannon's family had only succeeded in giving her a complex. Especially when her perfection haunted his every waking moment.

The elimination round flew by, the team from Canada the unlucky firsts to go home. All the while Shannon twisted her ring until he was certain it would leave a mark. Her anxiety was palpable. Made all the more intense by the dullness of her eyes and fake smile plastered to her face. He promised himself then and there that he would do anything to keep her from feeling that kind of defeat. That kind of disappointment.

And he kept his word for the most part.

They made it through cake week unscathed, landing smack dab in the middle and savoring the comfort. The competition bake had been illusion cakes, challenging their creativity alongside their skill. They made a pineapple cake shaped like the fruit itself. Using fondant, they had managed to sculpt the exterior into the desired texture before spraying the greens, yellows, and oranges on to perfect the look. Flavored with pineapple, coconut, and dark chocolate, their flavors would have quote, "taken the cake" had it not been for Samira and Chanda's bake which had looked so much like a fish, it made him sick to watch the judges consume it.

For pie and tart week, Shannon had knocked it out of the park with a Bakewell tart, while their competition bake had been a tiered pie monstrosity. It had been the ugliest thing Theo had ever made, his first real smile flashing at the cameras as he brought it to the judge's table. He couldn't help it. Better to laugh than cry over the state of their three-layer pie. Their only saving grace had been flavors which Daisy had said were life-changing as Darlington hummed his approval. And thank Lil's salt circle for that, because the bottom two teams had produced decent looking bakes, with terrible flavors. His spine still tingled with the shivers when he remembered how Charles had glared at the contestants before stating, "That's a shame." Those three little words haunted his dreams.

In the room, he and Shannon went back to business as usual. Practicing day in and out, building a rhythm that worked comfortably for both of them although it left them completely exhausted, crashing into their respective sides of the bed after dinner each night and falling asleep almost instantly. Thankfully, their weariness overwhelmed the tension.

It was the mornings that couldn't withstand the pressure. Oftentimes Theo would wake with one of Shannon's limbs draped over his body. Self preservation required him to wear a shirt to bed after her hand had been resting low on his abs one morning, evoking a flush of want so intense, it had taken him all of one minute to gently remove her hand, dart to the bathroom and come into the cold spray of the shower. His mind had supplied images of *her* hands on him instead.

Shannon liked to starfish, alright, and if half the king-sized bed was barely enough space for her to sprawl, he was glad she wasn't on the sofa anymore. Enduring the torture of her body so close to his was a small price to pay for her comfort.

But Christ he thought as his groggy brain zeroed in on her arm across his chest, *this is a torment.* Slowly, he began moving toward the edge of the bed, hoping to remove himself without waking her. The success rate had been pretty good save for one morning when she accidentally kicked him as his movements tickled her foot. The memory tried to penetrate his sleep-riddled mind. It was with a lazy kind of processing that the feel of her fingers at the dip of his shoulder tightened, holding him in place.

"Snooze," she murmured into the pillow. She was on her stomach, one leg kicked up, the knee brushing his side. Her upper body had to have been angled toward him as her hold tightened over his chest, her hand moving to the side of his neck. Theo's sleep fog burned off in an instant, all of his focus zeroing in on her hand at his throat. Her thumb traced sweet little circles along his skin before they stilled, her breaths growing soft and dreamy. It was a miracle the grinding of his teeth didn't rouse her from sleep.

Theo slid another inch, his fingers reaching up to gently pull her hand from his skin.

"Boo," she protested, gripping his neck and tugging. Shannon pulled herself closer and suddenly, she was everywhere. Her bent leg slid over him, hooking around his body and resting just over his crotch. Not ideal. Even less so was her breath on his neck as she nestled into the place where his shoulder dipped. Out of instinct, one arm snaked under her as she moved, holding her lower back while the other didn't know where to land. It belonged on her thigh. As she tightened around him and her breasts pressed against his side, separated only by a thin cotton tank, there was no doubt in his body that he should land that hand exactly where he wanted it to go. Squeeze the soft skin there and drive himself mad with need.

Too late. He was already hard, awake for all of two seconds and hot for the fucking woman.

"Shannon," he whispered. But it wasn't a whisper. His voice was a husky plea, begging his temptress to let him out of this situation alive. Clearing his throat, he tried again, ignoring the hand still awkwardly raised as if it would land on her thigh after all. "Lil, I'm just going to go make coffee." He tried the nickname thinking it would remind her who she was next to and rip her from sleep. Oh, but the gods were cruel. Instead of whipping awake and springing from his grasp, he felt the gentle slide of her thigh up and down his hips, pulling her closer and officially sending all of his blood shooting to his dick.

"Fifteen more minutes." An innocent enough statement had he not felt the brush of her lips against his neck.

"I can't," he said, the misery thick in his tone. "I…fuck." The feel of her thigh rubbing against his erection again had his protests stumbling over his thick tongue. He grabbed her thigh out of desperation more than anything, stilling the motion before he lost control. Every nerve ending in his body was a traitorous little prick. They begged him to focus on how good she felt in his arms, rubbing against him as her skin warmed under his fingers. "Wake up, Lil."

An unintelligible sound hummed from her lips. The same lips that had somehow found the spot just below his ear. All it would take was a tiny movement. A small turning of his head to connect their mouths and finish what they had started that first week. The image was easy for his mind to conjure. Running his cheek against her lips as he turned and gently, so gently, coaxed her out of sleep with his tongue. Feasting on the way she opened for him before taking it further and shifting so her weight was fully over him, their legs tangling together. She would press against him so perfectly, and he would have her moaning in record time.

He couldn't imagine a world in which he and Shannon together didn't cause fire and ice to clash to devastating effect.

But he couldn't let that happen. Moving slowly but steadily until pulled from her grasp, he nearly face planted from the bed in his haste. Shannon groaned in protest but didn't move, her sleep-heavy breathing starting up as he watched her for a second too long. Honey strands that escaped her braid fell over one cheek, the other smooshed into *his* pillow. He rubbed his chest down the middle, a strange ache spreading as he watched her fingers curl around the sheets where he had been moments before.

Probably heartburn from the previous night's dinner. The show had gone all out with a meal of pot roast and mashed potatoes seeing as it was their last dinner before they went on break. That's what he told himself fifteen minutes later as he sipped his coffee at one of the bar stools and a sleepy looking Shannon emerged from the bedroom.

"Morning," she said through a yawn, shuffling her feet towards the kitchen. "Thank the devil for you. I need this coffee. I feel way more exhausted than I should."

Theo's heart rose and fell at the realization that she had no idea what had happened that morning. It was for the best, he knew that. That knowledge didn't stop a strange feeling from creeping into his gut. "I would say that you have every right to be exhausted. We've worked non-stop for the past three weeks. Most of it as fifteen-hour days. That's nothing to scoff at."

She blinked at him from across the counter, nodding as she took a sip from the hot coffee. Sleep marks lined her left cheek in adorable little swirls. Waking up next to her for three weeks hadn't lessened the devastation of her beauty. She truly was a stunning woman, sleep marks or no.

"So, what are your plans today?"

Shannon shrugged, eyes closed as she leaned against the counter and blew on her hot coffee. "Not sure. Thought I might just get a car to the nearest town and explore."

"Hmmm." This reaction had her eyes opening, glaring at him from over her mug.

"Hmmm, what?"

"I'm just worried that you'll run into someone from the show, and they'll wonder why you're not hanging out with me."

"Yes well, I didn't exactly know what your plans were," she shot back, her annoyance shining through. "I didn't even know your mom lived close by."

"I know, I'm sorry." Her eyes widened with the apology, making him feel like a dick. Was it that surprising that he'd admit when he was wrong? "I didn't mean to spring that on you."

The surprise morphed into fire in an instant. "You're sorry that you almost slipped up in front of Samira, or are you sorry you didn't tell me?"

Theo set his mug down and leaned back, sweeping his eyes over her irritated face.

"Both?" he tried, unsure of why she was angry.

Her eye roll was a thing of beauty. "Forget it. I'm going to shower and head out. And maybe I won't tell you what I'm doing. Maybe I'll keep it all a secret just to balance the scales of our fake relationship."

"Hey," he said, falling from his stool in an attempt to block her from leaving. She breezed past his stumbling form without a second glance, sleep muddled jasmine scent hitting him square in the nose. "Wait a bloody minute."

"No, I don't think I will," she said without looking back. And then Theo's brain had a major malfunction as she tugged the shirt from her body, discarding it on the floor as she sailed through the dressing room. Gifting him a glimpse of her smooth, naked back before she reared back, kicking the door shut in his face. "I'm tired of waiting for you, Theo." That muffled admission was made just before the spray of the shower sounded from the other side of the door.

Mouth agape, he stared at nothing and fought the urge to scratch at his eyes. He would be seeing Shannon's naked back as if it were burned into his retinas. Giving in he removed his glasses to caress the bridge of his nose and attempt to ease the image of her smooth skin from his mind. He had imagined her whipping her shirt off an embarrassing number of times to admit—even to himself—yet he still hadn't been prepared for the sight of that damned plait resting between smooth shoulder blades. The iron grip of his control had been melted down and made into a dainty necklace if he was this churned up over a set of shoulder blades.

And it was about to get a lot worse.

Steeling himself for what he might see, Theo charged through the door. The small closet-like room was filling with steam, the swirling mass obscuring his vision from the bathroom beyond that held a claw-foot tub and Shannon's naked body. He tugged his glasses off as they fogged over, and his surroundings went even blurrier.

"I had a thought," he yelled over the spray of the shower.

Shannon screamed. "What the hell are you doing in here?"

"I'm blindly traversing your shoe pile so I can ask you to spend the weekend with me," he blurted before stubbing a toe on another stray sneaker. Leaning against the doorframe, he pointed his voice in the direction of the shower, the curtain blocking what would undoubtably be his undoing behind rose-covered vinyl. His chest did a little flip as he ignored every red flag and warning bell, making his request clear. "Come with me to my mum's. We can spend the weekend getting sick from all the beer and meat pies she forces upon us."

Silence filled the room as he let his invitation hang in the air. His fingers itched to run along the shadow and stars that swirled across his neck, a nervous habit he never did manage to control. And it struck him then, why that tic immediately jumped to the fingers that gripped his glasses like a lifeline. He was nervous. The idea of bringing Shannon to his childhood home—to meet his mother—it scared the shit out of him. Not because he was afraid of them not getting along, quite the opposite, actually. Shannon and Pearl would, without a doubt, love each other. A thought that should comfort rather than terrify him. Fear was a funny thing. Recognizing Shannon's fear of failure only brought his own trepidations into sharp focus and…he was choosing to ignore how that made him feel. Ignore how he was absolutely certain that bringing Shannon into this very personal, very private bubble of his life might make waves too strong to outswim.

The water's spray cut off and Theo straightened his back, eyes focused on one of the tubs gilded legs. One small section of the curtain pulled back, the space filling with Shannon's scarf covered head, cheeks flushed from the heat of the shower.

"Is that what you want?"

"To force-feed myself carbs to appease my mother?"

A small twitch of her lips was caught through his blurred vision. "To do that with me," she clarified, her mouth settling into a frown that had no business on her sunshiny face. "This is a weekend off, Lulu. Are you sure you want to spend it with me? No work. No competition. Just…"

"Just you and me," he murmured, bringing the glasses back to his face so he could see her clearer. "Chugging beer and glaring at anyone who dares flirt with my mum." His eyes ran over her face, skittering over the confused furrow of her brows before landing on cheeks, lips, the bridge of her nose. "Yes. I want that."

The wrinkles between her brows evened out at his confession but Theo's body refused to relax. Saying what was in his head, especially with Shannon, was quite difficult for him. Voicing his wants and needs was something he didn't do with people anymore. It made you too vulnerable. Desires could, after all, be used against you with startling effect. Even now, Theo's heart raced as he awaited her response, making him realize just how much he wanted her to say yes. The things she could do to him with that sort of power…

"Okay," she said, her mouth tipping up on one side.

"Okay?"

She nodded before tugging the scarf from her head, hair tied up in a loose knot. "Okay. Now get out before you catch a glimpse of my perfect—"

"Behave," he interrupted, at once turning himself around and fleeing. Her laughter could be heard all the way to the kitchen where he snagged his discarded coffee.

***

Shannon's gaze caught on Theo's grip of the stick shift for admittedly, the twentieth time in as many minutes. It was the only safe space for her eyes to land without heat crawling over her skin. She had been in the middle of a deeply inappropriate dream when woken by the feel of Theo's skin against hers. Sluggish from sleep, she had snuggled into that warmth, completely forgetting about the rules and their unspoken agreement to distance themselves from one another. There had been no distance between them then, and it would be a bold-faced lie to say she wasn't in control of her actions. She had been pushing it—just a bit. And unfortunately for her, her pushing backfired tenfold.

Her horny little body was screaming, no—*begging* for more of Theo Abbott. And not just sexually, although that was definitely leading the charge. Every inch of her skin vibrated with nervous energy as she finally got another glimpse behind the iron wall that was Theo's fortress of solitude. If the first glimpse had provided her with expert-level dirty talk and a praise kink unlocked, what the hell would this weekend unearth?

As they drove through town past sweet cottages of brick and wreathed doors, she tried and failed not to let her earlier feelings of hurt flood her body. His mother didn't just live close by, she was a brief thirty-minute drive from the château, a fact that Theo had actively decided not to share with her, just like everything else.

After the shock of hearing the word cock rasp against her ear, she realized there was very little she actually knew about a man she had spent more time with over the past six years than her own sisters. If she knew him better, maybe she would have been better prepared for his bedroom chatter.

But she didn't know him, and she wasn't prepared, and now all she could think about was a gravelly brogue saying *such a good girl* while looking at her like she was his last fucking meal. Desire to know more of him—to know everything—bounced off of her nerves like a pinball. And although she had hesitated, there was no way she would have passed up this opportunity to see behind the curtain. She was downright starving for it.

"We're almost there," he said while taking a corner, his left hand gripping the stick and downshifting. Jesus, his hand wasn't a safe space anymore either. The man had her all kinds of twisted up.

"Anything I should know about Pearl before I'm introduced? Does she glower at puppies like you? Maybe you get your hatred of fun, peppy blondes from her?"

He scoffed before slowing the car and Shannon's gaze slid over their surroundings. They had parked along a road filled with little shops and houses, every door, display window, and doormat decked out in fall colors. People moved through the streets, unhurried as they shopped or chatted outside of businesses.

"There's nothing to know about my mum. Seriously, I'm more worried about the chaos you two are going to kick up when you inevitably become thick as thieves." The wind tossed up a few orange leaves from a large maple tree, drawing her eye to a sign across the narrow street.

"The Tea Room," she read, recognizing it at once.

Theo paused, seatbelt snapping from his hand as surprised eyes shifted to her. "How did you know which one was hers?"

Shannon refused to blush as her eyes danced away from his, connecting with literally anything but his handsome face. "The tattoo on your back," she said, swelling with pride at how flippant she sounded, even as the memory of that cup and saucer on his shoulder blade reminded her of that last kiss they shared. That last, perfectly transformative, mind-blowing kiss.

"Right," he rasped, sounding like his thoughts had gone to the exact same place as hers. Then he was unfolding from the car, his long legs carrying him to her side and opening the door before she had her belt off. They were parked on the left side of the road, so she conveniently stepped out onto the sidewalk while avoiding looking directly at Theo's face.

Ear, she decided. That was her new safe space.

They crossed the road together, scurrying a little quicker to beat the oncoming traffic. The feel of Theo's palm was like a brand against the small of her back. His touch left her hot and tingly and Jesus—she was a mess.

The Tea Room ticked all of Shannon's convivial little boxes. The brick building was one of the largest on the block, its two ground-level windows strewn with warm fairy lights and fall gourds, the image instantly warming through the chill of an overcast day. The top half of a mossy green stable door was open wide, sounds of revelry and music reaching her just before the warmth. Theo's excitement was evident as he swung the bottom half of the door open for her, his eyes sweeping across the space with unfiltered affection. The look was…well it did funny things to her tummy before she too shifted her attention to the space.

"It's a bar," she blurted, taking in the long mahogany bar, patrons filling every inch of possible space.

Theo grimaced. "A pub," he corrected. "And inn. There are rooms upstairs along with mum's private apartment."

Placing his hand on the small of her back again, he eased them through the crowd, his bulky frame managing to block her from getting jostled while somehow managing not to touch her nearly enough. She registered the woodsy smell of the bar. No stale beer or tang of too many cramped, sweaty bodies. The place smelled of cedar and some sort of nostalgic dish, like meatloaf or something. Laughter and cheering cascaded from one corner that housed a dartboard, competing for supremacy with a small band crammed into the opposite corner. Theo steered her towards the end of the bar and away from the band, his eyes fixed on the woman pulling pints opposite them.

At once, Shannon was struck by her height. The woman had to be taller than her five nine, her curvy frame comfortable in jeans and a green sweater, silver-streaked copper hair curling around red cheeks. Moving around the bar with a smile locked on her face, sweeping hand gestures and oodles of enthusiasm blanketing her efficient movements, she looped up and down the length of the bar twice before they made it across the space.

Theo nodded to the only empty bar stool, his hand sliding from her back as she sat.

Lips pressed in close to her ear, their graze sending goosebumps along her neck. The chill made her look down to confirm she was in fact wearing the thick, cable knit sweater she had left in. "I'm going to say hi. I'll only take a couple of minutes."

She waved him away with a smile, her eyes wandering over every detail of the bar. "Take your time."

Theo circled the mahogany without a second thought, a rare smile already curving his lips. A whoop sounded over the noise as Pearl zeroed in on him, her wide smile a carbon copy of her son's. They embraced within seconds, a trilling, joyous laugh heaved from Pearl as Theo lifted her in his arms. In all honesty, the scene shocked the hell out of Shannon. She knew Theo talked to his mom and had a brother, but she never could have expected this kind of unadulterated affection. His broad shoulders, usually taught with stress, shook as he chuckled at something whispered in his ear. She was transfixed, watching as patrons yelled greetings and well wishes to Theo. Was absolutely spellbound at the lack of frown lines and scrunched brows

243

on his face. He looked delighted. Lucifer looked completely and utterly delighted.

The sight of it had Shannon's eyes burning with emotion. Not because she missed her own parents, that kind of loss and grief never went away after all, but she could handle it. It had been her constant companion for half her life. This emotion came from something else entirely. For the man who worked so hard and took so little, because the look on his face screamed relief, comfort, love.

Home.

She almost looked away, worried the scene would be too much for her to take. Wanting to see behind the curtain and facing the reality of what you find were two very different things.

Theo clasped hands with a bar back before leaning in to talk with his mom. Pearl clapped a hand over her mouth as her eyes widened, then snapped to Shannon. Theo's gaze followed, happiness softening his eyes as they connected with hers. And that's when she lost it.

Shannon's hand flew to her mouth as a tear streamed down her cheek, another not far behind. Theo's tear-blurred face crumpled before he moved, his long legs careening him to her side in two seconds.

"What's the matter, Lily girl?"

The nickname had her crying harder, an ugly sob heaving from her chest as strong arms encircled her, a broad palm cradled the back of her head.

"Happy…Tat…" she sputtered. Broken words ejecting from her body with each ragged breath. A smile stretched her lips, the tears streaming into her mouth as Theo shook his head in utter bewilderment.

"What? I don't understand, love."

"Happy," she hiccuped. "Happy Tat Daddy is really hot."

Theo barked a laugh, his smile bouncing back to his face as Shannon laugh-cried into his shirt. Pulling her close, his lips brushed against her hair, and she swore he had done the move a million times for how natural it felt. "Glad you approve," he murmured.

"Move it, Theodore!" Before Shannon could blink back a single tear, a flash of copper and cloud of perfume hit her like a blast of steam from the dishwasher. Pearl Abbott locked strong arms around her without hesitation in a perfect, lung-crushing hug. When she pulled back, Shannon scanned a set of irises almost identical to Theo's and shockingly filled with as many tears as Shannon had streaming down her cheeks.

"You're a beauty, aren't you? Lord have mercy! Why are we crying, darling girl?"

Shannon laughed, wiping a stray tear from Pearl's chin. "I don't know!"

"Well, that's good enough for me," she stated before pulling Shannon in for another hug, the two of them laughing watery laughs.

"Lord Jesus, this is what I was afraid of," Theo grumbled, shaking his head as he turned from the scene. But Shannon saw the smile stretching his lips and the happiness in those tawny eyes as he walked behind the bar and began pulling pints.

CHAPTER TWENTY-ONE

"Now, back up one step, and take two steps to the left."
Shannon eyed the man, a single brow raised. After abandoning her stuff at the bar and having the hottest man alive pour her an amber beer, she dried her eyes and immediately started up a conversation with one of the pub's regulars. Conor was the owner of an actual tea shop down the road and Shannon added it to her growing list of places to see before the weekend was through. She needed to stock up on the hard candies he had been handing her every half hour from the pocket of his tweed jacket. Adorable.

Hair half up, Shannon ran a hand down the light blue ribbon tied around her high pony, the silk smooth against her fingertips while her other hand clutched miniature spears of death. She had to give it to him; Conor was a patient teacher. The man was attempting to guide Shannon into a bullseye on the dart board, a feat that she was certain wouldn't be happening in her lifetime.

"Don't look at me like that, Miss," he scolded before taking a sip from his dark beer. Foam coated his mustache, cream blending with the salt and pepper of his beard. "Trust the process. You ever see *The Karate Kid*?"

Shannon winced, unable to focus on how cute the word karate was with his heavy accent. "No. And before this friendship goes any further, you should know that my movie knowledge will do nothing but disappoint, so it's best to assume I haven't seen anything."

"Come now, I have a feeling you don't disappoint very often, Miss Perry." The little charmer. "All I'm saying is, you have to trust the process. Now move to the left, off you pop."

Shannon did as instructed, her eyes locking briefly with Theo's from his spot behind the bar. With how busy it was, he had been helping his mother pour beers and run food for over an hour, movements practiced and efficient. Clearly, he had tended bar for her on more than one occasion, and to be honest, she needed to put a little distance between them. Unfortunately for her, the distance did zip-zero in terms of staving her attraction to the man.

Shannon was aware of Theo at all times, her eyes finding him instantly through the crowd. It was like she was drawn to him, even as she fought the pull.

Lining herself up with the left side of the dart board, Shannon stood in position, right foot forward.

"Good. Now, switch your stance. Put your left foot forward, take a deep breath like I told you, and chuck that dart at the bullseye."

Going against all instinct, she switched her stance, frowning in discomfort. *Trust the process.* Sucking in a breath, she allowed her shoulders to relax with the exhale before chucking the dart at the center of the board. It sailed directly into the thirteen. Literally. A laugh burst from her throat at Conor's wince. The poor man. If Shannon learned nothing else on this trip, she was walking away with the knowledge that she was truly awful at darts.

He gave her a sheepish smile. "At least you made it on the board this time."

"Progress," she agreed with a nod. "But I think I'm done for the day."

Taking the offered darts, Conor's eyes glanced behind the bar, softening for a split second before landing on the floor in a move Shannon had now seen a hundred times. A giddiness bubbled in her chest as she put in motion a plan that had been about an hour in the making. Finally, a game she could actually win.

"Join me for another drink?" she asked innocently.

His eyes brightened, accompanied by a nod. Taking their seats back, Shannon couldn't help but zero in on Theo as soon as her ass hit the stool. He was already watching her as he poured a beer, eyes intense and frown in its usual place. She smiled at him with a wink and basked in the comfort of his ticking jaw.

The band kicked up again, their music upbeat and happy, filling the half-full space with new life. Theo made his way towards them but froze at the subtle shake of her head. As much as she wanted to stare at his biceps while he pulled beer from the tap, she needed Pearl for the first leg of her plan.

Speaking of…the swing of the kitchen door was the only warning before Pearl cruised behind the bar, her copper hair glinting in the warm light. Spotting Shannon, she was in front of them in two strides, a smile stretching her mouth.

"Did you kick his ass?"

Shannon let out an elegant snort. "No, but I definitely showed the backboard who's boss."

"She did marvelously," Conor lied. The perfect lie as it provided her with what she needed.

"Not nearly as marvelous as you, Pearl. Conor here tells me you're a goddess with those darts."

Pearl's eyes widened, glancing to Conor who had gracefully choked on his stout. She slapped his back, her attention zeroed in on the blush creeping along the woman's cheeks.

"Oh, that's a bit of an overstatement…"

"Not the way he puts it. What was it you said Conor? 'Playing with Pearl is like watching the sunrise over a dew-covered field. At once beautiful and powerful.' Was that it?" Conor's cheeks flushed red beneath his beard; blue eyes wide with panic as Shannon grinned at the two of them. "I can't wait to see it. May I have another one of these?" she added, pointing to her empty pint glass.

Pearl peeled her eyes away from Conor who seemed to find everything and anything fascinating, and glanced at her glass, a dreamy look about her. She placed a full beer at Shannon's hands before a small smile dusted her lips and she turned to another patron. Shannon barely had time to register Theo's smirk before Conor rounded on her, hands grasping her shoulders.

"What the hell was that?" he asked, his voice shaking slightly.

"What?"

"Don't *what* me in that innocent tone. I never said any of those beautiful things. I just told you she was a great player."

"Yes, but your eyes were telling a different story. One where the sight of the bartender makes you think of sunrises and flowers." She eyed him as his hands fell to his lap, fingers moving restlessly. "Am I wrong?"

"Are you…oh bollocks. No. You're very much right, you little devil."

"Hmm." A smile threatened as she sipped from the cold ale, the tingle of bubbles dancing along her tongue.

"Devil indeed." Shannon startled at Theo's hand on her shoulder. After tracking his every move throughout the day, the nearness of him sent a shiver along her spine. She noted the beer at his hand, the other landing on her back, exactly where she wanted it to be. The fact that he was touching her again had a funny feeling tugging at her stomach. It was as if he relaxed entirely, and his comfort zone included her.

"Me? Never," She leaned into that hand on her back. It was a risky move, but one that ultimately paid off as his thumb brushed little circles over her sweater. "Cheers."

Theo brought his glass to hers with a small clink. "It's quiet enough to join you now. Sorry about that."

She shook her head, sweeping her gaze over the busy pub still rich with life. Locals and tourists mingled around a fireplace next to the bar, while a few enthusiastic folks danced in a small section near the door. Shannon had never felt more comfortably happy in her life, not since that first time she sat in Bloem with the softest cushion under her ass and the best coffee of her life coating her tongue. It was clear to her that Theo got his eye for aesthetics from his mother. Both of them had built such delightfully cozy spaces.

"Alright then, Conor," Pearl said, snapping Shannon's focus to the pair of them instantly. "Angie's here to take over for me. Let's go a few rounds, shall we?" For the second time that day, the poor man choked on his beer while Shannon fought the urge to whoop. The way Conor watched Pearl behind that bar might as well have been a billboard declaring his undying love. He just needed a little push.

"At the dart board," Theo growled beside her, the threat losing its fire as he fought his own smile.

"Yes, of course," Conor said, springing from his stool to meet Pearl at the board without a single word to Shannon or Theo, both of them forgotten.

Theo shook his head as he watched his mother lock arms with the man who was a good foot shorter than her, and sauntered away. "She won't take it easy on him. Mum has a habit of putting men in their place ever since my dad left." Startling at that little crumb of information, she immediately looked to Theo's jaw only to find it in a relaxed state as he sipped from his beer.

"When did he leave?"

"I was seven. I don't really remember much of him to be honest. Mum had always taken care of me, even when he

250

was around. She ran the pub while we were in the apartment upstairs doing schoolwork and studying. Thursdays were the best. Fish and chips day. She would run a big plate up to us for dinner during the first lull."

"Sounds wonderful."

"It was, yeah." He nodded with a ghost of a smile.

"Why did he leave?" She risked the question, thirsty for any information she could glean about the mystery man that was Theo.

"Why do any of them leave?"

Not exactly an answer, but she didn't press. Switching gears, she drew a finger over soft ink on his upper forearm. Delicately drawn trees in grays and blacks rose up to the cuff of his black sleeve hugging a muscled bicep. She had always wanted to touch those beautiful arms of his, and was two beers brave enough to finally do it.

"Tell me about this tattoo," she said, leaning in to be heard over the music.

He didn't hesitate. "It makes me sound like a total sap, but there's a huge garden that leads to a wooded area behind the pub, and when I was a kid, I used to lay amongst the flowers and stare up at the trees. Simon used to tease me because I thought the trees grew all the way to the sky, touching the stars."

Shannon's gaze lifted from her finger on his skin to the swirling constellations at his collar. Growing bolder, she ran a finger along his neck, right over those stars and grazing down his arm to the trees once more. Theo's eyes lifted from his beer and landed on her face, traversing a course across her features as that damn muscle kicked into a fluttering pulse.

"It's a comfort tattoo."

He nodded. "I can't see the stars in San Francisco anymore, as you know."

"And the only trees in my neighborhood are usually covered in pee. Not all of it from dogs."

"Precisely."

"So, this starry, forest scene covers your entire arm?" She asked, wanting to keep him talking more than anything.

"You know it does." His eyes burned into hers as they both remembered the last time Theo was shirtless in her presence.

Skin burning at the memory, she gripped his hand, rubbing her finger along a delicate rose at his thumb. "What about this one?"

He frowned down at the tattoo, something hardening in his gaze. "I got that when Sebastian turned two. Simon was always complaining about his crying one minute and smiling the next. But I thought there was something rather beautiful about it. To feel so much and be so young. It reminded me of a rose. Soft, delicate petals that bask in the sunshine, their thorns ever present below the surface."

Oh, for fuck's sake. "That's really beautiful."

"Yeah well, I told you I didn't need romance lessons from vampire tweens."

She snorted, her heart swelling as she refocused the image of the man sitting next to her. "Simon is Bast's father?"

"My brother," he confirmed with a curt nod.

"He left too." It wasn't a question. Krista had told her on a champagne-fueled girl's night all about Theo's asshole brother, picking up and leaving her alone with a two-year-old child. Leaving Theo. How anyone could walk away from family like that was beyond her. Especially when there was very little she wouldn't do to have one more day with her mom or dad. One hour to talk to her gran.

Theo glanced to where his mother was absolutely crushing the dart board just as she laughed, grasping Conor's arm. Shannon wanted so badly to know what he was thinking. To know how his mother's happiness was affecting him. But the silence stretched, filling the limited space between them as he turned back to her. Having readied herself to see the usual mask set comfortably on his face, she wasn't prepared when Theo landed sad eyes on her. He turned his hand over in hers and interlaced their fingers, the simple move somehow alighting her entire body with awareness.

"Are you okay—"

"I'm paying his child support," he blurted, fingers tightening in hers. "She doesn't know that, so please don't say anything." Shannon shook her head, mouth agape. "That's one of the things I didn't want you finding in the café's books. Simon's name is still on the account, and I have been ordering checks under it for years. I know it's not something I can necessarily afford, but I can't stop, Lil. I can't let them down. They're my family, and I just…I won't watch them drown because my brother decided to be a fucking coward."

Apparently, the shock of Theo sharing an intimate detail about his life was what tamed her smart mouth. Unable to formulate a proper response, all she could do was shake her head as she processed the latest information.

"We opened the café together, though everything that mattered in the end was in my name. My loans, my deed, my fucking debt. Simon managed to clear most of the accounts on his way out the door. But none of that truly mattered, did it? Not when the most precious thing he left behind was a loving wife and baby, just turned two." He searched her face, his eyes slightly panicked as he waited for her to say something.

"Lulu." It came out in a whisper, her brain unable to process the sacrifices made. Unable to ignore how happy and comfortable he was in this setting compared to San Francisco. It made her wonder if he would have left it all behind had it not been for the family he made there…but no. Aside from the fact that he loved Bloem, he would never want Krista to feel that kind of pressure if he wanted to move back home. "You should tell Krista."

"No." Pulling his hand from hers, he ran it through already tousled hair. "She'd be furious with me."

"No, she wont. Okay, maybe she would for a bit," she amended at his raised brow. "But she wouldn't stay mad forever. How could she when you are literally just trying to care for the people you love?"

"I can't tell her. She would blame herself for the position the café is in, which is bullshit. Giving her the money wasn't a problem until sales plummeted two years ago. No matter what I do, I can't seem to get back on even ground."

Shannon zipped her lips shut on the request to help. He had refused her once before, her mental stability would most likely wither in the face of another dismissal. But while her nerves were begging for self preservation, her desire to help Theo pushed passed the self-doubt and fear. Maybe what she had to offer wasn't enough, but she wanted—no, *needed*—to help. To try.

"Let me take a look." Shannon rolled the words around her tongue, ignoring her agitation at his potential rejection again. "It doesn't have to be anything more than that. I can at least run some numbers and see if this is viable with you still providing for your family. I can work out two separate budgets. One with the winnings from *Whisk Wars* and one…without." The last word left her lips as if it were vile. They would not be losing if she had anything to do with it.

Theo stared at her for a long moment, the pub's soundtrack completely at odds with their solemn conversation. A hollowed out feeling dropped in her stomach when he shook his head, lowered his gaze to the pint glass in his hand and wiped at the condensation with his thumb. Damnit. Even expecting the rejection, it still crushed her to see that shake of his head. Facing forward, she took a long pull from her beer, allowing the effervescence to dance along her suddenly dry mouth.

"You amaze me, Shannon." Snapping her gaze back to his, she found him angled toward her, eyes boring into hers. "Okay, yes. I would be grateful if you could take a look."

She almost swallowed her tongue. "Really?"

An odd smile curled his lips, bringing that happy glow back to his features. "Yes. But only if it's a proper transaction. What can I give you in return?"

Oh, she could think of several things. Her body heated in record time, causing her to wiggle on her stool. Theo narrowed his eyes.

"I know. *Behave,*" she said in a mocking tone. "You're no fun."

Tapping a nail against her chin, she thought about what Theo could give her that didn't involve getting him naked and came up empty. And you know what? Maybe she was tired of maintaining control. God help her, she wanted Theo before he ever opened up and now that he had, now that she got that glimpse behind the curtain that she had been craving, the wanting still lingered, growing ever stronger. Ever harder to fight. But it was different somehow. Pressure closed in around her as she fought for the high ground against her emotions.

Before, she had been just fine living out a hot-as-sin fantasy in the sheets with her boss, chalking it off to blowing off steam and returning to life as normal. No regret, pressure, or worries. She never anticipated actually caring for the devil. A real Beauty and the Beast conundrum. What if she did what she always did, and pushed? What if his control snapped for good and they took whatever this seed was between them and planted it? Allowed it to grow, and thrive?

Fear told her it would die. She'd never had a green thumb. How would she recover from the failure of loving and losing Theo Abbott?

Her eyes went wide in her head before she even registered what she had thought. *Love.* No, that wasn't going to be happening here. Of all the things that set you up for certain failure, falling in love was absolutely one of them. That's why it hurt the most when you disappointed friends and family. Letting down those that you love makes for the most brutal scars.

"How about a dance?"

Shannon jolted, glancing in the direction of his nod where a handful of people danced along to the band's cheerful music. That could be perfect. An innocent little dance to even the scales between them and clear her mind of ludicrous thoughts. A dance was simple. Safe.

A quick grin settled over her lips as she grabbed his hand and slipped from the bar stool.

"A dance would be perfect."

CHapter twenty-two

Well, this day was going to end him. Following Shannon to the dance floor, he noted the weight lifted from stiff shoulders. Felt the relief that came with sharing a bit of his stress with someone he trusted. Someone he cared for. Hell, while he was spilling his guts, he may as well drop some truth bombs to himself as well. He cared for Shannon. More than he should and definitely more than he should be admitting to her anytime soon.

When he had told his mum he brought her to the pub and saw the woman's face light up, Theo's disappointment burned his stomach like a scotch bonnet. He realized that he wanted his family to be meeting someone more than just a coworker. Dangerous titles swirled through his mind as he thought of introducing her as his teammate, friend, partner.

Lover.

The want he felt for the woman was dizzying. And when he glanced back and saw her crying tears of joy on his behalf…he hadn't been ready for the dull ache in his chest.

Shannon's feet hit the designated dance floor where she spun around, keeping a solid foot of distance between them as she released his hand. Hips swinging, she gifted him a brief smile before her attention darted to other dancers. A ludicrous inner voice suggested that she was nervous, and he kindly shuffled it out of his mind. He knew those tells, which started with deflection and ended with brutal honesty. Besides that, the woman flirted with him more than humanly possible without the slightest flicker of nerves. There was no logical reason for her to be nervous. Him on the other hand? Well, Theo was feeling reckless. The timing of it couldn't be pin-pointed, and why bother when the outcome was the same? At some point, between her hugging his mother and finding him every few seconds through the crowd, he decided to give in.

"Should I come up with a cookie pun real quick so you don't go through withdrawals?" she asked, her hips swaying deeper and drawing his focus.

Just a joke, he thought to himself. She's not deflecting. "Please don't taint the sacred walls of this pub. I will never forgive you."

Her laugh trilled as she spun, arms raising as the music kicked up. An answering smile puffed his cheeks when she faced him again, the blue ribbon attached to her pony trailing behind her. When the music launched into a chorus beloved by the surrounding patrons, the dancing intensified and before he could think twice, Theo pulled Shannon in at the waist, just managing to save her from an elbow to the head from a flailing dancer.

There was a slight hesitation in her movements before she closed her hand around his, bringing it between them to rest on his chest while the other found the hair at his nape. The song wasn't a slow one and he didn't give a fuck. They swayed slowly to the music, eyes locked in another heated staring contest he was destined to lose.

"Thank you."

258

He shrugged, almost managing to ignore the press of her body against his. Almost managing to not think about how well they fit together. "Lani is a notoriously terrible dancer. I saved us both from having to explain to Maggie why you came back from break with a shiner."

"Not for Lani," she mumbled through a rare frown. "For sharing something about yourself with me." The last bit was said in a hushed whisper, her voice so tender it made his teeth hurt. He cocked his head, confused. Not by her words, for Shannon had always been unafraid to say what she was thinking, but of the flash of something painfully close to worry he saw as his hand tightened around her waist.

"That's why you were angry with me. Because I didn't tell you my mum lived close by."

Lips quirking up in a small smile, she nodded. All signs of distress gone. "He's not oblivious after all, folks."

"Ha. In my defense, I don't understand why you want to know anything about me at all."

Gaze drawn to her lips, he watched as she pressed them together, taking her time to respond.

"You have to know the devil to defeat him," she teased, but there was something off about her smile. It was stiff and didn't quite reach the corners of her eyes.

He stilled, still clinging to her waist as an immediate thought simply spilled from his lips. "I'm afraid I was defeated a long time ago, love."

Shannon pulled her bottom lip between her teeth as his words circled them, drawing his gaze to her mouth. Maybe he didn't share every detail, but that didn't mean she didn't know *him*. Knew he hated fall décor but bought her new decorations every year anyway. Knew he left early on Thursdays to pick up Sebastian from practice, how he took his coffee and which pastries he loved to bake.

She knew what his lips tasted like. Had heard the filthy things he whispered against her ear. And every day, when she caught him staring, she had to see it—the longing, the need, the love. He didn't have to tell her the sad details of his life for her to know him. Not the important things, anyway.

But he would tell her, he realized. Because he wanted to. Because he wanted to share himself with her.

"Tell me what else you're thinking," she demanded, her eyes flicking to a spot by his cheek and back.

"I'm wondering why you're suddenly so serious." Not a lie. Not quite the truth either. "What are you thinking?"

Cocking her head to the side, she ran her thumb along the sensitive skin below his ear, and it took everything he had not to lean into the caress. He tightened his hold around her waist, their joined hands still resting against his chest. "I'm wondering if things have felt like this forever between us, or if it's new."

Well, shit. After all this time, he still hadn't been prepared for the blunt truth to roll from her tongue. Especially when it hit him like a punch to the gut.

"What does it feel like, Lily girl?" *Chicken shit.* Every one of his molecules fucking knew what this felt like between them. He just selfishly wanted to hear it from her. To know that wasn't just him feeling this obsessed and twisted up.

He needed to hear it, and he knew she would give it to him.

"Charged. Like we're suddenly magnetized and simply aren't strong enough to fight it."

"Is that what you want? To fight it?"

Air filled his lungs where it held, waiting for her reply. At some point his hand had traveled higher, tangling with her soft hair and the ribbon hidden among the strands. Their bodies were pressed together, slowly swaying to their own tempo and drowning out the sounds of laughter and slurred words. The crispest blue irises watched him, as if she were obsessed with his reaction.

"Not much of a fight. Didn't you say you're already defeated?"

260

"Yes," he huffed before letting her hand loose and cupping a reddened cheek. Reckless, that was exactly how he felt. "But somehow, I still feel as if I've won." Their lips met and Theo tasted *damnation*—soft and tender and irreversible. Jasmine mingled with the smell of the pub and he could taste the tang of beer on her tongue as he swiped it with his. A sort of pressure settled over his heart, either from her warm hand or the devastation of his feelings, he wasn't quite sure which. Peppering her lips with small kisses, she smiled against his mouth, the feel of it sending pleasure rippling through his nerve endings.

He pulled back just enough to press their foreheads together, turning those blue eyes into a single cerulean blob.

"I have a surprise for you, and that surprise doesn't have to involve me sleeping next to you this weekend but…tell me what to do, Shannon. Tell me what you want."

She hesitated for a moment before the most electrifying answer was delivered from just-kissed lips. "What I want is to sleep next to you like I've done for the last three weeks."

"Thank Christ," he gasped before leading her toward the doors that would take them to the back of the property. A glance toward the dart board showed his mum, waving at him from the lap of Conor Davies. He spared a thought to chat with the man tomorrow before he caught Shannon's eye again, her smile wide and crinkling the corners like he loved, reminding him of more important matters.

The walk through the back garden lasted a thousand years, he was sure of it. Now that the last of his resolve had officially withered and died, his patience was as thin as paper and just as frail. Waves of tension passed between them with every look, graze, and smile. It was the most torturous ten minutes of his life. She must have felt it too, after twisting her ring as they weaved through shrubs and dormant rose bushes, Shannon jerked to a halt.

"Our bags are still in the car," she said, glancing back down the path.

"Do you need something?" He sounded downright frantic, trying and failing to maintain his chill. Jesus, if he was any kind of gentleman, he would have asked *before* they traversed the wild. *What I want is to sleep next to you like I have for the past three weeks.* Insane how that one little admission turned him into an insta-alpha-douche. All of the blood draining from his head and reporting straight to his dick.

She raised a brow, her rolled lips clearly fighting a smile. "Eager to take a nap? I was thinking you might want to hang out some more. Play a game of darts with me or take another turn on the dance floor."

Theo brought his lips against her ear, not caring if his chill was officially vapors. "Very funny, Lily girl, but I need to get my hands on you within the next five seconds, and I'm not even sure privacy is a requirement at this point." She blinked at him, the wicked smile replaced with a look so heated, he was sure it would melt him to a puddle.

Without a word, they made their way quickly down the path, passing little signs reading Chamomile, Ginger, and Peppermint.

"Where does Peppermint lead to?" The question was muffled as Shannon craned her neck to look at the trees at the back of the property.

"To Peppermint," he said simply. "But I requested Hibiscus."

"Naturally."

When the familiar shape of the Hibiscus sign came into view, Theo had to fight a whimper. He snagged Shannon's hand again, tugging her along as he veered down the right path, gravel crunching under their shoes the only sound mingling with the swaying trees.

The tent was in view seconds later, its white canvas resting on a small wooden platform, the screens on either side revealing warm, inviting light.

He glanced at Shannon through his lashes, eager for a response to the scene before them. A little gasp escaped her lips before transforming into the brightest smile, a rival to any flower within the garden.

"Is there a *chimney* on that tent?"

"There is," he replied with a nod and mirroring smile.

"What am I looking at?"

"Hibiscus," he said as they ascended three little steps to the tent's—and this is true—patio. "My favorite tent at The Tea Room's glamp-site."

The sound she made was close enough to a giggle for him, the sound stretching his lips to their limit.

"Tea. Peppermint, ginger…" she trailed off, turning in a circle to take in the garden and towering pines from the view of their patio. "This is incredible."

Holding back the canvas, he unzipped their screen and held it aside for her. "Wait until you see the inside."

Watching Shannon absorb the interior of the tent was like witnessing an art lover traverse the Louvre. Seriously, she had as much enthusiasm over the king-sized bed and side tables as one had when gazing at the Mona Lisa. Big eyes scanned over the lit fire, temporarily providing the tent its only source of light, over the antique oak desk where writing materials and a few candles rested. Scanning the colorful, yet understated rug at their feet, the colors clearly inspired by the plant after which the tent was named.

He waited, taking in every inch of her face, every small laugh and gasped breath as she took in the space they would share for the weekend.

"Oh my god, I never thought I'd be so relieved to see plain white walls," she deadpanned, her voice cool yet brimming with something he wouldn't have been able to place had he not known her. She *was* nervous. And even as he scanned the room, passing over the blessedly solid-colored walls, he knew joking her way through it was her coping mechanism.

But that couldn't be possible, right? Turning from her perfect face, he leaned over to plug in the lights, his mind racing with the possibility. Shannon was an unapologetic flirt. Her nerves had never gotten in the way of a well-timed dick joke or some ridiculous Sexy Brit comment. What was it saying about this situation that she was nervous?

Just as the thought registered, a song started up from behind, startling him into fumbling with the light's plug. He turned to the sound, his heart hammering as Shannon leaned against the bed with "I Think We're Alone Now" trilling from her phone.

"No Maggie here to interrupt this time," she said gently over the music.

"No," he agreed, his focus returning to the lights before he asked, "Does that make you rethink things?" God, but he hoped that wasn't the case. White-hot need coursed through his body even as he readied to hear her say yes. Readied himself to walk away if she was the least bit apprehensive.

Early dusk filtered through the canvas, casting her perfect face in pink and gold before he slid the plug home. Soft, golden light bathed her features from the small fairy lights strewn around the space in lazy loops. A dramatic effect when combined with the shake of her head as she surveyed the space with new eyes.

His gaze didn't peel away from her. Couldn't, as he obsessed over whether that shake of her head said she wasn't having second thoughts, or simply meant she was in awe of the space.

"Jesus, my bar really was on the ground," she murmured, still looking anywhere other than him.

A shiver of satisfaction ran up his spine. "Your bar was in Hell." The statement packed a little too much heat as he unwillingly thought of her ex and ejected him from his thoughts all in one go. This moment wouldn't be tainted by that asshole. "Tell me, Lil. Are you having second thoughts?"

264

"No," she said slowly. "No, I very much want this."
Relief flooded his system as he chanced a small step
forward. "But…"

And that's where the relief shriveled and died. Shannon
worried her bottom lip, that idiotic song still playing from
the white-knuckle grip of her phone.

"But?" he pressed, nerves stiffening his spine as he
watched her. Lord, but she looked ready to bolt. Not what he
envisioned for this moment.

"I can't figure out what *this* is anymore," she blurted,
rising from the bed and setting her silenced phone on the
desk. Brows, hair, cheekbones, lips. His eyes roamed her
features, soaking up every little detail, every slight reaction
as she continued. "I'm afraid this has morphed into
something bigger than just blowing off steam, Lulu. I'm
afraid this is going to ruin our friendship, ruin us. It feels
like…"

"A lot," he murmured.

Afraid? He didn't like the sound of that yet couldn't
bring himself to say the damning words that crashed against
the walls of his brain like rogue waves. What he felt for
Shannon—yeah, it was a-fucking-lot. Catastrophic, even as
he was certain he would never recover from whatever she
was stirring up in his chest. What had she called them?
Magnetized? That was exactly what he felt. Drawn to her
against his will and losing more and more ground with every
day in her company. This woman, who worked tirelessly for
his dream—*fought* for his dream—had been pulling at his
resolve since day one, and it *was* a lot.

But even as he fought against saying those words aloud,
even as he watched her twist that ring on her finger with
those blue eyes glued to his jaw, he couldn't imagine walking
away from it now. Holding her in his arms was the closest
thing to home he had felt in a long time, and he couldn't
believe he had ever labeled it anything other than what it
damn well was.

Reckless, he thought as he took another step, leaving a foot of space between them. He had no idea what she saw in his features, but her eyes went wide and shot to his.

"You want to know what I'm thinking, Lily girl?" He barely waited for her nod before closing the distance between them, one palm cupping her cheek, the other caressing blue silk between his fingertips. "I don't know what this is, but I like it. Fucking hell, I don't make it through breakfast these days without thinking about all the ways I want you." She gasped, her lips parting so beautifully. "I think you're panicking because we're not getting each other out of our systems, yeah? You want more, and that scares you."

"Of course it does, Theo." The confession spilled from her lips as soft hands reached for his wrists, shackling him. "I'm feeling...this wasn't supposed to happen. I wasn't supposed to like you like this. What if it goes sideways? You will be able to go back to Bloem, carry on with your perfect biceps and apple tarts as if I never existed, and I—" She slapped her lips together, cutting herself off.

She what? God, he wanted her to finish that thought. Instead, he addressed the glaring issue with that little outburst. "You think I'd go on as if you never existed?"

Her fingers tightened around his wrists; chin lifted. "Wouldn't you?" Damned if those words weren't a dare. That stubborn chin and spark in those blue pools was a combination he was all too familiar with. A challenge she was certain he would lose.

"There is no Bloem without you." The words left him in a rush, and he barreled on just the same, hardly processing the wave of emotions that sailed over her features. "You want to know what's circling around in this relentless brain of mine? What I'm thinking about? You. Every second of every fucking day. I have been for a while, Shannon, and now that you're giving me more of yourself—it's not a gift, love, it's a fucking curse. Powerful, and unforgiving as I try

266

to get this new image of you out of my head. But I can't," he continued, his eyes burning with the release of so many emotions. "I've had too much of you, and now you're the light of the fucking moon and I'm one of those miserably helpless baby turtles, inexplicably *drawn* to your perfection."

She stared up at him, an indecipherable expression painted over familiar features. Her own eyes filled with moisture as she swiped a tear from his cheek and he gave in, leaning into her warm touch.

"Maybe…maybe we should take it slow," she whispered, tongue swiping out to wet her bottom lip as her gaze swept to his jaw again, expecting him to bite back the words that pushed past his defenses and straight from his tongue.

"Slow? Shannon, this couldn't have moved at a more glacial pace. We have been living one giant slow burn from your first pulled espresso at Bloem. I'm tired of slow. Tired of stalling when I know *exactly* what I want—"

His words cut off as soft lips crushed his own. Shannon moved, her hands leaving his wrists to circle him at the neck, tugging him closer as he angled his mouth over hers. One swipe of his tongue had her lips parting for him, the taste of her like crisp spring water to a parched mouth. Vibration tickled his lips as she hummed, pressing her hips against his as they took what they wanted.

It will always be like this. The thought struck him from nowhere as he fought through his desire for some semblance of control. Years from now, her kisses would still be carnal, filled with hours upon days of denied lust that was finally allowed release. Years, because Theo knew he would never stop wanting this woman.

A small sting at his bottom lip whipped his attention back to the present, Shannon's bite tingling as she licked over it. A groan rumbled his chest as he wasted no more time. His hands left her face, sliding over the delicate curve of her collarbone and lower, grazing the sides of her breasts on their journey. He'd circle back to those, he promised himself before reaching her thighs and lifting. Her legs came around his hips so easily, their kiss breaking for two seconds as they adjusted to the new angle before connecting once more, desperate and feral.

Setting her on the desk, the breath huffed out of him as the legs bracketing his hips pulled tight, his cock getting that first press of friction he had been all too close to begging for.

"Just like this," he groaned against her lips. "I have done nothing but think about getting between these sweet thighs since that day in the office."

"Hmm, I love it when you speak your mind."

Did she? His mind had run over all the inappropriate things whispered between them when his control snapped, and it did nothing but mortify him. Afraid he had said too much too soon—was too intense. Knowing she loved it lit a fire in his belly, his hips jerking forward for more pressure.

He was not embarrassed by the sound that left him as she rolled her body, her tongue licking into his mouth in the same rhythm. A shock zipped up his spine, pulling a whimper as she sucked his bottom lip into her mouth and smiled against it. The woman always knew her power, didn't she? He was a fool to ever think he had any of it.

Growing bolder, he inched his hands up, snagging the hem of her sweater and separating their lips long enough to lift it from her body. While his fingers found the clasp at her back, she explored, hands snaking down his chest and connecting with his own hem. Her fingers ducked under his shirt as the clasp gave, and it was heaven and hell to have her skin on his just to pull away as he discarded her bra. Heaven won out as his gaze trailed down to her breasts, and her fingers found his skin once more. Conflicting desires all-out raged within his body, begging him to rip the barrier of his shirt from his chest while another demanded he explore those perfect breasts. Taste the rosy peaks of her nipples and lap at the soft skin until she trembled.

Voice it, he reminded himself.

"I can't decide if I want to rip this shirt away and press those perfect tits against me, or play with those pretty nipples until you moan my name."

Her gasp was like music to his ears, the flush on her chest rising to the apples of her cheeks.

"Both, I think," she said before gripping his shirt and tugging it over his head. Sparing no time, she tugged him at the neck, connecting their mouths, hips and finally, pressing her bare chest into his. He whimpered into her mouth, the sound not nearly as dramatic as the moment deserved. The feel of her pressed against his skin was astonishing. Chilling and fever-inducing all at once. A shiver trailed over her body, releasing him of the thought that he was the only one completely losing it.

Gripping her back, he rained kisses along her neck, licking collarbone as it passed him by. Her heaving chest was no obstacle as his destination drew nearer, the desk creaking slightly as he shifted to lean a little weight against it. Pulling back, he gave her chest a last appreciative look before closing his lips around her nipple, swirling his tongue once, twice before giving it a little suck. A hiccuped breath caught, raising her chest in a staccato jerk before she arched, searching for more of his probing tongue.

He obliged, moving to her other side and whispering praise as he went. She was so beautiful, so soft. She was going to take him so well. They would be so fucking good together. Between the words and his tongue flicking over sensitive skin, he had Shannon squirming in her seat, legs tightening around his hips.

His rambling came to a stuttering halt when her fingers found the button of his jeans, tugging it free in one swift movement. Snagging her wrists, his heart pounded as he looked at her, flushed and swollen and begging for it. Fuck, she looked sinful. Sun-ripened forbidden fruit that he was more than eager to take a bite out of.

"I hate to tell you this, but we'll need your pants off in order to continue," she said in a husky voice he had never had the pleasure of hearing. It would run on a loop in his brain from that moment on.

"Not if we want this to last more than five minutes," he stated, only slightly embarrassed by the confession. Her smile was quick and vicious, eyes sparking with intent he decided he wanted no part in. Grabbing her hand, he pressed her palm against his hard length, the pressure causing him to choke back a full sob even as pure male pride flooded his veins when Shannon's eyes went wide, her gaze trailing down to where she palmed his erection through his jeans. "I'm going to need these thighs around my neck first, see if we can't get you at least one of those three orgasms you require before I sink inside of you."

She groaned, her hand getting one more caress before he pulled it to his face. Heavy lidded eyes watched as he laid an open-mouthed kiss to her palm, his other hand working the button of her jeans. Unable to help himself, he dipped his fingers down the front as soon as the zipper was down, his hand pressed at an awkward angle. He still managed to slip beneath her underwear, his cloudy mind managing to recognize that it was a mere swatch of cotton before he found her swollen clit.

Beautiful little moans escaped parted lips as he gently circled the delicate bud. His need was an electrical storm, zipping bolts of lightning through every nerve ending as he watched her. Leaning back, she lifted her hips for a better angle, his hand gaining an inch as he continued to caress. Bringing a hand up, she played with her own nipple. Gently brushing the hard peak and pinching it between her fingers.

Okay, he needed to get her naked and in that bed before his heart gave out. Without warning, he circled both hands to her ass and lifted, flinging her to the bed where she bounced with a laugh. Already shimmying her pants down her hips, he stumbled out of his own, his eyes roaming her face as hers meandered over his naked body.

It didn't make him nervous; he was comfortable with his body and had never shied away from his partners. Although she had seen him in a near naked state before, this felt different. Like if she started to ask him about his tattoos again, he would tell her. Give her every back story and all the meaning behind the ink. He wanted to give her bits of himself just like he craved bits of her.

Moving forward, he grabbed the bottom of her jeans and pulled. She huffed a laugh as her jeans and underwear went flying somewhere behind him, quickly followed by her socks. His gaze wandered from those stormy eyes, along her chest, down to her soft belly and finally to those bare thighs, thick and strong and *his*. "Look at you, spread out on this bed with nothing but a ribbon in your hair. You are sensational, Lily girl." And he would never be able to unsee it. "Get on your knees," he said, his voice low and rough.

Her breath hitched through parted lips, causing a twitch below his belly.

"Yes, *sir.*" A smile tugged at his mouth as it went dry, watching her maneuver to a kneeling position as he crawled onto the bed. A messy kiss, a clumsy roll and she was on top of him, their bodies flush together in ways he had only ever dreamed about in his deepest REM cycles. Her hair surrounded them, his hands diving directly to palm her ass, giving it a little shove.

She straddled him, rising to where his hands guided her over his chest before hesitating.

"You don't have to," she said, breathless. "This usually doesn't work for me if I'm being honest."

Head tilting on the pillow, he asked, "Doesn't work for you, or you don't like it?"

Her bottom lip worked between her teeth, gaze sweeping down in a clear appraisal. "I don't know?"

He pushed her again, his mouth practically salivating with his desire to taste her. "No harm in trying." A brief pause, full of panted breaths and the tightening of his fingers on her ass, before she moved, bracketing his face with her thighs and blessing him with a beautiful view. "Christ, this is going to wreck me, isn't it?"

Light trills of a chuckle reached his ears before he turned it into a gasp with a kiss to her inner thigh, teasing before he finally allowed himself to reach his greedy mouth to her core.

The sound that left him wasn't altogether human and completely out of his control. She tasted positively addicting. Somehow his dick got even harder as he squeezed the back of her thighs, encouraging her to relax so he could take her weight. He worked lazily at first, licking and sucking in delicate rhythms as her breathing became labored above him. Pride wouldn't allow him between those legs without delivering a mind-blowing orgasm, and as he heard a small moan from above, he raised his lids. Oh, he'd get her there. One look at those rosy cheeks and sex-stoned eyes and he was sure of it. He picked up the pace, something like ohmygodyesdontstop reaching his ears as he lapped at her pussy, sucking and savoring when her legs tightened around his head. It was a beautiful smothering. The most glorious way to die.

Shannon's hips jerked as she gasped out his name and he took the opportunity to lick up her middle, sucking on her clit as she came and not letting up until every wave of her pleasure was worn out. Peppering her sensitive skin with kisses, his eyes met hers, a small smile pressing against her thigh at the look of absolute devastation on her face.

"How…"

Gently shifting her lower, he sat up, back against the headboard and what he knew was the smuggest look on the planet painting his dopey face. "I've been practicing how to make you come in my dreams for years."

Fingers tugged at his hair, bringing their lips together and reminding him that the fucking moon itself sat in his lap, straddling his hips and grazing his dick. And when she ran her tongue over his lips, no doubt tasting her own pleasure on his skin, his brain snapped to attention immediately.

"I'm on the pill," she stammered out, and Theo allowed his whimper free reign that time, thrilling at the light it brought to her hooded eyes. "If you're good…"

"I'm good," he growled, his heart thumping at the idea of taking her completely bare. That was not something he did, yet the idea of sinking into Shannon with zero separation felt at once life-altering and exactly right. There would be no going back for him, he fucking knew it. The fact that he wanted that level of vulnerability with her was a pretty obvious sign of his feelings. This woman didn't just have his trust, she had his whole damn heart gripped in her tiny hand.

Voice it, he thought again, his eyes searching hers, trailing along her hair to her cheek, lips, eyes again. *Damn yourself to a life of loving.*

"I think I could love you."

Theo's heart stuttered and arguably stopped dead as he realized those words weren't his own. No, his sweet, brave little bundle of sunshine was the one to punch down her fears and spit out exactly what she was thinking because, of course she was.

"I'm starting to realize that love doesn't even begin to cover what I feel for you," he replied, his eyes burning with tears at an embarrassing rate.

"I don't,"—she murmured against his lips—"I don't think I'm working you out of my system."

Theo choked on his own tongue but kept moving, gripping her hips with a little too much enthusiasm and positioning her right where he wanted. Shannon lowered herself slowly onto him, her walls gripping tight and allowing very little movement.

"Fuuuuck," he said, drawing the word out as a shuddering breath escaped her lips and landed on his own. Another inch was gained, her breath catching and a whimper leaving both of their lips. Bringing them together so he could catch every stray moan and gasp in his mouth, he waited, giving her all of the control as she struggled to take his entire length.

"Such a good girl," he gasped as their hips connected. "Taking me so well."

"Theo," his name was a prayer, a muffled sob pleading with him to make sense of how good they fit together.

He couldn't, and as she started to move, Theo had to shuffle through a myriad of boring, menial tasks to keep from the shortest endurance of his life. Filling out tax forms, the *Whisk Wars* contract, reorganizing the POS menu—none of it actually helped as his hips rose to meet the gentle sway of hers and he buried himself to the hilt.

Rocking in a slow rhythm, Shannon's head rolled back on a sigh, a moan following close behind. The tips of her hair grazed his fingertips where they gripped her hips, the sensation sending a shiver through his body, gaze heavy and locked on her.

"Do you,"—twin moans escaped their lips as she rocked— "Should I go faster?"

Didn't matter, he was going to come quicker than he had in his life regardless of the pace. Bringing one hand to the back of her neck, he wrapped his hands around her hair and gave her a tug, panting into her mouth as she continued her lazy movements. Fairy lights and the flicker of the fireplace caressed her features as the word *mine* rang out in his mind like a battle cry.

"No. I want you just like this. Slow and *deep*. I want to feel nothing but you." He licked into her mouth, tongue coming back briny from the tears trailing down his cheeks with abandon. He would be embarrassed later, but none of that shit was for this moment. This was the moment he let himself feel, study, memorize. This was a moment he let consume him until all that was left was a burning ember fed and fanned only by the woman in his arms.

He was right there, Shannon's steady rocking providing more than enough friction to have him on the brink. "Can I come inside you?" he breathed into her mouth, their fingers clutching at each other as if they would spiral and fly away at any moment.

"Yes," she sobbed, her tears joining his in a wet mess, their lips slick and salty. When she tightened around him there was no chance in hell he was keeping it together. Hips jerking, release tore through him, soft whimpers interspersed with her clipped moans as he filled her. His brain scrambled to hold it together as she continued to move, the walls of her pussy gripping him in soft fluttering pulses. Reaching between them, he worked her clit with his thumb, as she murmured unintelligible praise against his neck.

Lifting his hips, he drove deeper into her, his heart racing as she tightened around him, a muffled scream delivered against his neck followed by the scrape of her teeth as she came. The pulsing around his cock almost bringing it back to life for another round.

As Shannon's limbs went completely limp in his arms, he collapsed against the back of the bed, heart thumping in time with hers. Her breath traveled over sweat-soaked skin, his neck tingling with sensation from each panted huff.

Slowly, she lifted herself from his lap and flopped onto her back. He followed immediately, his hand finding her thigh and squeezing as they both stared at the night sky through the tents net. "Well, shit," Shannon said, her breath evening out.

"Shit," he agreed, the crescent moon just visible in the patch of netting in the roof.

He practically heard the smile stretching her face before she even spoke.

"Helpless, baby turtle, Theodore?"

He groaned, rolling with a pillow to smother her before she could repeat that to anyone, ever. Her giddy laughter sailed through the tent and into the night, whirling through the garden and trees of his childhood.

CHAPTER TWENTY-THREE

Shannon eyed the camera wearily, her hair in a long braid down her back. Little wisps had escaped and were curling around her cheeks in a chaotic fluff.

"How do I feel about today's technical?" she asked, an unhinged giggle escaping her lips. "Well, that was a nightmare, wasn't it?"

"It's nothing we can't fix," Theo chimed in from her side, ever the stoic one. He gave her a worried look, his soft eyes melting her to a puddle of uncertainty and sadness.

"That's sweet, Lulu, but I don't think we can salvage this one." She sounded so sure of their failure. So defeated, even to her own ears. Theo was a sorcerer in the kitchen, but with the way she had royally messed up today, she had little hope of their success.

The smile Charles pointed in her direction was as fake as his white-capped teeth, pity practically caked on his skin. "Bread week is one of the hardest and I think this first challenge proved just how tough it can be. Any last-minute strategies going into the competition bake?"

"Listen," Theo said to the camera even though she just *knew* he was saying it for her. "We have an entire night to prepare for tomorrow. This is a minor setback, but I'm confident in our abilities." Funny that he said ours, and not his since he would be carrying the team on his back. "We *will* be going to the finals next week. I didn't endure all of these relentless baking puns just to go home now."

"So, how have you liked my little slice of England, Lily girl?"

Shannon dragged her gaze from Theo's flexing bicep as he fixed a leaky pipe behind the bar, her stomach back flipping as Pearl used the nickname as if she had been calling her that for years.

"It's wonderful. Truly, I never would have guessed such a curmudgeonly old Scrooge grew up in such a magically festive place."

"Bah," Theo grunted, his muscles flexing with each crank of the wrench. Pearl pointed a wide smile at him, her eyes softening even though he looked ready to snap the pipe in half rather than solve her problem.

After spending the evening tangled in the sheets, the fire casting amber light on their naked bodies, Shannon had been more than a little reluctant to leave the so-called tent. The evening's emotional rollercoaster had managed to leave her drained in the most unnerving way. Spent so deliciously, yet raw and exposed, all of her insecurities sun-dried and at risk of burning to ash by his hands. He could do it. With the chokehold he had on her heart, one little squeeze and he could completely destroy her. It was a truly damning place to be.

Yet as they emerged from their canvas haven, the day had unfolded like any other. She joked; he scowled. She danced; he scoffed. She poked, nudged, and leaned into him for

278

unwanted selfies, yet this time, he didn't shy away. He wrapped his arms around her and whispered sexy things in her ear. He kissed her cheek when she said something stupid and bought her things she had offhandedly mentioned liking. Reconciling the man she had known back in San Francisco with the one she knew in The Cotswolds was a fascinating task.

When they fell back into bed after spending dinner at The Tea Room, he had completely and thoroughly worshiped her body until her limbs had melted into the sheets. More tears were shed, more hopes of survival were crushed.

How did one recover from the realization that they were head over ass in love with someone?

Taking a bite of a jam-covered scone, she turned in her stool to face Pearl.

"Have you been to San Francisco to see the café?"

"Not since it first opened," she said like a confession, eyes darting to the floor along with her tone. Sore subject—noted.

"You should come out again," Theo grunted, his hands working the bolt one more time before a satisfied grunt accompanied a nod. Busying himself with cleanup, he didn't catch the wave of sadness that passed over her features before she schooled them away. Like mother, like son. "I'm sure Krista would love to see you too, Mum." This he delivered softly, his eyes briefly scanning her face before he turned to wash his hands.

"Alternatively," Shannon said before Pearl ripped out her own earring. Looked like the nervous gesture was very similar to her own as the woman whirled a silver stud in circle after circle. "We could all come back here. It would probably be possible after we win this thing."

"We?" Theo asked against her ear, startling and exciting her at the same damn time.

Pearl flashed a smile at her before winking, as if she and her son would forever be in on the joke.

"Oh, were you planning on taking Lip Filler? Because I'm sure I can facilitate that match." It was a joke, but one that tasted bitter all the same. The day she became Theo's matchmaker would be the day the flat Earthers were proven right.

"There's only one match I'm interested in," he said, his voice molten against her skin. "And that's one that you facilitated involving a one Conor Davies and the most beautiful redhead to ever grace these cursed lands."

Shannon squealed, unable to help herself as Pearl went a delightful shade of crimson.

"I'm sure I don't know what you mean. What's all this about a match?"

"Oh, that man has it bad for you Miss Pearl. And can you believe all of the beautiful things he said about y—" Shannon's words were cut off by a delicate snort.

Pearl eyed her over her coffee cup from two stools down, her face flushed but smug. "You expect me to believe that those words were ever formulated in Conor's brain? The man wouldn't be able to sing a lullaby without stumbling. I will give it to you though, Lily girl, I have been waiting for him to make a move for almost a decade."

"Ha!" Shannon laughed, her cheeks heating with excitement. "He looked about ready to keel over when you asked him to go a few rounds."

"Lord, save me from this torment," Theo mumbled, sliding into a stool and bracketing his thighs at her hips. When he tugged at her seat, bringing it flush with his and pressing his chest to her back, she sighed, leaning into the connection. He was warm and comforting at her back, his chin resting gently on her head. It felt so natural, as if they hadn't been avoiding the slightest graze for hours upon days upon years. Her brain told her she'd never get used to it, while her body relaxed, completely at ease in his arms.

"When do you two have to get going?"

"Pretty soon." Reluctance thickened his voice, his hands mindlessly sliding up and down her arms. "The bags are already in the car."

"And when you win this competition, then what? Can you swing back here for a couple of days?"

His hands tightened around her biceps for a brief moment. "Unfortunately, we're already cutting it close, Mum."

Shannon tried not to let the sadness she heard drag her shoulders down. She continued to stay bubbly half an hour later as they said their goodbyes, through the silence that met her as they drove on the wrong side of the road, the village passing her by in a collage of honey-colored buildings, cobblestone bridges, and fall leaves.

Her giddiness started to waver as the silence droned on and her own mind started turning on her. Why did it feel like they were leaving behind so much? Not just his family and childhood home, but whatever they built while there. Were all of her spilled emotions still coating the ridiculously nice floors of that tent? It sure felt like it. Her brain unhelpfully supplied thoughts of doubt. Was this where things went off the rails? Where reality sets in, and the fourth dimension they had entered when walking through that tent flap mirages into regret and panic? She didn't want Theo to regret her. The mere idea of that being the case set her heart skipping and stomach roiling, the ring on her finger sliding around and around as she fiddled.

"Are you okay?" Theo asked, his hand covering hers and stilling the movement.

"Me?" Why would he be asking that when he was the one who just left his family for God only knew how long?

"I can hear you spiraling," he said through a gentle smile.

"I don't want it to all be a dream," she blurted, never able to keep her damn mouth shut.

He gave her hand a squeeze before letting go, turning down the drive toward Châteaux Genevieve.

"Oh, it was a dream. One I won't soon forget. But it's not over for me, Shannon."

The trees opened up, the towering brick structure breaking over her horizon line, bringing them closer to their goals yet farther from where Shannon really wanted to be. Back at the pub, sucking at darts and laughing with Pearl. An overwhelming sense of homesickness waved over her as she realized she had missed this feeling for years without ever realizing it. Missed the familiarity and comfort of family.

The car slowed to a stop, and Shannon's eyes found that amber gaze trained to her face. They roamed, darting from one feature to the next as if lost and searching for the landmark that would lead to home. That uncertainty wasn't shared by her. She now realized that she had always thought it was Bloem that kept her grounded and safe. But it had always been Theo, hadn't it? He was exactly who she looked to for the right direction.

"You're my true North," she whispered, watching his lips part with the immediate softening of his features. "It's not over for me either."

***

"I'm so sorry," Shannon said for the hundredth time in a twenty-four-hour period.

"Shannon love, please stop apologizing and get the oven door for me, would ya?"

"Oven!" she called to the camera operator so he could swing around and catch a shot of Theo sliding a tray of bread onto the rack. He felt for her—he really did—but right now, he needed the apologies to stop before he threw everything on the ground and wrapped her in his embrace. He couldn't stand to hear her apologies.

282

Bread week would not take them down. The previous day had been sent straight from Hades starting with Shannon forgetting to turn on her oven and ending with bread that was very nearly raw. The nice thing to do would be to pretend it wasn't painful to watch but…it really was. Theo sat, helpless on the sidelines as her oven remained cold yet that stubborn cut of her jaw said she didn't have a care in the world. It had been heartbreaking to run over to her at halftime and break the news.

Still, as he worked on the next piece of their competition bake, he hadn't lost hope.

And even when Samira and Chanda managed to produce an insanely beautiful "bread painting" that mimicked a desert landscape—complete with a brioche sun setting over sandy focaccia dunes—he didn't lose faith.

No, it wasn't until the look on Darlington's face as he tried his cinnamon swirl sweetbread, breaking a piece from the painting and ruining the image of his mother's pub, that Theo's stomach flipped and fell. And when he and Shannon were called as one of the bottom teams to battle it out for a chance in the finale, Theo's heart nearly fell out of his ass.

They were so damn close.

***

Theo eyed the judges table, his station neat as a pin and the hum of refrigerators a full-on battle cry vibrating along his skin. Darting his eyes to the right, he caught the tremor in his opponent's hands where they rested on the butcher block in front of him. *Beardy*, that's what Shannon called him, and he never bothered to learn his real name. Didn't matter now since one of them was on a flight home tomorrow.

Shifting his focus to the left, he locked his gaze with Shannon's immediately, a small smile curling his lips in an attempt to wipe the panic from her sweet face. It didn't work. A crease formed between her brows as Daisy began the intro, drawing Shannon's worried gaze from his as he continued to have eyes only for her. Daisy's upbeat lilt was at complete odds with Beardy's tremors and the iron grip around Theo's stomach.

"Bakers, this elimination challenge will test your time management, organization, and ability to work under pressure." She paused as if they didn't already know what the challenge was. "Today, you will be making...classic muffins. For those of you watching from pretty much anywhere else in the world, we mean *English* muffins."

The little fuckers. He and Shannon stayed up well into the night practicing the bake. He knew them, had baked them, and *used* to like them. Now? Now he loathed the little shits almost as much as flavor syrups.

And he would bake a hundred of them if it meant Shannon never wore that worried look around him again.

"Sadly, whoever loses this challenge will not be moving on to the final," Jasper cooed, laying it on thick for the cameras before Charles took over.

"You have three hours to *rise* to the occasion."

Fuuucking hell. He would throw the whole thing just to never hear another fucking baking pun in his god-awful natural born...

"Bake!" Daisy called with a squeal, sending Theo into motion.

Now there was nothing particularly difficult about English muffins, they were just a labor of love. After blending the dough and bulk fermentation, he had to form the buns for the first rise, degas before shaping again, allow them to rise a second time before charring them on a griddle and baking. All of which needed to be carried out in three hours. Easy.

Easy.

Easy.

Beads of sweat dribbled down his temples, causing him to run his forehead along the crisp sleeve of his shirt as he actively ignored Jasper yelling out "Five minutes left!"

Fingers working at rapid speeds, he made quick work of choosing a dozen perfectly sized muffins and placing them on a slate platter. The clotted cream and strawberry jam—both recipes stolen from Conor's tea shop—set alongside them.

A glance to his right threatened to get his hopes all the way up as Beardy was barely pulling his tray from the oven. He wasn't going to make it…and that should have thrilled him. But as Theo glanced between his perfect platter and the man scrambling to get the hot muffins onto a bamboo board, he couldn't sit still. Jogging to his station, he asked, "What can I do for you?"

The man met his eyes, a look of utter relief splashing across his bearded face. "Can you pour the sauce on the burner into that pitcher?"

He could do that. In seconds, Theo and the man set his station up perfectly, his muffins still steaming as the pitcher was set out next to them with something resembling hot honey. Damn, that was a great idea. His opponent shifted the last muffin to line up perfectly just as time was called.

The breath that huffed from his chest was quickly cut off by strong arms, circling him in a death grip. Beardy was apparently *extremely* grateful for the help.

"It's nothing," he mumbled through the thank you's being thrown his way. "I was happy to…"

"May I cut in?" Shannon's voice was like the sound of rain in a drought. Peeling himself from one embrace, he circled around to clamp his arms around her like he dreamed of doing for the entirety of the challenge. "That was some good baking there, Lulu."

"I don't even care," he said honestly, his lips brushing over her hair, fingers finding the white ribbon in her braid. "I'd be happy to walk away right now if it meant I could hold you like this for the rest of my life."

It didn't feel strange, even though the act of saying exactly how he felt was completely foreign to him. The only indication of its scarcity was Shannon's soft gasp and wide eyes before their attention was caught by Darlington from the front of the room.

"The moment of truth!" He bellowed, his excitement filling the room as he glanced to Theo's left. "Who will be joining Samira and Chanda in the finale?"

One by one, the judges sampled Beardy's bake, their voices blurring into the background as Theo found himself lost in his own thoughts. Truth was, he didn't actually care— not when his hand was wrapped in a warm grip, gaze locked on a pair of ocean blue irises. He held Shannon's stare, barely registering his own voice as he explained his bake. There was giggling, the judges' laughter turning awkward when he didn't so much as glance their way. Even as they chewed, smiled, and threw playful remarks about prolonged eye contact his way, Theo's eyes never wavered. He didn't break. Not even when they announced Bloem the winners, sending him and Shannon to the finale and closer to that prize money, his attention stayed transfixed on what he really wanted. What he really valued.

"You don't care?" Shannon finally asked, her eyes lined with silver, the weight of the moment settling between them.

Theo exhaled, his voice quiet but certain. "Not when I've already won."

EPILOGUE

"Oh, that's horseshit, Darlington!"

Shannon choked on her champagne, her eyes feeling wide in her face as she turned them towards Krista's enraged expression. Had she ever heard her curse in front of Sebastian? Obviously not since the kid burst out laughing before yelling "Jar!"

Theo had been right. After spilling the beans to Krista, her eyes had held a level of murderous rage in them the likes of which Shannon had never seen. At once impressive and terrifying. But just as she predicted that murderous rage had been redirected, detouring away from her loving brother-in-law and landing on a more appropriate subject.

And now, it was pointed directly at Darling Darlington's pearly white smile.

The café was filled with life. Evie sat next to Max, her hands covering her mouth in shock, Max rubbing small circles on her thigh as he shook his head. Harper sat between Bast and Krista, her mouth pulled down in a frown as Elliot watched her reaction from behind her chair. Ben was frozen in place, his hands held in the air in celebration while his face appeared to be seconds away from tears. Juliette stood behind him, Vincent's plaid-shrouded arm draped over her shoulders. She quietly reminded herself to thank Krista for pushing that match along in her absence as she took in the rest.

A handful of Bloem's regulars sat alongside her closest friends, their disappointment evident as they looked between her, Theo, and the screen they had set up in front of the roasting room window to project the *Whisk Wars* finale.

It had been easier than she anticipated, keeping the results from their friends. After returning to a barely functioning café and relieving Krista of her duties, they launched into their work, coming up with an action plan and implementing steps discussed while they finished the competition and traveled home. By the time the first episode aired, Shannon had crossed so many tasks off her list she barely managed to feed herself.

Theo took care of that for her though. With renewed energy, he had hit the kitchen, tested recipes and managed to give the menu a major upgrade. The guests had been awed even before *Whisk Wars* filled their screens.

As predicted, the show turned the café into a certifiable madhouse. One week after the first episode showed a forty percent increase in first time guests, with that number growing to sixty percent by episode three. And although Shannon received her fair share of fangirling, it filled her with unadulterated glee to know that most of the guests came in to lay eyes on the sexiest frown on the planet.

Speaking of...

She peeled her gaze from her friends to find that beautiful frown exactly where she left it on the outskirts of the crowd by the pastry case. She knew he would already be watching her but still couldn't help the little gasp that left her lips as their eyes locked. Maybe she would never be able to help it.

After the semifinals, Shannon and Theo stayed glued to one another, practicing their bakes in nothing but their skin and constantly falling distracted by that fact. They made up for the years spent barely touching each other. They *really* made up for it. Just the memory of strong fingers working their way across her body sent a shiver up her spine, her cheeks heating.

Theo's eyes darkened across the room, his gaze jumping from point to point on her face in a pattern so familiar, it brought immediate tears to her eyes. They had truly been on a journey, hadn't they? Years of evading and ignoring—*denying* what was so completely obvious to her now.

A slap on her back broke their staring contest, Ben's deep voice grumbling into her hair.

"You're a winner in my eyes."

"Thank you, Benjamin. Your approval is truly all that matters."

Evie appeared on her other side, slipping an arm around her waist. "Dickhead Darlington doesn't know a parfait from a pop tart."

A laugh bubbled up and over, the sound pulling Theo's attention away from Harper, a quick grin passing over his mouth. She loved her friends, but the sooner they left, the sooner she could claim that mouth for herself and congratulate him on making it through the viewing parties she had forced him to host.

The apartment upstairs was only partially renovated, but the bedroom had been the first to get a facelift, and if she had it her way, they would be putting it to very good use as soon as the last guest cleared the doorway…

"You're mind-fucking Sexy Brit right now, aren't you?"

"Uh huh," she said, glancing to each of her friends without an ounce of remorse.

"So am I," Ben sighed, laying his head against hers as Evie cackled.

"You need us to shuffle the herd out of here so you can sneak off with your super hunky Pastry Daddy?"

Relief flooded her. "*Yes*. I will give you free apple tarts for a week."

"Done," Ben sang, delivering one more squeeze before he began coaxing people to the exit.

Evie paused, cupping Shannon's cheeks as her rich brown eyes searched her face.

"You lost." It was delivered in her chef voice, somehow gentle and firm at the same damn time.

"We lost," Shannon confirmed, mirroring her best friend, and cupping her cheeks. Evie's lopsided bun had come loose in her agitation during the episode, wisps curling under her hands where they framed her angel face.

"And you're...okay?"

Shannon grinned a toothy grin, her hands squeezing until Evie's lips puckered. "I'm perfect. We lost months ago, so I've had plenty of time to plummet into a deep pit of despair and lug myself up again before the episode aired."

Evie watched her for a few seconds before her face settled into soft angles, clearly satisfied with whatever she saw in her expression. With a nod, she kissed Shannon's cheek. "I'm proud of you," she whispered in her ear before turning to aid Ben with clearing the space.

Shannon smiled and held guests as they left the café, her attention never fully leaving Theo as he did the same from a few paces back, and as Evie and Max strolled through the door still fuming over the outcome of the show, she felt his gaze on her as if it were a caress.

Closing the doors, she turned the lock before making quick work of the drapes, pulling them shut and cutting them off from the surprisingly busy street. The minute the streetlights were blocked from view, tattooed arms circled her chest, tugging until her back ran flush with a warm, broad chest.

"I love you, but I am never doing that again."

Her heart fluttered at the flippant deceleration of love. He said it more often than not these days, the words seeming to flow from his mouth whenever they entered his brain. She would never get enough of it.

"Never traveling across the country for a baking competition? Or never hosting a large party where everyone we care about watches us get our asses kicked in high definition?"

He turned her until their chests connected, palms moving to cup her cheeks. "Neither. I would gladly do both of those things every year for the rest of my life it kept you by my side."

She pressed her smile to his lips, a hum issuing from somewhere in his throat. "Lucky for you, I would rather burn all the fall décor than go through that again. Either way, you're stuck with me, Lulu."

"Exactly where I want to be," he murmured, his hands shifting into her hair, soft lips brushing over hers. "No, I meant never connecting this shirt to my skin ever again. I can actually feel the pun through the cotton."

She didn't need to peel her body from his to know what he meant. Ben had shown up with custom shirts, her and Theo's faces plastered over pink lettering that read "Batter Together."

"Fair enough," she said, tone serious. "We should get it off of you immediately." One swift tug and she pulled the shirt over his head, walking him backwards towards the stairs that would take them to the apartment above. "Batter?"

"Not quite." A giggle escaped as he snagged the hem of her shirt, slowly raising it up and off, his fingers grazing her breasts along the way. Her skin already burned as they reconnected, the feel of his bare chest still managing to feel foreign and familiar all at once. No time to think too hard on it when his tongue licked across her lips, spreading them eagerly and groaning at the first taste.

When his foot hit the bottom step, they separated, darting up the stairs past the office from hell, and falling right back into each other's arms as the apartment door was kicked shut behind them. Within seconds, Shannon's bra and pants were on the floor, scattered amongst painting supplies and tools, her underwear the only barrier as Theo skipped out of his jeans, not bothering to ditch his socks as he followed her down the plastic lined hallway to his bedroom.

"Tell me, what were you thinking about when that pretty little blush appeared earlier?"

"I was thinking of all the ways you made me come over the last few months," she said, her lips trailing to the stars along his neck. "And how I wanted to return the favor with my tongue. I want to taste every single tattoo on your body." She pivoted, pressing a kiss to his ink covered chest, over the hard lines of his stomach and trailing back up, lingering on the lilies tattooed on his rib, her head rising and falling with his rapidly increasing breaths.

"When did you get this one?" She licked the lilies from stem to petal, smiling when he grunted her name. Her feet were swept from the floor, coming around him automatically as he pushed her against the wall, the chilled surface pulling a gasp from her lips. Pinning her hips with his own, she moaned against his mouth as his cock rubbed against her wet panties. The pressure made her desperate, grinding her hips into his and chasing the angle she needed.

"Your birthday," he said through clenched teeth, his hips pressing her against the wall accepting every rock of her own as his hand found her chin. "I got that one on your birthday three years ago."

She froze, her eyes scanning his face for a sign of deception she knew she wouldn't find.

"Why?"

The kiss he pressed against her lips was soft and slow, as if he wanted to savor the taste of her reaction. "You know why, Lily girl."

The breath whooshed from her lungs as rapid blinks attempted to windshield wiper the moisture from her eyes. Three years ago?

Theo sucked her bottom lip into his mouth before running soft kisses over her pout. "Say something," he breathed.

"I love you, but you need to stop making me cry during sex."

He chuckled, the sound huffing against her lips and bringing lust slightly ahead of the shock from seconds before. She pressed against him again, knowing the move would wipe the no-doubt smug look right from his face. This man would never stop surprising her. Never stop pulling emotions she never even knew existed straight from her heart to barrel from her tear ducts, but she wouldn't allow him to fully get away with it unscathed. She reached between them, pulling her panties to the side and rubbing herself up and down, a smirk of her own appearing when he whimpered in her ear.

It didn't take long before he thrust fully inside of her, their cries bouncing off the walls as he buried himself deeper and deeper with each drive.

Her arms looped around his neck, bringing his ear to her lips. "Tell me," She panted, her orgasm building with each delicious pulse of his hips. "Tell me everything you couldn't three years ago. Tell me all of it, Theo."

And he did. Through gritted teeth and moans of pleasure, he rained praise down in a torrent of confessions. How he dreamed of having her, taking her just like this until his name left her lips on a scream of pleasure. How he longed to taste her lips and kiss her smiles. How he bought the blue coffee mugs because they reminded him of her eyes, the same eyes that he chased day in and day out from the roasting room.

Whispered words rolled from his tongue, against her ear, lips, throat. Words telling her how good she felt, how well she took him. The way his heart stopped when she smiled at him and how his hands trembled with their need to graze her skin—confirm that she was truly in his arms and not just another dream. He had dreamed of her so many times.

But this was very much real, and as he followed her over the peak of their pleasure, arms clutched tightly around one another, the best truth spilled against her lips between soft kisses.

"I love you." A delicate press of his lips against hers.

"Yeah?" A gentle caress of his tongue. "And how long do you intend to love me, Lulu?"

His smile curled against her mouth. "Every day for the rest of your bloody life, Guv'na."

ACKNOWLEDGEMENTS

How do I properly thank all the people who helped get this story out of my brain and onto the page? I guess I just…start?

So, David. Obviously. Thank you for always encouraging me to follow this wild dream. You're my favorite person, and the blueprint for at least three book boyfriends. Maybe four. Who's counting?

Mom. Katie. Thank you forever and always.

To Kelsey, Liana, Ali, and Darcy: you beta read like it's a competitive sport, and honestly, you deserve medals. I still don't know how I spelled altogether wrong that many times, but thanks for saving me from public shame.

Sam—you wizard. This cover makes me giddy every time I make eyes at it. You are so insanely talented, and I will always be your hype girl.

And finally, to the reader: thank you for picking up *Whipped* and giving Shannon and Theo a chance. This book was a beast for me to write, which naturally makes it completely and utterly invaluable to me. Thanks for spending time with something that has my whole heart. Appreciation floods my body anytime I see *Whipped* on those Goodreads shelves.

ABOUT THE AUTHOR

E. J. Hopps is a restaurant-obsessed, perpetually dehydrated romance writer hailing from the Northern California coast. When she's not spinning her daydreams into written word, you can find her pouring sake at the restaurant she runs alongside her husband or cozied up with a good book and her dog, Dozer.

With her heart firmly rooted in both the world of fine dining and the promise of happily ever afters, Hopps seeks to captivate readers with steamy restaurant romances, inviting them to savor the magic of her world with every turn of the page.